"As readers follow Kathi Macias's characters through intense spiritual warfare, set against the backdrop of the Mayan culture in old Mexico, they will find themselves encouraged to trust the working of a sovereign and good God in their own lives, and to follow His will—wherever it leads."—James H. Pence, coauthor of *Terror by Night*

"Once again, author Kathi Macias delivers a powerful novel that explores the tensions faced by those who seek to honor Christ but who live in a world marked by violence and despair. Painting the lives of the Mayan people in richly hued detail, Macias transports readers into a world of shamans (curanderos), siestas, and spiritual warfare. An undercurrent of suspense draws readers from scene to scene as, one by one, characters are forced to face the reality of their relationship with God against a backdrop of evil. From first page to last, *More than Conquerors* reminds us that even when circumstances appear to be at their most desperate, God is at work in and through all things."—Shelly Beach, Christy Award–winning author of *Hallie's Heart* and the sequel, *Morningsong*

"Kathi Macias writes from the heart of faith and hope. In *More than Conquerors*, she weaves together the lives and faith of people who meet not by chance, but by divine appointment—and at a cost. She reminds us we all have a part to play in the arena of faith, and that God sometimes calls us to places that require us to count fully on Him in order to be more than conquerors. Curl up with this book, and let Kathi Macias take you to that place."
—Bonnie Grove, author of *Talking to the Dead*

More New Hope books by Kathi Macias

No Greater Love

Mothers of the Bible Speak to Mothers of Today

*How Can I Run a Tight Ship When I'm Surrounded by
Loose Cannons? Proverbs 31 Discoveries for Yielding to
the Master of the Seas*

Beyond Me: Living a You-First Life in a Me-First World

More than *Conquerors*

Book 2 in
the "Extreme Devotion" series

Kathi Macias

NEW HOPE
PUBLISHERS
Birmingham, Alabama

New Hope® Publishers
P. O. Box 12065
Birmingham, AL 35202-2065
www.newhopepublishers.com
New Hope Publishers is a division of WMU®

Library of Congress Cataloging-in-Publication Data
Mills-Macias, Kathi, 1948-
  More than conquerors / Kathi Macias.
      p. cm. -- (Extreme devotion ; bk. 2)
  ISBN 978-1-59669-283-1 (pbk. : alk. paper) 1. Mexico--Fiction. I.
Title.
  PS3563.I42319M67 2010
  813'.54--dc22
                                    2009046160

Cover design: faceout®studio.com
Interior design: Sherry Hunt

ISBN-10: 1-59669-283-9
ISBN-13: 978-1-59669-283-1

N114129 • 0410 • 5M1

To my dear husband and best friend, Al,
who is both my strongest critic and most loving supporter;

To those whose selfless lives of love and service
inspire me to press on;

To the One who enables us to be "more than conquerors"
because we know that He has gone before us
and made a Way.

Prologue

PASTOR HECTOR MANOLO RODRIGUEZ SIGHED with relief, as his dilapidated, once-blue station wagon crawled and chugged through the final inches of the hourlong event known as a border crossing. The international station between San Diego and Tijuana saw the heaviest traffic of any crossing in the world, with about 300,000 people making the trek every day—some to work, some to play, some to shop or visit relatives, and some to conduct illegal activities of various kinds. For Hector, it was strictly a venture of love, one he made regularly and yet was relieved when it was over.

It wasn't that Hector didn't appreciate the beauty and modern conveniences of his sister city to the north, but he preferred the slower, quieter pace of his humble home on the outskirts of Tijuana, even now in 2008 when crime increasingly encroached on the peace of their existence. He had lived there his entire thirty-eight years, the middle child in a family of nine offspring, and had later married the beautiful Mariana Lopez, who had grown up right next door to him. That she had even noticed Hector never ceased to amaze him, and that she had agreed to marry him was nothing short of a miracle. Now, still living in the same neighborhood where they grew up, they did their best to feed and clothe the three children God had given them, as well as minister to the fifty or so members of their beloved *Casa de Dios* congregation. To supplement their income, Hector worked part-time in his younger brother Jorge's shoe repair shop. Though their financial situation did not allow for luxuries, it did provide a roof over their heads and food in their bellies.

It was a good life, Hector thought, as he coached and prayed the twenty-five-year-old car through the undisciplined crush of traffic on Avenida Revolucion, the main drag in this burgeoning city of nearly one and a half million people. As always, Hector was anxious to break away from the city's hub and escape to a quieter, more navigable thoroughfare. Though the quality of the roads would deteriorate the farther out he went, he would be glad to leave the hustle and bustle of the Tijuana tourism trade behind.

He would also be glad to leave behind the sadness that seemed to cling to him each time he crossed the border. And yet he knew his need to continue making the trip would end far too soon...

Then, of course, there was the situation in Chiapas, which seemed to grow more desperate and dangerous by the day. And his sixty-three-year-old mother, Virginia Correo Rodriguez, was living right outside San Juan Chamula, right in the middle of it all.

Hector pleaded with his mother to return with him to their home in Tijuana.

Chapter 1

THE AREA IN AND AROUND THE SMALL MAYAN village of San Juan Chamula, nestled in the Chiapas highlands just six miles from the city of San Cristobal de las Casas and home to several shamans and healers, known as *curanderos*, was not friendly to outsiders or to evangelical Christians. Virginia Correo Rodriguez was both.

Devout, dedicated, and determined to fulfill her calling to spread the gospel wherever and whenever God gave her a chance, she had come to San Juan Chamula with her pastor-son, Hector, on one of his rare trips to bring Bibles to the unevangelized areas of Chiapas State. While in Chamula, she distinctly sensed God calling her to remain there with one of only a handful of evangelical households in the community that openly acknowledged Christ as Savior and struggled to practice their faith in an increasingly hostile environment. Though Hector pleaded with his mother to return with him to their home in Tijuana, she had instead chosen to obey God's directive and stay behind.

That was nearly two years before, in the summer of 2006. Now, as the early days of spring 2008 unfolded and the first rays of sunlight began to peek over the tops of the trees in the rain forest that surrounded the small, dilapidated, mud and wood hut Virginia called home, she welcomed the new day with a prayer of thanks to the Creator of those trees and the Source of all light. Though it would be more than an hour before the sun dispelled the damp chill that nearly always settled over the village and its outlying areas during the night, Virginia would rise early to start the fire, and then spend some time in prayer and Bible reading before preparing a meager breakfast of homemade corn tortillas and vegetables from the garden for the family of seven who had so graciously adopted her.

She shivered as she sat up on the side of the rickety cot in the corner of the house's main room, which served as kitchen and living area. Sliding her feet into her well-worn but functional *zapatas*, Virginia grabbed the heavy wool *serape* from the foot of the bed and threw it over her shoulders, as she thought of the family who had become so dear to her over the last couple of years. The parents, Diego and Eldora Campos, slept with their newborn son in the smaller of the two bedrooms, while the four older children shared the larger one. There was no indoor bathroom, only a shabby outhouse with holes in the walls big enough to poke a fist through, and no running water or electricity. Yet the size of the home made it one of the nicest in the area, despite the fact that it was a step down from where Virginia had lived in Tijuana. These were hardships Virginia now took in stride, however, though it had required some serious adapting when she first made the commitment to stay. It had also been a challenge to adjust to the 7,200-foot elevation after living her entire life in the nearly sea level city of Tijuana.

But God had brought her here—planted her, as she liked to say. And she had every intention of blooming right where she was planted. As a result, the adjustment had been nothing more than an inconvenience when compared to the joy she felt at being used by God in this late stage of her life. Just when she had thought her usefulness was nearly over and she was ready to pass the baton of ministry to the next generation, God had graciously surprised her with the chance to teach her new family, along with the few other evangelical families—disparagingly known as *los evangelicos*—in the area, to read. Since the Bible was one of the only books at her disposal, she happily used it as her primer. As a result, even a few women in nonevangelical families who also spoke Spanish had dared to come for reading lessons and were now hearing the Scriptures for the very first time.

What an amazing ministry, she thought, lighting the kindling that had been stacked in the woodstove the night before. *And what an amazing God You are that You would entrust it to me! Thank You, Father.*

With the fire going and the area around the stove beginning to radiate a welcome warmth, Virginia settled back on her cot and opened her Bible to the Book of Psalms.

O God, You are my God; Early will I seek You . . .

Virginia smiled as she read the familiar verse. *Oh yes, Lord, You are my God, and I will rise up early and also stay up late to seek You!*

It seemed the older Virginia got, the less time she spent sleeping and the more time worshipping the Lord. And instead of making her tired, her new schedule left her energized.

For the next hour she alternated between reading from the Bible that lay in her lap, and closing her eyes to respond to God in silent, sometimes whispered, prayer. It wasn't until she heard the baby's cry and Eldora's responding coo of reassurance that Virginia realized it was time to put her Bible aside and get on with the breakfast preparations.

"That's all right, Father," she whispered, closing her beloved book and rising from the bed. "We will find more time to be alone together throughout the day. Meanwhile, thank You for giving me this little flock to love and care for. I know that most of the people around here don't know You or worship You—though they think they do in their mixed-up Mayan version

13

of Catholicism—and therefore they don't welcome me in their midst. But I also know You love them more than they can ever imagine. Use me, Father, any way You wish, to conquer their fears and superstitions with Your great love."

Hector was never happier or more at peace than when he was at home with Mariana and their three children. Their house might be modest, even by local standards, and desperately in need of paint, but at least they had running water, electricity, and indoor plumbing, which was more than his mother now enjoyed living on the outskirts of the quaint village of San Juan Chamula, home to approximately 80,000 people, most of Mayan ancestry. Perhaps if she had moved in with a family who lived in town she would at least be able to enjoy the more basic luxuries of modern life, but she had chosen instead to live in the exact spot where she believed God had called her.

Sitting on the sagging stoop and watching his children play ball in the small, fenced dirt yard, with only patches of dry grass and a few healthy rosebushes that Mariana had planted along the fence line, Hector took a sip from the glass of cool water his wife had brought him and sighed. Hadn't he always told his congregation that there was no better or safer place to be than in the middle of God's will, even if that meant living and ministering in a dangerous situation or location? And who, in fact, had taught him that? His mother, of course. Certainly not his father, who had deserted the family when Hector was still a child and who, even now, in what was most assuredly his last days on earth, continued to deny God's existence, though Hector chose not to believe his avowals of atheism. No, it had been Hector's mother, the strongest, most faithful human being Hector had ever known, who drilled that great truth into him. It was primarily her influence and example that had brought not only Hector but also his eight siblings to give their hearts and lives to Christ and to lead their own families in the same way. So how could Hector now challenge his mother's right—and yes, her responsibility—to follow God's call, despite the danger involved?

A slightly deflated soccer ball landed with a thud in front of Hector, pulling him back from thoughts of his mother and the hardships she was undoubtedly enduring. Glancing down at the ball, which had failed to roll beyond the spot of its original plop, and then back up at his children, who were now eyeing him expectantly, he scolded himself for getting caught up in worry and letting his mind wander when he should be enjoying his family and leaving his mother in God's capable hands.

"So," he said, rising to his feet, "you want your papa to play with you, is that it? Why didn't you just say so?"

The three youngsters giggled and squealed with delight as Hector used the scuffed toe of his brown cowboy boot to send the not-quite-round ball rolling gently back in their direction. The scramble was immediate, as each tried to be the first to reach the ball and kick it back to their father. The firstborn, Hector Jr., who was nearly ten, won the race and promptly kicked the black and white ball in the desired direction. When it sailed up and into Hector's chest, he exaggerated the effect and howled in mock pain as he fell to the ground. In seconds the three were upon him, climbing and laughing, urging him to get up and quite obviously not believing his ruse for a moment.

"All right," Hector gasped. "I give up! You got me. The three of you are just too strong for me. I'm going to have to tell Mama to quit feeding you so much. You're getting too big for me to handle."

Lupita, the youngest child and only daughter, who was sitting on her father's stomach by then, squealed with joy and bounced up and down, evoking a very real grunt from Hector.

"Enough!" he cried. "I told you. I give up! Have mercy on your poor papa!"

When that didn't work, Hector grabbed the four-year-old girl and tickled her until she rolled off him onto the ground, only to be replaced by six-year-old Manolo. "Oh, no, you don't," Hector insisted, immediately dislodging the boy and getting to his feet before he could be attacked again. "What's the matter with all of you? Do I look like a horse? Or maybe a *burro*?"

The laughter level rose as Manolo began to prance around the yard, whinnying and hee-hawing, and sending Lupita into near convulsions of giggles. When Mariana stepped outside to investigate, Hector grinned at the pleased look on her face. He knew there was nothing his beautiful wife liked more than seeing her brood enjoying one another.

"All right," she said at last, raising her hand in silent command. "Time to stop and come inside to eat. The *frijoles* are done, and I've made fresh *tortillas*. Though I don't know why I bother." She shook her head, even as the dimples in her cheeks telegraphed amused approval. "All of you, inside...now." Her sparkling brown eyes settled on Hector. "That means you, too, *Señor* Rodriguez. Honestly, I can't leave any of you alone for a moment, can I?"

With a giggling Lupita attached to his left leg, Hector slipped his right arm around Mariana's still slim waist and limped into the house, dragging his delighted daughter with him while the boys followed closely behind. "You most certainly cannot, *Señora* Rodriguez. We wouldn't manage for an hour without you."

She smiled up at him with her large brown eyes, and he kissed the top of her head, enjoying the fresh scent of shampoo in her thick, wavy dark hair, gathered neatly in a jeweled clasp at the nape of her neck. Life was indeed good, Hector thought, as he did so often. God had blessed him beyond his wildest dreams, and he couldn't be more grateful.

The wasted remnants of an exhausted, pain-racked human being lay in his bed at the hospice facility, drifting in and out of consciousness, glad for the "out" times that took him away from his agony. How much longer? And what would happen then? In his lucid moments he hoped he was right that there was nothing beyond his last ragged breath—just peaceful oblivion and escape from the hell his life on earth had become. But in his heart he sensed there was something much worse, some type of existence after this one, a reckoning of sorts. If that was truly the case, there was little doubt he would not be happy with the results.

Sixty-five years old, but looking much older, Alberto Javier Rodriguez fought the memories that danced through his mind, swirling together in confusing storylines that tormented an already guilty conscience. But each stabbing memory only reinforced his determination to blot out the past and deny the need for repentance or confession. If there was a God waiting to judge him, Alberto ricocheted between wanting to spit in His eye and curse Him for creating him in the first place...and lamenting that it was too late to seek forgiveness and restoration.

The pictures of his family were the clearest, and the most painful. How had it ever come to this? He knew, of course. After all, he was the one who had made the choices that led to such a tragic outcome. He had no one to blame but himself. If only he could bring himself to admit that to someone, but even when the chance had been offered him—more than once, for that matter—he had hardened his heart, sealed his lips, and refused to confess his faults and ask for forgiveness. Now he would no doubt die alone, unloved, unrepentant, and unforgiven. And deservedly so, he reminded himself. But oh, what a comfort it would be if just one of those whose hearts he had broken would be there with him when the time came!

For now, the only comfort he had was the drip of morphine that flowed at preset intervals into the vein in his right arm. He had, indeed, reaped what he sowed in his life, and now he wrestled with the fear that things were only going to get much worse.

A young Mayan woman named Imix, or Water Lily, had shyly asked if she could join the group.

Chapter 2

AS HAPPENED MOST EVERY DAY IN HER RELATIVELY quiet, tucked-away corner of the world, Virginia's morning had passed quickly but peacefully. Now, in the middle of the afternoon with many of the nearby residents of San Juan Chamula observing one of the few Mexican traditions occasionally practiced by the Mayan people—that of afternoon *siestas*—Virginia's "classroom" was full, as she and the other women took advantage of the brief break in their daily routines. Eldora Campos, of course, was there, sitting on the floor, holding her sleeping baby, Rudolfo, in one arm and balancing her Bible on her lap with the other. Maria and Concepcion, Virginia's other two regulars, were also in attendance, as were their children, who sat together with Eldora and Diego's older four, listening intently. The men of the families did not come, as they felt it was inappropriate for a woman to teach a man under any circumstances. Still, Eldora had confided in Virginia that oftentimes, in the quiet of the early night, after the children were all asleep and husband

and wife had retired to their room, Diego would ask Eldora to show him what she had learned in her reading class that day. Virginia smiled at the thought. She couldn't help but wonder if Maria and Concepcion's husbands did the same, though doubtless she would never know for sure.

The most exciting thing for Virginia was that today she had another new student. A few weeks ago a young Mayan woman named Imix, or Water Lily, had shyly asked if she could join the group. Virginia and the others were stunned but had welcomed her with open arms. After all, Mayans did not mix with or even accept *evangelicos* in their communities; it was almost unheard of for a Mayan woman to want to join such a study group, particularly when the object of study was a Prot-estant version of the Bible, even if the purpose ostensibly was learning to read. But many of the Mayan people, even those in San Juan Chamula, spoke Spanish as a second language, so Virginia's reading class was certainly a viable option for Imix and anyone like her.

As a result, Imix had attended regularly for several weeks now, but this week she had arrived with a friend in tow. Kawak, whose name meant "storm cloud" and whose counte-nance mirrored her name, sat stoically beside the soft-spoken Imix, as Virginia read a couple of lines from the eighth chapter of the Book of Romans, reminding herself to focus on teach-ing her students to read and allowing God's Spirit to speak to them about anything else during the process.

It wasn't easy, of course. Virginia was not a trained teacher, of reading or any other subject. And yet, it seemed as she read one or two verses each week, slowly working her way through a chapter, that most of the group followed along as she taught them to sound out the words within the verse. Today's lesson was verse 37, which read, "Yet in all these things we are more than conquerors through him who loved us." As Virginia sat on the floor, facing her students, she read the words aloud, preparing to break down the verse word by word, letter by letter, sound by sound. But almost immediately upon complet-ing the initial reading of the verse, she heard a stirring from the spot where the two Mayan women had settled themselves. Lowering her book to her lap, Virginia looked over the top of the reading glasses that were perched on her nose and locked eyes with the new visitor to the group. In that instant, Virginia caught a glimpse of how this Kawak, whom Virginia imagined to be in her mid- to late-twenties, had lived up to her name. Her very face looked as if it were a storm cloud, gathering force and preparing to unleash its fury on anyone who got in its way. Imix, on the other hand, appeared upset and confused, as her eyes darted from Kawak to Virginia and back again. Even Eldora and the other ladies were squirming a bit, as Virginia prayed for an explanation to the sudden reaction.

More than conquerors... Of course! She should have realized how those words might sound to her Mayan guests, many of whom were still sensitive to reminders of the Spanish *conquistadores* and even the Aztecs who had fought for and won much of the land the Mayans considered theirs by right of having been there first.

Virginia felt the heat climb to her cheeks, and her initial reaction was to apologize profusely, but she knew it was best not to focus too strenuously on her gaffe. Instead, she moved on to the next two verses: "For I am persuaded that neither death nor life, nor angels nor principalities nor powers, nor things present nor things to come, nor height nor depth, nor any other created thing, shall be able to separate us from the love of God which is in Christ Jesus our Lord." She knew they wouldn't get past the first few words that day, but at least it might help get everyone's mind off the word *conquerors* and on to something else.

As the undercurrent of agitation subsided a bit, Virginia sighed, offered up a silent prayer for God to use even her mistake for His glory, and moved on.

Marty loved San Diego. In his opinion, it deserved its repu-
tation for being one of the finest cities in the world, with the
most perfect climate anywhere. But even more than all the
upper class neighborhoods and renowned beaches or tourist
hot spots for which the area was famous, Marty liked the quiet
suburb of Imperial Beach the best. He especially liked the fact
that from certain vantage points on the beach, he could see
Tijuana in the distance.

Anytime Marty had a few spare moments between classes,
homework, and his part-time job at a local convenience store,
he headed to the beach and walked along the sand or out to
the end of the pier. Today he had chosen the pier; once at the
far end of it, he parked himself on a bench and settled in to
watch the people as they strolled past or fished over the pier's
railing—and while he watched, he prayed. This was his quiet
time with the Lord, something he had to fight for in his busy
life. But here, at the end of the pier in Imperial Beach, it was
peaceful, as he listened to the waves roll in and the seagulls
screech overhead. Occasionally the delighted squeal of a child
punctuated the otherwise predictable sounds, and Marty knew
life on this earth couldn't get much better.

As he sat under the noonday sun and communed with God
about his own life, seeking direction for the future as his college
days drew to a close and graduation loomed, ready to launch
him into the next phase of his life, he also prayed for the people
he watched and heard. How many of them knew the Lord—
and how many scarcely even knew *about* Him? Marty's twenty-
two years of life, twelve of which had been spent as a dedicated
Christian with a certainty that God had a special call on his
life, had taught him that most people contended they believed
in God, but very few of them actually lived accordingly. Therefore, Marty could only conclude that they really didn't believe
in Him at all.

He sighed, taking a sip from his water bottle as he considered yet again what his next move would be. Because he had
doubled up in many classes, he would be graduating early—in
a couple of weeks, as a matter of fact—and he saw no reason to

continue working at his part-time job when he would then be free to move on to something else. And yet nothing had opened up with any clarity as far as a future career or ministry. The only thing that came to mind each time he prayed for direction was a visit to his friends, Hector and Mariana Rodriguez. The devout Christian couple had been Marty's hosts each time he had gone to Mexico during the past three summers to minister to the young people in the area, and they had told him he was welcome any time. Though Marty had enough money saved up to stay in San Diego for a few months as he continued to seek God for direction, he was beginning to think God was telling him he could just as easily seek that direction from the Rodriguez home south of the border.

He smiled at the thought, just as a couple of bikini-clad teenage girls swaggered past, casting teasing glances toward him and giggling with each sway of their overexposed hips. No doubt the immature yet admittedly lovely young girls had misinterpreted his smile as a flirtatious overture on his part. Nothing could have been further from the truth. Marty had no time or place in his life for romance, at least not yet. And when the time came, it certainly wouldn't be with someone who so casually advertised her wares to everyone who crossed her path.

No, Marty had known since he was ten years old that he would someday, somehow, dedicate his entire life to God's service, wherever that might lead and whatever it might entail. If God saw fit to bless him with a wife to share such a focused and self-sacrificing life, she would also have to be a dedicated Christian whose heart was first and foremost after God and who had no time for the distractions of a materialistic or hedonistic world. Marty's only concern with the two giggling teenagers and so many others like them was to lead his life in such a way that those who saw him would want to know and serve the Lord as he did. Until God brought a woman with equal passions and dedication into his life, romance would simply have to wait.

With a fresh picture of Hector and Mariana's humble but welcoming home in his mind, Marty rose from the bench and began his trek back to the parking lot at the other end of the pier, where his dinged-up '84 El Camino, with its once-white paint job, sat waiting for him, gleaming in the Southern California sunshine.

Mariana's eyes opened wide at the news. "Marty's coming?"

Hector nodded, and Mariana felt her heart leap, as her husband waved the letter in front of his face. The three children were already jumping and twirling around the kitchen, rejoicing at the top of their lungs over Hector's announcement. The very fact that the young man had written a letter, rather than called, endeared him to Mariana that much more. She loved the old-fashioned nature of the handsome Bible student who had girls swooning in his presence yet seemed unfazed by the attention. Marty was so focused on ministry that he scarcely noticed the female frenzy that followed him wherever he went.

What a catch he'll be one day, Mariana mused. *Not so much because he's handsome, but because he's exceptionally dedicated and faithful.* She had thought more than once how nice it would be if Marty noticed her younger sister, Susana, who had quite obviously developed an immediate crush on the San Diego student the moment he first set foot in Hector and Mariana's home. But Susana, though quite lovely and mature beyond her nineteen years, was quiet and bashful. As a result, she and Marty had scarcely spoken a dozen words over the three summers the young *Americano* had visited with them.

Now he was coming back, and Mariana knew Susana wouldn't be the only one excited about his return. Everyone in their neighborhood would be ecstatic, even as Hector Jr., Manolo, and Lupita obviously were already. From Marty's first visit to the family, the children had christened him *Tio Marty*, and the young man had quickly adapted to the familial term of affection. As such, he never failed to observe his adopted niece or nephews' birthdays or any other holidays when he could send them a special card or treat. There was little doubt in Mariana's mind that the gracious young man would once again show up bearing gifts when he arrived in a couple of weeks.

Mariana kissed Hector on the cheek. "That is wonderful news, *mi esposo*. How long will he stay? Did he say in the letter?"

Hector shook his head. "No, *mi amor*. He said only that he needs a quiet place to work and minister, even as he prays about what God wants him to do next." He broke into a wide grin, his even white teeth showing beneath his thick mustache and his dark eyes twinkling with mischief. "A quiet place. And so he comes here, to our household, where we haven't had a quiet moment since the little ones came into our lives."

Mariana laughed and threw her arms around her husband. "Maybe we can't offer him a quiet place, but we can offer him a home filled with love while he waits to hear from God. What better gift can we give anyone?"

Hector pulled her close, his laughter mingling with hers, though nearly drowned out by the shouts and squeals of their rejoicing offspring. "None, *querida*," he said. "You are absolutely right. There is no greater gift that we can give him at this point in his life. But something tells me we will receive an even greater gift in return."

She knew, of course, where he had gone,
but there was nothing she could do about it.

Chapter 3

VIRGINIA WAS TIRED BUT PLEASED AS SHE FELL INTO bed at last. Despite her earlier cultural faux pas of reading a verse that reminded her Mayan guests of the conquests of their country and the resentment that still flourished within their culture, the study time had seemed to end on a positive note. Virginia was hopeful that Imix and Kawak would return for another reading lesson, and that she and her two new acquaintances could somehow develop a meaningful relationship, one in which she could carefully introduce their need for the Savior.

How truly blessed she was, Virginia thought, as she considered the simple ministry God had entrusted to her at this late stage of her life, as well as the loving family He had provided in this quiet but lovely area so many miles from her Tijuana home. The little house was quiet now, except for an occasional giggle from the children's room, followed by a responding "hush" and a loving command to go to sleep from one of the parents. It was a routine Virginia had come to love over the nearly two years she had lived near Chamula, though it never failed to evoke a touch of nostalgia as it brought back memories of the many years when she had tried to settle her own children into bed—all nine of them—after a hectic but joy-filled day. For no matter how busy or difficult those days had been, knowing that she had all of her children with her— happy and healthy—supplied all the joy and strength Virginia needed to continue on.

True, her life had not been easy, particularly after her husband deserted them, leaving her to care for the children on her own. She knew, of course, where he had gone, but there was nothing she could do about it. Alberto had met the beautiful, wealthy *Americana* with the golden hair when she vacationed at the beach resort where he worked, and he had never again been the same. Soon after that initial meeting, Alberto had begun disappearing on his days off, often being gone overnight and offering no explanation when he returned. Money for household expenses disappeared as well, leaving Virginia struggling to make ends meet, even as she hoped and prayed her suspicions about another woman were wrong. And then she had seen them together, strolling down the street just blocks from Alberto and Virginia's home, laughing and carrying on as if they had nothing to hide, and the shame had nearly killed her. When he finally left yet again and this time failed to return, she told herself she was glad it was over and that God would take care of her and her children. And He had, of course, though she worked long and hard in the interim, without so much as a *peso* of support from her departed husband. But though she heard the beautiful *Americana* had eventually dumped Alberto for a younger man, Virginia never heard from him again—nor did she rejoice at the news of his abandonment. She had instead continued to pray for the father of her children, as she had each day since becoming a Christian soon after they married, asking God that He would reveal Himself to Alberto and give him a heart to love and serve the Savior.

There were many times, like tonight, as she lay on the cot in the Camposes' home, with nothing but a sliver of moonlight showing through the tiny, curtainless window above her bed, that she wondered if she might one day see Alberto again—if not in this life, then in the next. For that, after all, was what really mattered. And then, despite the lingering pain of his betrayal and abandonment, she gave herself over to praying for him—wherever he was and whatever he was doing.

Hector lay awake long after Mariana and the children had fallen asleep. His wife slept with her head on his shoulder, breathing softly against his chest. But though there was nowhere he would rather be than lying beside the love of his life and holding her close as she slept, his thoughts were elsewhere. What had it been like, he wondered, for his parents when they first married? Surely they had once been in love, even as he and Mariana were now. After all, they'd had nine children together! And though it had been many years and Hector had been quite young at the time, he could still remember the few occasions they had all gone somewhere together as a family—his parents walking arm in arm, with their brood of nine, one still sleeping in the broken-down stroller pushed by Hector's oldest sister, scampering along behind. Weren't their parents happy then? They had seemed so. And what a handsome couple they had made! How was it possible that his father had simply stopped loving his mother and run off to live with another woman, leaving his entire family behind to fend for themselves as best they could?

Hector sighed, shaking his head in the darkness. He was a man who, like his father, wasn't blind to the beauty or temptation of women other than his wife. But he had made a vow before God to have nothing to do with anyone else, and he had never even considered breaking that promise. In his opinion, Mariana was the finest and most beautiful woman in the world, and his responsibility to care for her and the three children they had produced together was paramount in his life—almost as overarching as his desire to please and obey God.

And that, he thought, was the difference. Hector's mother had instilled a deep faith in God in all nine of her children, both before and after their father's departure. And she had lived that faith and modeled that selfless love to them in such a way that all had made their own commitments to Christ and now walked with Him unswervingly. Their father, however, had never known or practiced such a faith. Though he had attended church occasionally as a child, it had never impacted his life in any meaningful way. When Virginia had "become a fanatic," as Alberto termed her heartfelt conversion, it had no doubt driven a wedge between them, even if Hector and his siblings had been too young to recognize it.

Now his father was gone, dying alone in a charity hospice north of the border, without his family—and without God. Hector knew he had to visit him again soon and try once more to open the man's eyes to the truth of his need for a Savior, but he also knew he was overdue for a visit to Chamula. He had promised to bring more Bibles, as well as some personal things to his mother, including her blood pressure medication, and he just didn't trust the mail service to deliver such precious cargo. The trip to Chamula would be costly—nearly $200 and two days on the bus each way—but his car would never make it. Thanks to his small salary as a pastor and the money he made working part-time in Jorge's shop, Hector had just enough money saved up to make the trip. But if he was going to get to San Juan Chamula and back before Marty came in less than two weeks, he must leave in the next day or two.

Hector sighed again and kissed the top of his sleeping wife's head. His father would just have to wait until he returned. In the meantime, Hector would ask Marty to please stop by to see the ailing old man in San Diego—and Hector would continue to pray that God would spare Alberto Javier Rodriguez just a little while longer.

Kawak had thought about it all night, these meetings where they learned to read the symbols on the paper. She knew she shouldn't have gone, but Imix had insisted, over and over again, until curiosity lured Kawak to a meeting. Now that she had been there and heard what this foreign woman had to say, Kawak knew she had been right about everyone in that house. It wasn't that Kawak had never seen a Bible before, since many in her Mayan culture considered themselves Catholics and occasionally kept a Catholic version of the Scriptures in their homes, though they seldom if ever read them. But the Campos family, like other *evangelicos*, had rejected everything the nominally Catholic Mayans considered sacred—and that made them evil, just like the stranger they allowed to live with them. The woman had no doubt already cast her spell over them and was now pulling in Imix as well.

Kawak could not allow that to happen. Imix was her friend. She was one of them, unlike the Campos family and their foreign guest. Kawak must rescue her friend before it was too late, and before this sorceress cast a spell on others in the village and drew them in as well. Tomorrow Kawak would talk to *la curandera*. Kawak would tell the shaman of the strange version of the Bible that spoke of *los conquistadores* and how the woman who lived with the Campos family taught them from it. Surely the holy woman would know what to do to stop this spread of evil in their community before it defeated what was left of their ancient culture and practices, the remnant of a great civilization that had nearly been destroyed by the invaders so many years earlier.

The pain was worse tonight, blinding as a white-hot poker in his eyes, causing him to grind what few teeth he had left until he was sure they would soon dissolve to powder. Oh, when would it end? No! It mustn't end, for then there would be no more hope. But was there any . . . even now?

Alberto drifted back and forth from his hospice room to the world of memories and nightmares, illusions and temporary escapes from reality. It was impossible to decide which was worse. Occasionally he awoke to find a young woman with soft hands touching his forehead or his cheek and speaking softly to him. At other times she adjusted the tube that hung from the bottle beside his bed or jotted a note on his chart. Her dark hair and rosy lips reminded him of Virginia—but that had been so long ago. By now she must have aged, even as he had. Perhaps she was even dead. He had not had the nerve to ask Hector the last time he came.

Would he come back again? If he did, what would they talk about? Alberto longed to tell him what was in his heart, but he dreaded it as well. Would he have the nerve . . . this time? Last time he had locked it down inside, ignoring the pleading he heard in his son's words and saw in his eyes. Would it be any different if Hector returned and spoke to him again? And what of the other eight children Alberto had left behind? Should he ask about them? Beg Hector to encourage them to come? But why? So they could see him as the pitiful, wretched shell of a man he had become?

No. Better that they remember him as a young, strong, handsome father—even if he had played the fool and abandoned them when they needed him most. Perhaps they would find at least a scrap of good in their memories of him, though he couldn't imagine what it would be. He was indeed the poorest excuse for a man—for a husband and father—who had ever lived. And now he was too much of a coward even to die with dignity.

La curandera never failed to strike terror into Kawak's heart.

Chapter 4

KAWAK HAD KNOWN LA CURANDERA FOR NEARLY twenty years now, ever since Kawak was a little girl, and she had always been in awe of the special powers ascribed to the woman who was never seen without the small square mirror that she wore on a chain around her neck to ward off evil. But even with the colorful attire displayed by the shaman, including the bright red shawl she wore at all times, regardless of the weather, *la curandera* never failed to strike terror into Kawak's heart, particularly when she heard the woman speak of the Mayan prediction of the end of the world, less than four years away.

Still, there was no choice for the young Mayan but to follow through with her visit and report to the holy woman on the goings-on at the Camposes' home. And so Kawak pushed one foot in front of the other as she continued down the street toward the shaman's house, dodging chickens and even a couple of turkeys on the way. When at last she stopped in front of the low building made of breezeblock, her heart raced with anticipation—and dread. Her hands clammy and her heart racing, Kawak passed quickly through a cypress leaf archway and into the realm of spirits and darkness that had always frightened yet intrigued her.

Sensing that she was no longer alone, Kawak called out, her voice shaking. "Evita? Are you here? It is I . . . Kawak."

She waited, but there was no answer. Could it be that the woman had gone out? If so, why was the smell of candles and incense so strong and heavy? No, she must be there. Kawak tried again, taking one tentative step inside the open doorway as she spoke. "Evita?"

The woman was in front of her so quickly that Kawak gasped. How had she not seen her approach? And yet it was fairly dark inside; perhaps that explained it.

Swallowing, Kawak tried to steady her heart and her breathing. "I . . . I came to see you," she said. "To . . . tell you about the foreign woman at the Campos' house. And about . . . *los conquistadores*."

Even in the semidarkness of the oppressive room, where candlelight danced against the walls and oxygen seemed hard to come by, Kawak could see *la curandera*'s eyes narrow.

"*Conquistadores?*" Her voice seemed to crackle when she spoke, though Kawak knew it wasn't from old age. The woman was, at most, in her early fifties, though she had an ancient quality about her. Evita grabbed Kawak's arm, sending a shiver down the young woman's spine. "Come with me," Evita ordered, and without another word they made their way to the center of the room, where they sat down on the thick blanket of pine needles that stretched out in a circle in the center of the floor.

"Tell me what you have learned about this outsider," Evita said. "I have watched her for some time now, and I believe she is an evil presence in our community."

Kawak nodded. However frightening the shaman might be, Kawak trusted her far more than the foreigner who spoke of *los conquistadores* and pretended to teach others from what

Kawak was certain was a perverted version of the Bible. It was important that Kawak not fail in her attempt to convey to *la curandera* her concern over the seriousness of what was happening in the Camposes' home and how it was affecting Imix. As the headiness of the burning candles and incense enveloped her, Kawak poured out the story of her attendance at the reading class the previous day, noting with satisfaction that the shaman was listening intently to every word.

Though the breeze off the ocean was a bit cool that morning, Marty didn't mind. Walking along the sand, just far enough from the ebbing waves to keep his shoes dry, he breathed in the salty smell of the ocean and absorbed the warmth of the sun on his face. He'd already completed the first half of his walk and was on the return journey. He couldn't imagine living anywhere that didn't include a beach, but then, who knew where God would send him? He would just have to enjoy the beauty of the Southern California coastline while he could, and then adjust when his assignment became clear.

How glad he was that Hector had responded to his letter so quickly, extending a full and complete welcome to him from the entire Rodriguez family. Though staying in their home meant bunking with Hector Jr. and Manolo in their already cramped bedroom, Marty didn't mind. A bedroll on the floor with such a loving family was a welcome retreat from the lonely studio apartment he'd been renting since starting school almost four years earlier. Many of his friends preferred being in a quiet place with no one around when they were spending time praying and seeking God for direction, but Marty needed the wisdom and guidance of an older, more mature Christian, someone he admired and respected, and no one filled the bill like Hector Manolo Rodriguez. And Hector's wife, Mariana, was the kindest woman and best cook Marty had ever met —

his idea of the perfect wife. He could only pray that God would someday bless him with such a life partner.

He kicked a pebble and smiled at the thought of Hector and Mariana's children. They were a handful, but being around them was like catching a glimpse of what it would have been like to grow up in a loving, Christian home. Marty had never had that experience, his father having died before Marty's first birthday, leaving Marty with no siblings and with a mother who was too busy with her society friends and activities to pay much attention to him. When Marty had become a Christian while visiting a local church with a friend from school, his mother had advised him not to get too carried away with his new religion, assuring him his enthusiasm would wear off quickly. She was wrong. Marty's enthusiasm and excitement at the new life he had found in Christ only grew with each passing year, as did his determination to go to Bible school. When his mother had refused to pay the tuition for what she considered a frivolous waste of time and money, he had taken the money bequeathed to him by his father and kept in trust until his eighteenth birthday and left San Francisco in the rearview mirror of his beloved El Camino, heading south to San Diego and the Bible college of his choice. Now, near the end of his senior year, it was time to put that education to use.

The sound of swooping gulls and laughing children brought him back from his daydreams, and he looked up to see that he had come full circle and was nearly back where he had left his car.

Good, he thought. *I'm getting hungry. Think I'll grab some breakfast and then head over to the hospice facility to meet Hector's father. Lord, please go ahead of me to prepare the way and accomplish Your purpose in this visit.*

The fever burned hot…and yet he was so cold. Many times, at least when he was lucid, Alberto wondered if he would ever be warm again. He dreamed of the warm sunshine that had characterized his life, both in Tijuana and San Diego, and he longed to feel it on his decaying skin just one more time before he took his last breath. And yet he knew that would never be. Wherever he was—and he had long since forgotten the name of the place or how he came to be here—he had accepted that he would never leave there alive. And so, as awful as his existence was in this lonely room where he lay, hour after hour, racked with pain, he dreaded the moment when he would pass from this agony to one he was sure would be much worse.

Voices. One of the nurses, no doubt, and maybe a doctor or another lab tech, come to poke him with yet another needle. If it eased his pain, Alberto didn't mind. For any other reason, it was pointless.

For a moment his heart leaped, as the thought crossed his mind that the male voice might be Hector, that possibly his son had returned. But he knew better. Hector had been here enough times now that Alberto recognized his voice. The words he heard now did not belong to his son.

"Mr. Rodriguez?"

Alberto sighed, wondering if it was worth the effort to open his eyes. He could easily feign sleep, and maybe the voice would go away and leave him alone. But curiosity got the better of him, and he willed his eyelids open.

The tall figure standing beside his bed came into focus slowly. Blond hair. Young. Handsome. Well built. Apart from the hair color, everything that Alberto once was but would never be again. So what was the handsome young man doing here? He wasn't wearing a white coat and didn't appear to be a doctor or any other medical person. What did he want with him? It would take too much energy to ask, so Alberto would just wait and let the man talk when he was ready.

His visitor smiled. "Hello, Mr. Rodriguez. My name is Marty Johnson. I'm a friend of Hector's—of his whole family, actually. He asked me to stop by and see how you were doing."

Hector had sent him? Why would he do that? Why hadn't he come himself?

39

Alberto opened his mouth, trying to remember how to utter the words that were formulating in his mind. "Wh— Why?" he croaked, the effort leaving him too exhausted to say more.

The man named Marty smiled again. When he spoke, his voice was soft, caring, soothing even Alberto's aching spine with the words. "Because he's concerned about you. He cares about you very much." Marty paused, as Alberto absorbed the message, waiting anxiously for the young man to continue, to give him more words to cling to.

"He wanted to come himself," he said, "but he had to go to San Juan Chamula first—to see his mother."

Alberto felt himself frown. Virginia was in Chamula? Why? What was she doing there? Didn't she know that wasn't a safe place to be, especially for a woman alone? And then another thought pierced him, like a slice of burning lightning to his heart. Perhaps she was no longer alone. Perhaps she had met someone, started a new life...

As if the young man could read his thoughts, Marty said, "She's been living on the outskirts of San Juan Chamula for almost two years now, with a family named Campos. She teaches reading to some of the people who live there. Hector visits her occasionally, and he's overdue to bring her some supplies and medicine, so he said he had to go there first. But as soon as he returns, he plans to come and see you. Meanwhile, he asked me to check on you now and then, and...to pray for you."

The words hung in the air, as the revelation that the mother of Alberto's children lived in a place where she had no business being, a place that was unfriendly—even hostile— to outsiders. Didn't Hector realize that? Why had he allowed his mother to go there? Alberto had heard stories of people disappearing in that remote Mayan village, where past resentments festered and superstition ran deep. No. Virginia— his *esposa*, his wife, as she would always be in his heart—had no business being there. But what could he do about it? Even if he were able to get up and walk out of this building and back across the border into Mexico, what right would he have to go to the woman he had deserted so many years ago and demand that she come back home where she belonged?

For the first time in longer than he could remember, Alberto felt hot tears squeeze out of his eyes and roll down his gaunt cheeks. His visitor, undoubtedly mistaking what he saw, laid his hand on Alberto's shoulder and began to pray, sending sparks of fear shooting through the old man's body. Would God kill him now for such a sacrilege? Would Alberto be ripped from his tenuous hold on life and plunged into what was surely a hell much worse and more deserved than he had ever imagined?

His body shook with painful sobs as the young man continued to pray, with Alberto catching only a word here and there. Why had Hector sent this Marty Johnson to torture him? Why couldn't he have left him alone with what little peace he had? Now he would have to bear the added burden of knowing that the woman he had once loved and later betrayed was in great danger and could possibly die even before he did. The revelation was crueler than anything Alberto had endured to date, for he knew that if he hadn't deserted his family, Virginia would be safe and sound, growing old side by side with him as they'd originally planned.

Would the consequences of his foolish choices never stop haunting him? He shuddered at the vision of what awaited him when he passed on, and he had his answer. Forever was a very long time indeed.

Hector was too stunned to move.

Chapter 5

GANG VIOLENCE WAS AN ESCALATING PROBLEM ON both sides of the border, and Hector wasn't blind to its dangerous potential within his otherwise family-oriented neighborhood. But to have it permeate his *Casa de Dios* congregation was nearly incomprehensible to him.

It was Sunday evening, and the service had been drawing to a close. Hector planned to stay and pray with anyone who wanted to linger, and then lock up and go home to get ready for his trip to San Juan Chamula in the morning. But even as the final notes of the closing worship song hung in the air, gunfire erupted on the street outside, turning worshipful voices to gasps and screams as most of the congregation fell to the floor in an effort to dodge any stray bullets that might penetrate the church walls.

Hector was too stunned to move. Instead he stood, still and silent, facing his terrified, cowering flock and staring at the closed door that led to the street. It never even occurred to him that he should lock that door to prevent an invasion from warring factions that seemingly became more brazen with each passing day. This was a church, a place where people gathered to worship God and fellowship with each other. Never was it meant to be a fortress to protect those within and ban others from joining them. But now, as he realized that his own dear wife and children were among those huddled on the floor, praying for God's protection, Hector was no longer quite so sure.

No. He shook his head. He could not allow fear to manipulate him. He, as well as those gathered together with him, had no reason to fear. They were, according to Romans 8, more than conquerors through Him who loved them. God was their Defender, their Protector. Jesus was their Savior. And nothing, not even death, could separate them from that love.

"Brothers and sisters," Hector called, realizing the gunfire had stopped and sirens were already wailing in the distance, even as he lifted his arms as if offering a benediction, "do not be afraid. All is well. God is with us. Please, let us come together and pray—not only for ourselves, but also for those involved, whether victims or perpetrators. They all need a Savior. They all need the hope that only Jesus can bring."

Soon the thirty-plus people who had gathered for the evening service stood in a circle, hands clasped and eyes closed, as they prayed for God's intervention in whatever had transpired outside their little congregation. They prayed that God would spare anyone who might have been injured, and that He would send the gift of repentance and turn the hearts of everyone involved toward Himself. By the time Hector uttered the final amen, the sound of the sirens had increased until they drew up to the church and then stopped. Hector wondered if he should go outside to offer his assistance, but before he could step to the front door, a light touch on his right arm stopped him. He turned and looked down into the troubled eyes of one of his oldest parishioners, *Señora* Antonia Mesa, referred to by nearly everyone who knew her as *la abuela*, or "the grandmother."

Her dark eyes, nearly hidden behind decades of wrinkles, were sadder and more frightened than Hector had ever seen them. He laid his left hand on hers and smiled. "Are you all right, *Abuela*?"

The woman shook her head, her gray hair covered almost completely by a worn scarf. "No," she whispered. "*Ayúdame*. Help me, Pastor. Pray for me—and for *mi familia*."

Hector frowned, shocked at the depth of frailty he sensed in the woman's trembling hand. He nodded toward some vacant chairs. "*Por favor, señora*, please, let's sit down, and you can tell me what's on your heart. Then we will take it to the One who already knows the answer."

The tiny woman nodded, as a flicker of hope passed over her face. She allowed Hector to help her to a nearby chair, where she sank down in obvious relief.

As he waited for the woman to speak, Hector offered up a silent prayer for wisdom. As so often happened, his sense of inadequacy in such a situation warred with his belief that God would somehow give them the answer they needed to whatever the situation might be.

"It is *mi nieto*," the woman whispered at last. "My grandson, Roberto." Tears squeezed their way from her eyes then, but she ignored them as they trickled down her withered cheeks. "The gangs, they—" She stopped, seemingly unable to continue.

Hector waited, but when the old woman continued to struggle to speak, he said, "Do you mean the gangs are giving him trouble? Are they after him? Are you concerned they might hurt him?"

The ancient *abuela* fixed her eyes on his, and the ache he sensed there filled his heart with a burning pain. "No," she said, her voice as shaky as the hands she held out in supplication. "I am not afraid they will hurt him. I am afraid he will hurt others. He is . . . one of them. Part of the gangs." A sob rose up then, convulsing her body as the flow of tears increased. "A murderer," she cried. "My Roberto is a murderer. The worst of the worst. My fear is not for his life . . . but for his soul."

The groan burst forth from Hector before he could stop it, his tears following right behind. More than once he had

45

counseled families who had lost a loved one to gang warfare, but never had one of his own flock come to him with such a confession, such a grief or agony!

Aye, Dios, he prayed silently. *Ayudame! Ayudame! Help me, Father...*

And with the little *abuela*'s hands clasped in his own, Hector began to pray.

The hot, crowded bus rumbled and ground through occasional gear changes, as it agonized along its way from Tijuana toward Mexico City, where Hector would change buses for the second leg of his journey. If he'd had more money, he could have flown instead, arriving at his destination in a matter of hours, but he also would have had to pay extra for all his cargo. Though he hated spending two days on the road each way, it was his only viable option for getting the Bibles and medicine and other personal items to his mother. And so he sat—along with at least thirty other passengers, most of them humans, but with a couple of chickens and a very loud, obnoxious rooster thrown in—bouncing his way toward Mayan country in Chiapas.

He stared out the window at the passing countryside, but little of the scene registered in his mind. His thoughts were still with the little woman, the *abuelita* who was so concerned about her grandson and the destructive lifestyle he had chosen. Hector tried to imagine how he would feel if one of his own boys got involved in something so hideous, but he just couldn't picture Hector Jr. or Manolo participating in such crime and violence. And yet, had *Abuela* Mesa ever imagined her sweet little grandson turning into a murderer—the "worst of the worst," as she had called him?

Of course not! She had no doubt bounced him on her knee and talked to him of Jesus, teaching him to pray and to love

God with all his heart. How, then, had the once sweet young child turned so far from goodness and truth?

Hector shuddered, shifting in his seat. With his two boxes and one small suitcase piled on the floor at his feet, he couldn't stretch his legs, and the woman in the seat next to him seemed determined to take up all of her seat and as much of his as possible. His overweight seatmate also appeared sleep-deprived, as she had so far spent the majority of the trip snoring loudly and occasionally drooping her head over onto his shoulder. He had long-since given up trying to move it and had decided instead to pray for the woman who reeked of garlic and sweat. It was all part of the crossing-Mexico-on-a-bus experience that Hector had survived more than once.

He had, in fact, brought his mother with him on a similar trip a couple of years earlier, never dreaming she would not return with him. Had he known, he might have put up a bigger fight when she insisted on coming along in the first place. He might even have slipped out during the night and gone without her. But he hadn't, and now his mother had settled into an area that was a throwback to the Mayan culture and even hostile to the Mexican government, so much so that the nearby village of San Juan Chamula had its own independent police force and paid no attention to the country's laws. Those very oddities, coupled with the fact that the superstitious people of San Juan Chamula—who considered themselves Catholics though they continued to practice many of their Mayan religious customs—were less than welcoming to strangers, made for a potentially dangerous living situation for the woman who had so faithfully raised Hector and his eight siblings. And yet, the very essence of Virginia Correo Rodriguez's being established her right to remain where she believed God had called her.

Hector sighed. He accepted that truth about his mother in his mind, but would he ever get to the place where he could accept it in his heart? Seeing her, of course, would help, but leaving her behind yet again would simply add to his pain. If only his father hadn't left them so many years earlier! Surely then his mother would be living safely in her little home in Tijuana, the one that now served as a meeting place for the *Casa de Dios* congregation, growing old with her *esposo* and enjoying the many *nietos* God had given her.

But he did leave, Hector reminded himself. *And now he's dying. Oh Lord, I should be much more concerned about him than about my mother. Her salvation is sure. She walks with You and serves You with every beat of her heart. I have no doubt of her eternal destiny. But my father?* Hector closed his eyes and shook his head. *Oh God, have mercy! Have mercy on him, Lord!...*

Virginia was excited. She had seen her son only twice since she settled into the Camposes' home in Chamula, and she desperately missed him and her other children and grandchildren. But God had blessed her with a surrogate family for however long He had called her to minister near this little Mayan village lost in time; knowing she was right in the middle of God's will for her life made all the rest bearable.

She had awakened long before the sun rose that morning, a song in her heart even before she swung her legs over the side of the cot. Her time with the Lord had been especially sweet, and when the children had come bouncing and squealing from their bedroom, nearly as overjoyed as she that Hector would arrive before day's end, she had found herself nearly too thrilled to eat.

But now breakfast was over, and it would soon be time to walk into the village to the spot in the town square where the bus would deposit her son. It was a walk she always enjoyed, particularly as the midmorning sun warmed her bones and dispelled much of her arthritis pain in the process. It also gave her extra time to commune with the Lord—to thank and praise Him for His goodness to her, and to pray for the precious people of San Juan Chamula who so desperately needed to know her Savior.

And yet, though she had been in the area for nearly two years now, she understood that she was still regarded as an outsider. An occasional smile from a Chamula resident warmed her heart, but they were few and far between. She was much more apt to receive suspicious glances and even hostile glares from the people she so desperately wanted to get to know.

As she entered the block where the centuries-old Catholic church stood—a church that hadn't heard a mass in thirty years and where the statues of Catholic saints had been replaced with those of Mayan gods and goddesses—Virginia felt the warmth of the sun dissipate, as the spiritual darkness that hung over Chamula seemed to seep into her skin. And then she saw her, *la curandera* known as Evita, standing across the street in her multicolored dress and red shawl, the bright colors belying the sinister presence that surrounded the woman. Though Virginia had never spoken directly to her, she sensed the shaman was well aware of her presence in the community. Even now it seemed she was staring at Virginia, sizing her up somehow—and the look that passed between them made the skin on the back of Virginia's neck crawl.

For a moment she thought of crossing the street and introducing herself to the woman who was so highly thought of among the Mayans in San Juan Chamula, but then Virginia heard the familiar screech of grinding gears and a rumbling engine, and she turned her attention to the approaching bus. Hector had come, and all the rest no longer mattered.

Marty was restless.

Chapter 6

HECTOR GROANED AND RUBBED HIS EXTENDED stomach, emphasizing his refusal of yet another plate of food. "No more, Mama," he insisted. "I'm about to explode already!" The four older Campos children, sitting cross-legged around the low-slung table at the center of their gathering, giggled at Hector's protestations.

Virginia frowned. "But you only had two helpings, *mijo*, and after such a long bus ride—"

"I told you, Mama," Hector said, laughing as he interrupted his mother's well-intentioned urgings, "Mariana packed me plenty of food before I left. I didn't go hungry, Mama, not for a minute. I promise!"

Virginia appeared skeptical but accepting of his explanation, and Hector turned his attention to Eldora Campos, who sat beside her husband, while baby Rudolfo slept peacefully in her arms. Hector marveled that the woman was still slim and attractive after bearing five children in such a short time, particularly when she lived in an environment that seemed to age its inhabitants prematurely.

"*Señora* Campos," Hector said, nodding his head in her direction, "the meal was delicious. I so appreciate your hospitality and all the work you put into preparing such a fine meal. Thank you."

Eldora's cheeks flushed in response, and she smiled shyly. Hector had noticed she said little in his presence, leaving the conversation to her husband. Hector also knew this wasn't the type of meal the Campos family enjoyed often, making the offering even more precious.

"Eldora learned how to prepare the armadillo from her mother," Diego offered, speaking up for his wife who appeared too shy to do so herself. "Her family is from Bolivia, where it is quite a specialty."

Hector was well aware of those facts, as the family had explained them to him on his previous visit, when they had also prepared an armadillo feast. But he smiled and nodded, adding, "And a delicious specialty it is. If you would be willing, *Señora* Campos, I would like very much to take the recipe home to *mi esposa*, Mariana, and ask her to prepare it for me."

From the corner of his eye, Hector glimpsed his mother's grin, and he knew she was wondering what Mariana's reaction might be to such a request. Eldora, however, smiled and nodded. "I would be honored to share the recipe with your wife," she said, her voice scarcely above a whisper.

The children were becoming restless by then, though Hector marveled that such young ones had sat still for so long. He pictured his own three in such a situation and knew they would have been pressing to go outside and play long before this.

Fixing his eyes on Diego and Eldora, he said, "I brought the children a small gift. May I take them outside and show it to them?"

The excitement level around the table elevated immediately, though still the children managed to stay in their seats. Hector's brief glance in their direction, however, showed their dark eyes were wide with excitement and expectation.

"That is very kind of you, my friend," Diego said, and then turned to the children. "You may be excused to go outside with Señor Rodriguez, but do not leave his presence to go anywhere else."

Cries of "*Sí*, Papa" and "*Gracias*, Papa" erupted from their lips, as Hector excused himself to grab the package from his overnight satchel, which had already been stashed next to Virginia's cot. The bedroll he had brought with him and placed on the floor beside his mother's bed would be Hector's resting place for the three nights he remained in the San Juan Chamula area.

Leading the way out the door, package in hand, Hector smiled at the squeals of delight that followed him. He imagined the Campos children would soon feel like royalty, with their very own soccer ball to share between them. And it wasn't even flat like the one his own children played with every day.

Marty was restless. He had taken his usual morning walk on the beach, sat at the end of the pier for a couple of hours, and prayed, and still the restless sensation nagged at him, even as he now sat alone at the table by the window, staring out at the rolling breakers and ignoring his half-eaten salad.

The restlessness had been there ever since his encounter with Alberto Javier Rodriguez. The brief visit with Hector's father had cut him to the heart. To see this hardened, pitiful old man lying there in that hospital bed, racked with such obvious pain and guilt and yet still refusing to repent and turn to the only One who could help him, had nearly crushed Marty's heart. Perhaps it was that he had never stopped to consider the toll that a life of selfishness and sin could take on a human being—and the awful fate that awaited such a stiff-necked, unrepentant soul. That the very God of the universe, who owed His rebellious creation nothing, would deign to join them in human form and take upon Himself the punishment that only He did not deserve, and then to have such an unspeakable gift refused by the very ones who had no other hope, was more than Marty's mind could fathom.

And yet he had seen it with his own eyes. Alberto, suffering in his body and tortured in his heart, had pressed his lips together, refusing to pray with Marty, though the young man had nearly fallen to his knees to implore him to do so. The only memory of the visit that encouraged Marty was the fact that the old man had cried. Tears had coursed down his cheeks and his body had convulsed with sobs as Marty prayed for him, but that had been the end of it. Quite obviously Hector's father felt remorse for the choices he had made in his life, but equally obvious was the fact that he refused to truly repent and ask God for forgiveness.

How much longer would the old man wait? Marty wondered. And how much longer would the faithful Father give him to make that turn?

Marty sighed. What a reminder this was that no one is promised tomorrow—or beyond this moment, for that matter. Though Marty had long since repented and made the about-face from following his own way to walking after God's, he still needed to hear from the Lord daily—and especially now that he was seeking clear direction for his life's work. How he looked forward to his time in Tijuana with Hector and his family! The moment Hector contacted him and let him know he was back from visiting his mother, Marty would fire up his El Camino and head south. Meanwhile, he would try again to reach the old man with the hardened, broken heart.

Tossing his napkin onto his plate, he dug out his wallet and headed toward the cashier. Before talking with Alberto about God, he knew he needed to talk to God about Alberto.

The visit had gone so quickly, and now Hector would be leaving in the morning. As Virginia lay in the darkness, knowing her son slept on his mat beside her cot, her heart ached. Though she rejoiced to know she was blooming right where God had planted her, she also longed to get on the bus and go back to Tijuana with her son—back to her other children and her grandchildren and all that was familiar to her. And yet, wasn't her former home now serving as a gathering place for the *Casa de Dios* congregation? If she were to return to Tijuana, she would have to live with one of her children.

That wouldn't be so bad, she thought, smiling at the thought. She knew without asking that any of her brood would gladly open their home to her. God had blessed her with such loving children! And that each one served the Lord was the greatest joy any mother could hope to experience in this life.

She shook her head. No. She must not allow herself to start dreaming about going back to Tijuana—not until God released her to do so. For now, He had placed her right here with the Campos family, and they had welcomed her and made her feel as if she truly were one of them.

"Thank You, Lord," she whispered. "You always provide exactly what we need to fulfill Your purpose and calling."

"Mama?" Hector stirred and then sat up, his outline barely visible in the moonless night. "You are awake?"

Virginia smiled. "*Sí, mijo*. I was just thanking God for His goodness to me. He has blessed me so abundantly."

Hector paused, and when he spoke softly in reply, Virginia detected the catch in his voice. "*Sí*, Mama. You are right, of course."

Virginia sat up on her bed and lowered her feet to the floor, then patted the cot beside her. Her son needed no further coaching to join her. As soon as he settled in next to her, she took his hand, relishing his closeness. "You, my son, are one of my greatest blessings—you and your *hermanos y hermanas*, who so faithfully serve our Lord."

"It is because of you, Mama," Hector whispered, the struggle to control his emotions evident to Virginia. "It was you who set such a good example and led all your children to the Father's heart. How could we not follow?"

Virginia smiled. Could a mother receive a more beautiful benediction? She doubted it, though she questioned that she deserved it.

She swallowed. "I will miss you." She raised his hand to her lips and kissed it. "It is hard to let you go."

"It is harder for me to leave," he answered, "especially knowing you are in a place where the people do not welcome those who believe as we do."

Virginia's heart squeezed. She never wanted to cause her loved ones any fear or concern, and yet she had to obey God above all else. She knew Hector understood that, but she also knew it would not be easy for him to climb on the bus in the morning and leave her behind.

"I will be fine, *mijo*," she said. "God is my Provider and Protector. Look how He has placed me in such a loving family. And now He has provided me with a ministry besides. As I teach reading to my little flock, I am able to read God's Word to them as well." She squeezed Hector's hand as a note of excitement crept into her voice. "And now he has brought two Mayan women to join us. Imix has been coming for a few weeks now, and recently she brought her friend Kawak. Just think, *mijo*. God has opened the door for me to be able to share the words of the Bible with two women who otherwise might never hear them!"

This time it was Hector who squeezed her hand. "Oh, Mama, I'm glad for you. Truly I am! But I am worried too. Be careful, please. I've heard stories about outsiders disappearing in these forests, never to be heard from again."

Virginia chuckled, and she hoped her son hadn't noticed the nervous lilt mixed in. "Aye, *mijo*, I've been here for two years now. Surely I am no longer an outsider to these people. They've all seen me, many times over, and no one has even uttered a word of complaint."

"Not that you know of," Hector said, the fear in his voice breaking through the darkness of the night.

"God knows," Virginia said quickly, wanting to reassure him. "He knows where I am; He knows what others think or say about me; and He knows what He has planned for me tomorrow. So long as I stay in the middle of His plans, I will be in the safest possible place. Am I right, my son?"

Hector's sigh rolled through her heart as she waited for his reply. "Yes," he said at last. "You are right, Mama. Truly you are."

Virginia smiled. "Then let's spend some time together, praying and praising the One who holds our life in His hands."

After only a brief hesitation, she heard her son's voice. "Father," he murmured, "thank You for Your goodness to us. Thank You for Your love. And thank You for Your perfect plan for our lives...whatever it may bring."

Despite the morning sun, she shivered, pulling her serape more tightly around her shoulders.

Chapter 7

WAITING FOR THE BUS TO PULL AWAY WAS THE hardest part of saying good-bye to her son. After their time of prayer together the previous night, Hector had returned to his mat on the floor and, judging by his light snoring, had fallen asleep almost immediately. Virginia, however, had continued to stare at a ceiling she could not see, talking to the God she could not touch but whom she knew without question was there with her. *Protect him, Father*, she had prayed silently, more than once during those long hours. *Take him home to his precious family safely. And thank You, Lord, for allowing me to spend time with him again.*

Now the all too brief visit had come to an end. She had risen earlier than usual, after little more than an hour or two of restless sleep, and lovingly prepared fresh corn tortillas and wrapped them around the last of the armadillo meat so her beloved Hector would have a healthy meal to take with him on the bus. She knew the ride home would be difficult for him, as he had made no secret of the fact that he wished she were coming with him. But he also understood why she could not. And she understood that he must return to his wife and children, as well as to his congregation. But knowing all these things didn't make the pain any easier to bear.

They had walked arm-in-arm in the early morning sun, making their way from the shack Virginia now called home to the town square where the bus would once again become Hector's rolling abode for the next two days. They spoke of family members, the everyday joys and sorrows of life, and even the weather as they strolled to their destination. And of course Virginia had thanked him yet again for the box of ten Bibles he had brought to her to disperse as God gave her opportunity. But all too soon they were standing in front of the bus, and it was time for Virginia to bestow a final kiss upon the son of her heart, and then place him once again in the faithful hands of God.

Her eyes had strained to see every final movement as he climbed aboard the bus and found a seat by the window, where he could wave to her one last time. Then the bus had rumbled to life, belching smoke from its tailpipe as the familiar grinding of the gears signaled her son's departure. Virginia raised her hand to return Hector's wave, the heaviness of her arm nearly equaling the lead weight in her heart.

And then he was gone. The waiting was over at last, and she could return to her life with the Campos family. She knew that in a few days the pain would lessen and she would smile again. But for now, she could only turn away from the vanishing bus and begin the lonely trek homeward.

Trudging along the roadway, the thought came to her that she was getting old and that her life on earth would soon be over. She was surprised at the comfort that realization brought to her, though it was tempered by the darkness she sensed in the atmosphere of the otherwise quaint village of San Juan Chamula. Despite the morning sun, she shivered, pulling her *serape* more tightly around her shoulders and quickening her pace as she continued on, humming a praise song as she walked.

Evita had risen early and spent her time communing with those who lived in another realm. The incense and candles were still burning when she felt the need to go outside and walk to the town square. As a shaman, she had long since learned to obey such urges, and so she had slipped out and made her way nearly unseen in the early morning light. Taking a seat on an old crate at the edge of an alley, she had waited patiently until she saw the old woman and her son walking toward the bus.

Her eyes had narrowed and her heart beat faster as they approached and then passed by within a few feet of her. Though they smiled at one another as they spoke, the sadness that hung over them was nearly palpable, and Evita quickly recognized the sorrow of parting, for she, too, had experienced it many times.

When at last the young man had boarded the bus and the vehicle had rumbled out of sight, Evita watched yet again as the old woman who lived with the Campos family began her journey back home. Her shoulders seemed more hunched than usual, and Evita knew how the heaviness of a heart could pull the shoulders forward. Still, she felt no sympathy for her. After all, the woman was a stranger, an interloper who had no business in San Juan Chamula. She had come uninvited and was now stirring up trouble with her talk of *los conquistadores* who had long ago invaded and disrupted the life of Evita's ancestors. *La curandera* knew it was now up to her to end this disruption and to stop the poisoning of the minds and the stealing of the hearts of the Mayan young people.

Sensing she had been released from her assignment, she abandoned her post and returned to her house to seek those who would guide her next actions and give her strength to carry them through.

Hector was usually a very patient man, but the last two days had seemed interminable. At last he could see the outline of the building where the bus would stop and his journey would end—and his reunion with his wife and children would begin. Though he had suffered great pangs of regret and concern over leaving his mother behind in San Juan Chamula, he knew deep down it was where God wanted her—and where she wanted to be. And so, as the worn tires had continued to turn and to bring him closer to home, his heart had turned as well—from the pain of leaving his mother to the anticipation of returning to his family.

The squealing brakes announced their arrival, even as Hector stood to his feet and stretched the muscles in his cramped body. Though the aisle seat next to him was empty, he still had to wait, as passengers woke their dozing companions and gathered their belongings, jostling for position until the driver finally opened the front door.

Moving slowly with the line of exiting travelers, Hector's anticipation mounted. He could see Mariana and the children standing just a few feet away from the front of the bus, peering anxiously at the stream of exhausted but relieved humanity pouring out of the vehicle. The closer Hector got to the door, the fresher the air that infiltrated the stuffy bus, dissipating the rancid smell of sweat and smoke.

At last he was down the steps, and the welcoming squeals of his children washed over him like refreshing waters. But before he could scoop them up and into his arms, Mariana nearly knocked him down in her rush to greet him. Kissing her first and reveling in the warmth of her embrace, he then turned to the three bouncing children who surrounded their parents. In an instant he had Lupita in one arm and his other arm around Mariana's waist, while Manolo and Hector Jr. followed behind, all of them chattering and carrying on as if he had been gone for months rather than days.

Hector's heart swelled with joy and gratitude as they walked the six blocks to their home. And how good that home looked! As humble as it was, the unpainted little house resembled a mansion compared to the hovel where his mother now lived, so many miles away.

His heart squeezed at the thought, but he shoved it away and refocused on the laughter and conversation that circulated around him. He was home with his family where he belonged, and nothing could steal the happiness that flooded every corner of his being. He was indeed a wealthy and blessed man.

Marty was excited. Just two more days and he would be heading south to the Rodriguez home. Though he wasn't sure what he expected to discover while he was there, he sensed it would be meaningful—life-changing even—and he was anxious to get started.

He had tied together most of his loose ends in San Diego, quitting his job and even giving up his apartment and putting his belongings into storage. He was down to a bedroll, a television, and an ice chest, and the emptiness of his apartment nearly echoed with every step he took.

Marty smiled. There was something freeing about living simply and traveling light that he really enjoyed. What would it be like to live such a simple life all the time, free of the encumbrances of modern conveniences and material possessions? He supposed he wouldn't find out until his time on earth ended, but it was nice to imagine.

He locked the front door behind him and headed down the stairs two at a time, determined to make at least one more stop at the hospice to visit Hector's father before he bade a temporary farewell to San Diego and relocated for an indeterminate time south of the border. But first he would head to his favorite beach restaurant and treat himself to a couple of the best fish tacos east of Maui.

Saturday had been one of Alberto's good days, if indeed there was such a thing at this stage of his life. At least the pain hadn't been as excruciating as the day before, and for that he was grateful. The downside, of course, was that it provided him with more clarity and lucid moments to think—and thinking was his enemy. No matter how hard he tried to focus on the good memories, his rebellious mind and tortured conscience always returned to the selfish choices he had made that had ultimately ruined his life—and the lives of those he loved.

Virginia and the children topped that list, but hadn't he also loved Miranda? Miranda with the sea-green eyes and the wild red hair that blew in the breeze and smelled of perfume and roses... Oh, she had been so beautiful and exciting, so alluring and tantalizing—everything Alberto's life had long since ceased to be. And she had invaded his dreary existence at the most vulnerable moment imaginable, right after a fight with Virginia when he had stormed out of the house, trying to drown out the demands of an emotional wife and nine rambunctious children. He had been nearly running down the street in his effort to escape, cursing his life and bemoaning his troubles, when he looked up and saw her for the very first time, standing not five feet from him, her pale pink dress blowing in the breeze, right along with her long, copper-colored curls. When she turned her emerald eyes on him and smiled, he knew he didn't have a chance. And then he discovered she was vacationing at the resort where he worked. It seemed too good to be true.

He told himself he would end it—soon—before Virginia or anyone else found out. But each time he tried, the memory of the way he felt when he was with her, as if he'd suddenly had twenty years restored to his life and hope coursed through his veins, he slipped further and further from his commitment to his family. When at last Miranda begged him to come away with her, to live with her in San Diego and enjoy the "good life" she could provide with the money her father had left her, he followed her like a sheep to the slaughter, only to be discarded a few years later when she met someone younger.

No, he thought. *I didn't love her. Not really. And she certainly didn't love me. But she made me feel so alive, so...young again.* A shudder passed over him at the absurdity of it. *Now look at me. A foolish old man, sick and dying and all alone—just as I deserve.* When the hot tears pricked the back of his eyelids, he didn't even try to hold them back. What did it matter? Even his miserable days in this lonely hospice room would soon be over. And then what?

He shuddered again at the unspoken answer.

Surely this was as bad as pain could get . . .
wasn't it?

Chapter 8

SUNDAY EVENING HAD ALWAYS BEEN MARTY'S favorite time to attend church, ever since he'd become a believer and started going with friends. He knew a lot of churches had discontinued the Sunday evening services, but he was glad the congregation that had become his church family while he lived in San Diego was not one of them.

As the final worship song drew to a close, Marty lingered, knowing this would be his last time at this church for a while. He had no idea where his time in Tijuana with Hector and his family would lead him, but he trusted that God would give him clear direction while he was there. The very thought of it sent a surge of excitement up his spine and set his stomach to churning. Would God lead him to serve in Mexico? Would He send him back here to the States? Or would Marty find himself flying off to some remote corner of the world where he knew nothing of the culture or the language? Whatever God's assignment for his future, Marty knew it would be right. It would be the place he would find fulfillment of purpose and abundant joy, regardless of the challenges or hardships it might also contain.

The voice at his side jerked him back to the present, and he turned, surprised to be reminded of his surroundings. People were filing out of the sanctuary, streaming toward the back doors, and Marty hadn't even realized the service had been dismissed. Quite obviously it had, since the pastor was the one standing at Marty's elbow, drawing his attention back from his daydreams.

Marty smiled. "I'm sorry, Pastor. I guess my mind was wandering."

Pastor Rick returned his smile. "No need to apologize. I do that a lot myself. I just thought we might take a few moments to talk a bit and pray together. I know you said you'd be leaving soon."

Marty nodded. "Tomorrow. I put everything in storage yesterday, and I'm packed and ready to go. I'll be staying with my friends, the Rodriguezes, down in Tijuana for a while."

"The family you stayed with when you were down there on short-term mission trips in the summer, right?"

Marty nodded again. "Yeah. Great people. Like a second family to me." He smirked. "A first family, actually. I have no brothers or sisters, my dad died when I was a baby, and Mom is…well, she's Mom. Her social life and her friends are everything to her, and since Dad left her with plenty of insurance money and a trust fund, she never had to work. So…" He shrugged. "Sorry. I didn't mean to ramble. I just meant that the Rodriguezes have pretty much become my family, especially since they're such committed believers, and when I talk and pray with them, they understand."

"What a great gift," Pastor Rick commented. "I can't imagine not growing up in a Christian household. I was really blessed to have that situation when I was young. But the Bible does say that God places the solitary in families, and it sounds as if that's what He's done for you with the Rodriguezes."

Marty smiled. It was good to know his pastor understood. "They're going to be a big help to me in seeking God for clear direction for my life now that I've graduated."

"They certainly will," the pastor said. "In fact, why don't we agree together in prayer for that very thing?"

Sitting down side-by-side on the pew, Marty and his pastor joined hands and began to pray, as Marty's feelings of excitement became tempered with a strong sense of peace.

Monday unfolded in a haze of gray, as a steady mist dripped down the outside of the hospice windows. The pain had come roaring back, as if trying to reclaim the few hours of respite Alberto had experienced the day before. Even breathing hurt, and he wondered how much worse it could actually be once he died. Surely this was as bad as pain could get...wasn't it?

If only Hector would come again before it was too late. Though it was difficult to admit, even to himself, what Alberto really wanted was to see Virginia one more time. That was impossible, he knew, particularly now that she was living in some primitive Mayan village where outsiders were unwelcome except to deposit their tourist dollars and then leave. Somehow he could picture her there, though he knew she was much older now than when he'd last seen her. In his tortured mind, her dark hair had no streaks of gray, and her brown eyes were still wide and clear. The softness of her skin called to him, drawing him back to his youth and to the dream-filled beginnings of their life together.

His memories were interrupted by a voice, and Alberto frowned. He did not want to leave his daydreams behind, not today when those dreams had been of more pleasant times. He didn't mind being interrupted when he was in the middle of being tortured by his past mistakes or his present misery, but his visions of Virginia had been so soothing.

With great effort he opened his eyes and did his best to focus on the nice-looking blond man who stood beside his bed. Why did he look familiar? He had seen him before, but where? When?

Kathi Macias

Then he remembered. Of course. The young *gringo* who claimed to be a friend of Hector's—who, in fact, had recently told him he was going to visit Hector and his family in Tijuana. How long ago had it been since the boy was here and told him that? A day? A week? A month? Time was without measure to Alberto, except that it dragged interminably when he was in pain and flew too fast when he thought of his ultimate destination.

"Hello, *Señor* Rodriguez," the *gringo* said. "How are you doing today?"

How am I doing? Alberto thought, believing he was speaking. *I'm dying. Can't you see that?* He realized then that he hadn't spoken after all, and he decided that was a good thing. Instead he just nodded and waited. After all, he owed the young man nothing. He hadn't invited him to come.

After a moment the visitor cleared his throat and tried again. "I...wanted to stop in and say good-bye before I leave for Tijuana. I'm on my way there now. I thought you might have a message for Hector and his family."

A message for Hector? *Sí*, Alberto thought. *Yes, please tell my son to come and see me while there's time.* But he clamped his lips shut and said nothing.

Again, after a pause, the young man said, "I'm sorry if I've come at a bad time, sir. I'll leave now so you can get some rest. But first...may I pray with you?"

No! Alberto wanted to scream, but though his mind cried no, his heart longed to say yes. Oh, if only there were hope for him that God would listen, that He would answer...

But no, it was too late. Wasn't it?

If it wouldn't have hurt so much, he would have sighed in resignation. *Let the boy pray*, he told himself. After all, what could it hurt? If talking to an invisible God made Hector's friend feel better, so be it. And then, when he was gone, Alberto could return to his dreams of Virginia and their early days together. It was all he had left.

70

Hector had gone to Jorge's shoe repair shop to help out for a few hours, and Mariana was busy preparing for Marty's arrival. The boys were in school, and Lupita was helping her mama, sweeping with a broom that was at least a foot taller than she. But the little girl loved her *Tio* Marty and was nearly as excited about his arrival as was Mariana. The two Rodriguez ladies had already baked a chocolate cake, which was now cooling while they finished straightening up. Mariana knew they would just have time to finish the cleaning and frost the cake before their guest arrived.

The knock at the front door stopped her in her tracks, dust rag in hand. Surely that couldn't be Marty already! He wasn't due for a couple of hours yet.

Glancing at Lupita, who had dropped her broom at the sound of the knock and now stood, eyes wide and sparkling at the possibility of Marty's early arrival, Mariana hurried to welcome her guest, with Lupita scarcely a step behind her. When Mariana pulled the door open, she breathed a sigh of relief to see her beautiful young sister standing on the stoop.

"Since when do you knock?" Mariana asked, ushering her inside and closing the door behind her. "Are we no longer family?"

Susana's cheeks flushed pink, and her eyes turned downward. "I...thought you might have company," she stammered. "I didn't want to interrupt."

Mariana smiled. So that was it! Her little sister was here to greet Marty. Mariana's suspicions about Susana's feelings for the handsome young *gringo* were right!

"So," Mariana said, talking over Lupita, who had grabbed her *tia*'s hand and chattered excitedly as she led her into the kitchen, "you came to help us prepare for our guest. We welcome the help, *mi hermana*."

"We made *Tio* Marty a cake," Lupita announced.

"So I see," Susana answered, glancing at the chocolate offering that sat in the middle of the table. "It's beautiful."

"Do you want to help?" Lupita asked. "Mama won't let me frost the cake by myself, but I can do it if you help me."

Susana laughed, and the sound of it reminded Mariana of starlight on a clear night.

"I would be happy to help you," Susana said, glancing at Mariana questioningly. "If that's all right with you, *hermana*."

"Of course it is." Mariana retrieved a large bowl from the cupboard. "Here, you can use this. You know where everything else is. Help yourselves. I'm going to go finish dusting in the other room."

Humming to herself to keep from giggling with delight, Mariana exited the kitchen with her trusty dust rag in hand. Hector was always warning her not to get involved in matchmaking, but it was so obvious that Susana and Marty would be perfect for each other.

And then he saw Susana.

Chapter 9

MARTY'S EL CAMINO RUMBLED TO A STOP IN FRONT of the Rodriguez house, and he scarcely had time to turn off the engine before the front door burst open and children exploded out into the yard, whooping and grinning in welcome. No wonder he so enjoyed coming here! There was never any doubt that his hosts were happy to see him.

As Hector Jr. yanked open the door on the driver's side and Manolo and Lupita argued over who would open the passenger door, Marty did a quick comparison of welcomes between this one and those he received when he drove to the Bay Area to visit his mom. There he was always greeted by a perfectly manicured lawn, trimmed shrubs and blooming flowers, and an immaculate room set up just for him. But often it would be hours before his mother returned home from her current social event or cause of choice, leaving Marty to spend the first portion of his visit virtually alone. Of course, the house keeper was always lurking nearby, ready to meet any need he might have, but he still felt like an intruder and found himself looking forward to leaving and wondering why he had bothered to come at all.

It was never that way when he headed south of the border to *"Casa Rodriguez,"* and today was no exception. By now all three children had gathered on the driver's side of his car and were bouncing up and down and chattering at him in Spanish, with words and phrases that swirled around him like an excitable gathering of honeybees. Marty's Spanish was more than passable, but he preferred it at normal speed and one person at a time.

Unfolding himself from the front seat, he stood and gathered all three Rodriguez children into a crowded embrace, glad he had remembered to stop and buy them gifts before crossing the border. But before he could retrieve the bag of presents from behind the seat of his vehicle, Hector and Mariana had joined the welcoming committee and were quickly pulling him toward the house.

Marty's heart was light as he found himself surrounded by laughter and love and complete acceptance. Even if he was having trouble sorting through everyone's talking to him at once, he sensed he had come home. The burdens of school and work, of maintaining an almost one-sided relationship with his mother, and even of wondering where God would send him next seemed to lift from his shoulders, as he reveled in being connected to people who cared.

And then he saw Susana, standing off to herself and watching all the gaiety. When their eyes met, she quickly dropped hers and Marty was sure he saw color rise to her cheeks. *Funny*, he thought. *I never realized how really attractive Mariana's sister is—until now. When did she stop being a teenager and turn into a young woman?*

He waited for her to look back at him so he could smile in welcome, but instead she turned and hurried into the kitchen. Had he offended her in some way? Embarrassed her, perhaps?

Marty hoped he would have a chance to find out very soon—and to make it right if possible. Meanwhile, he was just relieved to be with people who loved him and who shared his passion to serve God. What else mattered? Nothing, he thought, smiling to himself and clicking off his cell phone. It was certain he wouldn't need it anytime soon, so why even keep it on?

The spiritual darkness of San Juan Chamula seemed to deepen daily. At least it was more pronounced to Virginia, even when her little group met at the Camposes' home for their weekly study. Imix and Kawak continued to attend, and Virginia was concerned that Kawak never spoke or contributed to the lessons in any way except to intimidate Imix simply by her presence. Before Kawak had started coming to the group, Imix had seemed more relaxed and interested, if not talkative, but now it appeared she was following the lead of her sullen companion.

Eldora Campos had commented on the situation as well, so Virginia knew it wasn't just her imagination. Throughout the lesson today she had tried to be especially attentive to her two Mayan guests, smiling warmly each time she caught them looking at her, but her gestures had evoked no response, leaving Virginia to wonder why the two women even bothered to continue attending.

Perhaps it is just to keep them in my thoughts so I can pray for them, she deduced. *And so I shall.*

When the group left that afternoon, Virginia took her Bible and retreated to a quiet spot behind the house where she often went to find a few peaceful moments during the day. Sitting on her *serape* beneath the trees, she began to pray in earnest for the two young women who seemed so closed to learning anything she might have to teach them. But the clouds that soon drew across the sun overhead caused her to shiver, and she pulled the *serape* from beneath her and wrapped it tightly around her shoulders as she continued to pray.

The voices of the Campos children, playing in the yard in front of the house, eventually drifted all the way around to Virginia's quiet place, and she smiled. It was time to go back inside and prepare dinner. She would stop on her pathway toward the house to check the small garden where the family grew most of its food. Whatever offerings she found there would serve as the primary ingredients of their evening meal.

Thank You, Father, Virginia prayed, *for providing for me so bountifully—even here where the people are so poor, and yet they willingly share whatever they have. I am so grateful, Lord!*

Once again removing her *serape*, she used it to carry the vegetables into the house, stopping long enough to speak to the children before going inside. By the time she stood in the tiny kitchen area of the home, ready to begin the meal preparations, she was humming a praise song, overwhelmed with the joy of knowing that she was serving God exactly where and how He had purposed for her to do. And here, in this godly little abode she now called home, the light of God's love dispelled any darkness that might have lingered earlier in the day.

Marty was sure he would never be hungry again—not if he lived to be 100! Mariana had stuffed him with her delicious *arroz con pollo* until he felt as if his stomach would explode with the chicken and rice meal, and then—much to the delight of the three Rodriguez children, who had obviously been waiting for this very special dessert—she had placed right in front of him the most tempting double-layer chocolate cake Marty had ever seen. How could he possibly consider eating even a bite? And yet he had—several, in fact—and now he wondered how he would ever find the strength or energy to get up from the table. He might just have to sleep right where he sat!

The children had been excused to go play with their new toys—the small race car set Marty had presented to Hector Jr. and Manolo, and the baby doll that cried and was now absorbing Lupita's motherly interest. The four adults were at last alone at the kitchen table, with the intriguing Susana sitting directly across from Marty. He just wished she didn't have that annoying habit of looking down at her plate each time he glanced across the table at her. He knew her eyes were beautiful, and he would enjoy having the chance to gaze into them for a few seconds.

But just when he thought he would finally have the chance, now that the children had taken their giggles and chatter to the next room, Susana quickly rose from her seat and busied herself with clearing the table.

"*Hermana*, you don't have to do that," Mariana protested. "Come, sit with us and visit with our guest. We can do the cleanup together in a little while."

Marty watched the color rise in Susana's cheeks once again, but still her eyes remained downcast, even as she obediently returned to the table. It was obvious that getting this girl's attention was going to be more difficult than Marty had realized. But why did it matter? Why was he even trying? At a time in his life when all he wanted was to hear from God about his next direction in ministry, he certainly shouldn't be concerned with this young woman named Susana, no matter how lovely and sweet she might be.

Help me, Lord, to stay focused on You, he prayed. *Susana is a beautiful girl, and I know she loves You, but...I also know I have no business even thinking about her. Not now, anyway.*

And then he reminded himself that God could do anything—which was needful to remember at the moment, since Marty couldn't help but consider how difficult it would be to avoid seeing someone who was so closely related to his gracious hosts. He realized, too, that his restful time at the Rodriguez home had already become much more complicated than he had anticipated.

Virginia was exhausted when she finally fell into bed that night. It had been a lovely evening, with the family sitting together and visiting with one another over their simple meal. And, as always, they had included Virginia as if she had been one of them from the very beginning.

But now, at last, the chores of the day were completed, and the Campos family had retired to their tiny rooms. As much as she loved these dear people, Virginia also relished the night hours, when she had the slightly larger main room of the house to herself. Lying on her back on the cot, she stared at the ceiling, the sliver of moonlight from the one small window over her bed enabling her to identify shapes and outlines in the familiar house. Though still missing Hector, as well as the rest of her family, she sighed contentedly, appreciative of the full day she had experienced. Her life was truly blessed, despite—

An image of Alberto rose unbidden in her mind, interrupting her musings and grabbing her full attention as she considered the update on his condition that she had received from Hector during his visit. It grieved her to know the man who had been her *esposo* now lay dying in a faraway place where she could not go to comfort him. But she could pray for him right where she was, and God was able to reach anyone, anywhere, anytime. For that she was grateful, as she began to intercede for the man who had once shared her life and who still held such a big part of her heart.

Nearly an hour later, she was at peace, sensing God had heard and would answer—in His way and in His time. She had been obedient to do her part, but only God could do the rest.

She was just drifting off when she heard it—a nearly indistinguishable but sharp crackling noise from somewhere outside, as if someone had stepped on a branch or a twig. That in itself was not unusual, as stray dogs occasionally roamed the area at night, scrounging for scraps of food. But something about the noise and the jolt of alarm it sent up Virginia's spine as she was yanked back from her near-sleep condition convinced her that the sound had not been made by one of the neighborhood dogs. She didn't have to look outside to know that someone was there, watching and waiting. For what? She had no idea, but she sensed it had to do with her.

Once again she closed her eyes and began to commune with her Father, asking for wisdom and protection for herself and the Campos family—and for salvation and deliverance for whomever might be lurking outside the walls of their little home in the shadows of San Juan Chamula.

She was on her knees in her little room off the kitchen when she heard Roberto arrive.

Chapter 10

LA ABUELA'S STEPS HAD GROWN SLOWER AND heavier through the years, but never more so than when she'd learned of her grandson's involvement in a gang. Her first reaction was that Roberto was a victim, lured or forced to participate in such unspeakable and violent acts. In the beginning she had tried talking with him, and though he was always respectful of her, it was obvious he didn't take her words to heart. It had taken nearly a year for *Señora* Antonia Mesa to accept the unacceptable—that her beloved *nieto* was indeed a criminal without shame or remorse—and to finally commit herself to ongoing intercession for his salvation and deliverance. If that meant he would be arrested and even spend the rest of his life in prison, so be it. She could not bear the thought of his continuing his life of crime—or the people who might be destroyed in the process.

The hardest times were when Roberto came to see the family. Antonia had lived with Roberto's parents for many years now, and though she tried not to play favorites with her grandchildren, young Roberto had been a daily part of her life from the time he was born. When she remembered the sweet little boy who used to play at her feet and sit on her lap, it was all she could do not to weep at the image of what he had become. Yet she knew that God loved Roberto even more than she. And where she was powerless to change her *nieto*'s heart, God was not.

She was on her knees in her little room off the kitchen when she heard Roberto arrive. Antonia's daughter and son-in-law were not home, so her *nieto* let himself in. The sound of voices told the *abuela* that he had not come alone. Though she tried to tune them out and remain in prayer, it was impossible not to hear their words as the voices continued.

"Here, have something to eat," Roberto said, as Antonia heard the refrigerator door open and close. "And tell me what we're going to do about the little one who saw us on Saturday."

The answer was somewhat muffled at first, indicating that the speaker was talking through a mouthful of food. Antonia could almost picture him shrug as he spoke. "What is there to do? You know we can't leave any witnesses. No loose ends, *verdad*? Am I right?"

"True," Roberto agreed, the accompanying scraping noise telling *la abuela* that he had pulled out a chair and joined his companion at the table. "But how do we do it? She is almost always with her family. We might have to take all of them out."

"So we do it. What does it matter? What I don't understand is why she had to pick that one night to be hiding outside, watching. Everyone else was in the house where they belonged."

"It happens," Roberto said. "We plan things the best we can, but sometimes..." He paused, and Antonia's heart raced at what he might say next. "Sometimes there are just loose ends. And we have to cut them off, like you said. And the sooner, the better."

The little *abuela* could stand it no longer. Rising stiffly to her feet, she shuffled to her bedroom door and pulled it open. Though her heart ached at the words she had overheard, she knew her eyes were blazing.

"Roberto," she exclaimed, glaring at the boy who used to bring her flowers from the garden, "shame on you! What have you done? And what are you now planning to do because of it? May God have mercy on you both!"

The look of shock on the young men's faces was quickly replaced by anger and resentment. "We didn't know you were here, *Abuela*," Roberto said quickly, rising from his chair.

"Obviously," Antonia answered, her eyes narrowing as she shifted her glance from one to the other. Was it possible these two young men, eating tortillas and cheese at the kitchen table, were murderers? How could it be?

"So you...heard us?" Roberto asked, taking a step closer to Antonia.

"Of course I heard you," she answered, her indignation overshadowing any sense of danger. "I may be a *vieja*, an old woman, but I am not deaf!"

The look of distress on Roberto's face passed quickly, and he turned back, exchanging glances with his companion. When he refocused on Antonia, his face had softened. "Go back to your room, *Abuela. Por favor.* Please. And stay there."

"You know what we have to do." The hard, icy words came from the young man sitting at the table, and for the first time Antonia felt a chill of fear pass over her. Surely her own *nieto* would not—

Before she could finish the thought, Roberto came toward her and gently but firmly pushed her back into her room. "Stay there," he repeated. "I will come and talk with you later."

Eyes wide, the little *abuela* watched her *nieto* pull the door shut, leaving her standing alone on the inside. What would happen next? Was her life here on earth to end that very day; would she go to be with the Father before another sunset passed over their home—and at the hands of her own flesh and blood?

If so, she decided, she would do so on her knees, interceding for Roberto and his cohort. And so she turned back toward her bed, determined to pray—even to her last breath—not only for the two young men in the other room, but also for all the "loose ends" they planned to cut off.

The weather was cool and the beach less crowded than usual, though the tourists still strolled the quaint village of Puerto Nuevo, searching for the best lobster meal or the perfect souvenir to take back to the States. And there were plenty of both to choose from in this Mexican town known for its scores of restaurants, all serving the same specialty. It was nearly unheard of to go inside one of these eateries and order anything other than "lobster, Puerto Nuevo style," with sides of beans, rice, and flour tortillas. Hector and Marty would indulge soon enough; for now they were content to walk the softly packed sands and watch the waves roll in under the gray fog that had settled over the area.

"What do you think?" Marty asked. "About the mission field, I mean. I know common sense—not to mention my mother—cautions me about heading for any far-flung areas right now. After all, there are plenty of relatively peaceful and safe places full of people needing ministry and teaching, so it isn't like I have to travel thousands of miles to find a need. But you know I can't just pick a place based on expediency or safety. I have to know beyond a doubt where God is calling me—and then go there, regardless of the price or the risk."

When Hector didn't answer right away, Marty turned his head slightly to the right, catching the pensive look on his friend's face. Obviously he was thinking and praying about his answer, so Marty would be patient. That was one of the things he loved about being in Mexico with the Rodriguez family. No one seemed to be in a hurry. They had time to enjoy life, to cultivate relationships. Just an hour north everyone rushed at breakneck speed to make it to the next appointment, cram in one more meeting, or cross off one more item on their to-do list, all so they could collapse into bed at the end of the day, grab a few hours of sleep, and then jump up in the morning to start all over again.

Marty sighed. He needed this time to rejuvenate, to reflect and refocus on what was really important. Even walking the beach here was different than it was in San Diego, though the skateboarders and surfers had invaded many of the havens south of the border as well.

And the tourists! Always there were tourists—everywhere, it seemed. Even on this cool and slightly damp afternoon, the visitors prowled the towns of Tijuana and Puerto Nuevo and Ensenada, searching for bargains or entertainment—or even illegal activities. And most of the time, there was no shortage of each. Marty sometimes wondered if he needed to go deeper into Mexico to experience the real feel of the country.

No, he reminded himself. He was right where he needed to be, at least for now. And he was grateful for that. Even as three shirtless teenaged boys raced by, kicking up sand as they tried in vain to get their kite aloft in the windless sky, Marty smiled. It hadn't been that long since he was that age, racing toward adulthood and waiting for a good updraft to give him a lift.

"I understand exactly what you're saying," Hector said, pulling Marty back to the present. "When God spoke to my heart to start the little church of *Casa de Dios* in my mother's house, it made no sense to me. There were several bigger churches within a few blocks, and what did I know about being a pastor? But the more I prayed and waited on God, the more I knew I would be disobedient if I didn't follow through."

He flashed a smile at Marty before returning his gaze to the sand in front of him. Without missing a step, he said, "It was the same when I sensed God calling me to bring Bibles to Chiapas State—to San Juan Chamula, to be exact. I knew, being an *evangelico*, I wouldn't be welcomed there, but when I stepped out in faith and took that first bus ride to Chamula, God opened every door. He put me in touch with the Campos family right away, and they took me into their home and allowed me to stay there for several days. Their house became my base of operation when I was there, and soon we met a few other families who, like the Camposes, had long prayed for Bibles and other Christian literature, even though most of them don't read very well. The true believers are so few in the area, and yet they are so faithful."

He paused, and again Marty waited, knowing Hector would continue when he was ready. Finally he spoke again, this time with a slight catch in his voice. "I had no idea that my mother would also feel the call to go to San Juan Chamula, but she insisted, so I took her with me. She never returned. As you know, she lives with the Campos family to this day, ministering to her little flock as a teacher, using the Bible as her primer." He shook his head. "It's an amazing thing to think that my elderly mother is off living in such precarious conditions when—in the natural, anyway—she should be growing old with her husband by her side and her grandchildren in her lap, right there in Tijuana, in the house where we were raised. But God had other plans. And that"—he interrupted himself, swallowing before speaking again—"that's what makes it so hard. I know she has to do what God has called her to do, just as you and I have to. But she's my mother, and she's in an extremely dangerous place. It is very, very difficult to leave her there."

Marty nodded. He could only imagine how Hector must feel about his mother being in such a distant and, in many ways, a primitive location, where Bible-believing Christians who practiced the faith taught in the Scriptures were not welcomed. What he could not imagine was the joy of having a mother whose commitment to serve God was the most important thing in her life. How he would gladly trade all the comforts and possessions his mother enjoyed to see her living her life for Christ! Much better to have a loved one in physical danger than spiritual, he reasoned.

Hector clapped him on the back then, and Marty started. "Sorry," Hector said, grinning. "I didn't mean to get off track. I should be helping you find your own answer, not giving you mine or my mother's."

Marty returned the smile. "You didn't get off track at all, my friend. You told me exactly what I needed to hear. You confirmed that we cannot allow situations or circumstances to dictate how or where we live our lives. We must determine to hear from God—and then obey whatever He speaks to us."

Hector's eyes shone with understanding. "A message we all need to be reminded of—often. If we would remember and follow that great truth, we really wouldn't need to know much else, would we?"

"Absolutely," Marty agreed, and then turned his gaze from Hector to the row of restaurants and shops behind them, nodding his head in their direction. "And now that we've been reminded of that basic fact, are you ready to let me buy you some *longasta*?" He rolled his eyes and smiled, remembering how only the evening before he had thought he would never want to eat again. Apparently he had been wrong. "I've been dreaming about Puerto Nuevo lobster for weeks now," he confessed. "I couldn't wait to get here and have some with you."

Hector laughed. "*Longasta* is a treat I will never turn down. Come, my friend, I know the best place in town. The *turistas* haven't discovered it yet."

Roberto stood in front of his house, leaning against his car and watching the sun sink below the horizon. He was angry. He was also scared, but he would never admit it. Why hadn't he realized his *abuela* would be in her room and that she would hear them? Just because his parents weren't at home didn't necessarily mean the house was empty. When would he learn to think before opening his mouth? Now he had a problem—a serious problem. He had sworn to cut off any loose ends, and now his *abuela* had become one of them. He knew what he was expected—even sworn—to do, but how could he? Strangers were easy; they meant nothing to him. True, the first time he had killed a man who was looking directly into his eyes and begging for his life, Roberto struggled. But he did what he had to do, just as he had the first time he'd had to kill a woman.

Now he was faced with taking out a witness who couldn't be older than nine or ten—and his *abuela*, a member of his own family. He wasn't sure if he could do it.

The child was bad enough. She had been outside when she shouldn't have been—at night when kids her age were supposed to be sleeping. But she had seen Roberto and Paco murder that cowardly snitch, and Roberto wasn't about to end up in prison because a little girl saw something awful and decided to tell.

But his *abuela*? Someone in his own *familia*? Paco had urged Roberto to take her out right then, as soon as they'd realized she overheard them. But Roberto had stalled until his parents returned, and he managed to buy his *abuela* at least another day. Now Paco was pushing him, telling Roberto that if he wasn't tough enough to do what had to be done, then he would. Roberto didn't doubt for a moment that his cold-hearted companion would follow through on his threat.

He slammed his fist down on the hood of his car. Why? Why did she have to be there and hear them talking? And why did she have to come out and confront them about it? Why couldn't she at least have waited until Paco left? Then she could have talked to Roberto when they were alone. Maybe they could have worked something out. But now, with Paco nagging at him and threatening to tell the rest of the gang what had happened, Roberto knew he had to choose—between the *familia* he was born into and the one to which he had sworn his allegiance. And he had to do it quickly.

Rosa knew she had been very bad
to go outside at night after dark.

Chapter 11

THE LITTLE GIRL NAMED ROSA LAY STIFFLY IN HER
bed, staring at the closed door to her room and wondering
when they would come for her. When they killed her,
would they also kill her two younger sisters, who shared her
room? What about her parents and her brothers?

Rosa knew she had been very bad to go outside at night
after dark. She was supposed to be sleeping, but she had
always loved being outside after everyone else had gone to bed.
Their neighborhood wasn't as quiet as it once was, but still it
was peaceful to sit under the tree and watch an occasional
neighbor stroll by, unaware of being observed. She also spent
the time talking to God, who, though invisible, always seemed
to be right at her side.

Now she wasn't so sure. Though she had talked to God for
as long as she could remember and had always trusted Him
to take care of her, she had never imagined He would allow
something like this to take place right in front of her eyes. At
first she had thought they were just a few young men who'd

had too much to drink, stumbling their way back home. But as they drew closer and their voices escalated, she had realized that one was begging the other two for his life. Horrified, she had watched from the shadows as the drama unfolded before her. Suddenly the one who had been pleading for mercy broke away and began to run, but shots rang out and he had dropped to the ground, just a few feet in front of where Rosa cowered, too frightened even to breathe. When the other two caught up to the unmoving victim and Rosa saw their faces in the moonlight, the little girl jumped up from her hiding place and bolted for the back door. She was sure the two gunmen had hollered at her to stop, but she had raced to her room and slid under her bed, praying for God to make the killers go away.

Miraculously, He had. Within seconds of scooting under her bed, she had heard an approaching siren. When the gunmen did not follow her into her room, she decided the siren must have scared them off. Still, she wasn't foolish enough to think they wouldn't be back.

Should she tell her parents, warn them of the impending danger? True, she would probably be reprimanded for being outside, but that seemed a small price to pay compared to being gunned down by the two who had ended a life right in front of her house. But would telling her mother and father help or make the situation worse? She knew it wasn't always wise to talk to the police about the crimes that went on in their neighborhood, and no doubt her parents would do just that if she told them she had witnessed the murder. Was it possible the killers and their gang would leave Rosa and her family alone if she didn't say anything?

Still staring at the closed bedroom door and listening to her sisters sleeping peacefully, she was almost sure they would not. It was just a matter of time until they came for her. For now she would continue to pray for a miracle.

Roberto drove, with Paco in the passenger seat, as they slowly approached the spot where they had eliminated the suspected snitch on Saturday night. Paco had his automatic weapon at the ready. They had determined that the room where the little girl slept faced the street, so it would be an easy task to silence her once and for all. If some of the others in the household were killed in the process, so be it. That was just collateral damage that went with the territory.

Roberto tried not to think about the little girl, whose image as she raced away from them toward her house still burned in his memory. She seemed so skinny and fragile, with her dark hair streaming behind her. If only she hadn't been there!

But she had, and that's all there was to it. Though the thought of murdering her as she slept grated on Roberto's heart, he hardened himself against the emotion, telling himself that not only was it necessary to kill her, but possibly his involvement in the killing might make it easier to argue for sparing his *abuela*.

Maybe. But he doubted it.

There it was — the house where the little girl and her *familia* slept. Though he cursed himself for his weakness, he hoped she would die quickly and without pain.

As they drew even with the house, a streak of darkness flashed before them, and Roberto jerked his head to the left to see its origin. As he realized it had been nothing more than a cat, possibly racing to avoid their oncoming car, he felt himself catapulted into the steering wheel and beyond as his vehicle rammed into a tree near the curb. The force of the collision knocked the air from his lungs, even as his head exploded with the pain of impact against the windshield. As warm liquid began to drip down his face, he heard Paco groan a few times — and then he was silent.

What had happened? How had it happened? He had only turned his head for a moment, and now —

With every movement an agony, he turned toward Paco. "We've got to get out of here," he said. "They'll be coming for us soon. We can't let them find us here with a gun."

When Paco didn't move or answer, Roberto reached over and grabbed his shoulder. He was surprised he was able to move as well as he did. Perhaps he wasn't hurt as badly as he thought.

"Wake up," he ordered, using what little strength he had to shake the man who still sat motionless beside him. Instead of responding, Paco fell to the left, landing almost on top of Roberto. And Roberto knew. Paco was dead.

A couple of lights had come on in nearby houses by now, and Roberto realized he was running out of time. Pushing the dead man away from him, he managed to pry the gun from Paco's lifeless hands, then shoved the driver's door open and rolled out. He was sore and bleeding, but nothing seemed broken. Thankfully the car was stolen and there was no way to connect it to him. If he hurried, he could get out of the neighborhood before the *policia* arrived.

As he pulled himself to his feet and hobbled away, he couldn't help but wonder if the little girl who had watched them kill a man on Saturday had any idea that she had once more escaped death herself.

Susana was confused. Though nearly twenty years old and accustomed to attention from young men—much of it unwanted—she had never found herself so nearly obsessed with thoughts of someone the way she was with Marty Johnson. Ever since the handsome *gringo* had started spending his summers with Hector and Mariana, doing mission work in the neighborhood and surrounding areas, Susana had felt drawn to him. But now the attraction was stronger. She lay awake at night thinking of him. She tried to resist going to her sister's home when she knew he was there, but the harder she tried to stay away, the stronger the pull to go.

So why did she have to behave like a schoolgirl once she got there? Why couldn't she remain calm and simply have a conversation with the man? After all, he spoke passable Spanish and she spoke enough English to get by, so there was no reason they couldn't speak to one another. But every time he looked at her with those sky-blue eyes, her heart raced and her palms got sweaty, and the next thing she knew she was staring at her feet. The good-looking *gringo* must think she was a dunce.

When she had finally stopped fighting with herself and given in to her desire to go to Mariana's home once again and see Marty, she had been disappointed that he and Hector were still gone to Puerto Nuevo. But Mariana had said they would be home soon and insisted that Susana wait with her until they arrived. Though Susana had protested, Lupita and the boys had joined in, declaring that *Tia* Susana must stay and visit with them for a while.

And so, with only halfhearted resistance, she had finally conceded to their pleas and waited until the rumbling of the El Camino announced Marty and Hector's arrival. They had walked in the front door laughing, accompanied by the three delighted children who had raced outside to greet them.

Once again, Susana had found herself sneaking peeks at Marty, only to drop her eyes when he returned her glance. They had spoken little when she finally excused herself to go home. When Marty insisted on escorting her, Susana's feeble attempts to decline his offer fell on deaf ears, and the awkward couple had at last found themselves alone together.

"How have you been?" Marty asked, as they strolled a bit stiffly down the three blocks from Hector and Mariana's home to where Susana still lived with her parents, right next door to the house where Hector had grown up and which now served as a meeting place for the *Casa de Dios* congregation.

Susana swallowed and shot up a silent prayer that God would calm her heart and steady her voice so she wouldn't look like a complete fool. "I've been...well," she answered, with only a slight tremor betraying her. "And you? You are finished with school now, yes?"

"Yes, I am," Marty answered, and Susana found herself thrilling at the solid timbre of his voice. If only she could be as confident as he! But he was a sophisticated college graduate from a well-to-do family north of the border. How could she ever be like him? What did they possibly have in common? And why had she allowed herself to get thrown into this situation? If it were anyone but Marty, whom Hector and Mariana considered family, Susana knew her brother-in-law would have insisted on accompanying them on this short walk in the darkness of night.

"Now I must decide what to do next," Marty said. "That's why I'm here—to spend some time seeking God for direction." When he spoke again, Susana could hear the smile in his voice. "And, of course, to see all of you."

Susana swallowed again. "I'm...glad you came," she said, nearly faint with the utterance of what seemed such a bold statement. Holding her breath, she waited.

"So am I," Marty said. "Especially because..." He paused, and Susana wondered how much longer she could hold her breath, waiting for him to finish his thought. "Because it means I can spend time getting to know you better."

Susana exhaled, stunned at the sense of joy that washed over her at his words. Could it be? Was it possible that Marty Johnson was as attracted to her as she was to him?

Though they completed their walk in near silence, Susana's heart didn't stop racing until long after she had arrived at home and Marty had said good night and started his return trip to Hector and Mariana's house.

Maybe today will be different, Hector mused, turning on his blinker.

Chapter 12

HECTOR HAD BEEN BACK FROM HIS TRIP TO SAN Juan Chamula for a week now, and he felt badly that he hadn't been able to break away sooner to cross the border and visit his father. But he'd had a lot of church business to attend to, particularly involving *la abuela* and her family, as well as working at his brother's shop and spending time praying and talking with Marty. The time had simply gotten away from him.

Now it was Monday morning, though not too early. Hector had opted to wait until the main crush of people heading north to start a new workweek had passed. Instead it was slightly after ten, a time he thought would be good for Alberto as well.

Then again, how can any time be good for someone dying without hope? he pondered. *What does my father think of as he lies there, day after lonely day, night after terrifying night, drawing closer to the inevitable and knowing deep in his heart that his worst nightmares can't begin to equal what he will face for all eternity?*

Two more car lengths and he would be on the other side. He coached his ancient chariot forward a few more inches. *And he does know it*, Hector reminded himself. *Despite all his denials of a belief in God, he knows. Everyone does. The Bible says that God has put the knowledge of eternity into the hearts of all men. Burying the truth doesn't change it. We each have an appointment with death—and with judgment.* Hector shuddered. *To face it without Jesus as our Advocate—*

The neatly uniformed border guard waved him through, interrupting Hector's thoughts. Hector accelerated slowly and thought once again of how different it could be for his father if the man would simply stop rejecting the free gift being offered to him from a loving, forgiving God. But each time Hector tried to broach the subject, his father had shut him out, either with an angry outburst or a simple refusal to listen or respond.

Maybe today will be different, Hector mused, turning on his blinker to merge into the ever-crowded freeway traffic of Interstate 5. *Maybe today...*

His heart contracted at the finality of his father's decision should he continue to choose his own stubborn way. Hector had been blessed to lead many people to the Lord during his years of ministry and service, but never one so adamant in his refusal to believe as Alberto Javier Rodriguez. But even now, as despair threatened to overwhelm Hector and he faced what seemed the impossible, he reminded himself that nothing was impossible with God—and it was not God's will that any should die without first receiving Jesus as Savior. That so many chose to do so must grieve the Father's heart more than Hector's or anyone else's.

Reminded of that great fact, the humble pastor began to pray as he moved north with the flow of traffic, beseeching a faithful God on behalf of his not so faithful father.

Roberto had been sleeping at his parents' home more often than usual lately, and he knew that made his *abuela* nervous. He also knew she was spending more time than ever in prayer, but he doubted it was for her own safety or protection. Deep down Roberto knew the tiny woman who so many times had held him on her lap, dried his tears, kissed his scrapes and bruises, and told him stories of Jesus was even now praying for the eternal soul of the grandson she loved so dearly. That Roberto had rejected her teachings and chosen a life of crime and violence had not seemed to deter her prayers or dissipate her love. And that made what he had to do so much more difficult—and necessary.

Lying in the darkness on the bed where he had spent nearly every night of his life before moving out to live on the streets and sleep where he could, Roberto stared upward and wondered if an invisible God truly did exist—somewhere. And if He did, what did that matter to Roberto? Why should he care what some distant Spirit thought about him? His *abuela* might talk about Him like He was her best friend, the One who cared for and watched out for her, but Roberto knew there was no one he could count on other than himself. Even his fellow gang members, who had sworn to give their lives for their "*hermanos*," might turn on him when he needed them most. Why should it be any different with a God he couldn't even see or touch or hear?

No. Even Roberto's parents had seen the futility of trusting his *abuela*'s God and had long since stopped going to church except for an occasional Christmas or Easter visit. Even then they went more out of a sense of obligation than of faith. Roberto figured he had just taken it to the next step— denying God's existence altogether. And if God didn't exist, then Roberto owed Him nothing. So what did it matter if he killed a *vieja*, an old woman whose life was nearly over anyway?

Pain shot through his chest at the thought. Though killing his *abuela* might be of no major significance, it certainly wouldn't be easy. Roberto had witnessed a lot of killings and had even participated in many of them, but never had he been forced to kill someone he loved. And he loved his *abuela*, despite the fact that he was honor-bound to eliminate her.

As he had done so many times since the day she overheard Roberto and Paco's conversation, he silently cursed his *abuela* for being there at the wrong time—and then for confronting them about what they had said. If only she had remained silent! But of course, she hadn't. And though Paco could no longer force Roberto to act and no one else knew of the incident, Roberto understood only too well what it would do to him if he didn't follow through—the weakness that would creep into his heart and ruin his life if he allowed his *abuela* to live, even if she never said a word to anyone about what she had overheard.

So far the *policia* had apparently not made the connection between Paco's accidental death and Roberto, but the gang knew without asking. If they knew, was it possible that others would figure it out? Would the fact that it happened in front of the very house where another gang member was executed only days earlier trigger an investigation that would lead to Roberto?

The chances were slim, as the police were overwhelmed with crime, many of them involved in it themselves. But every day that Roberto's *abuela* still lived increased the possibility that he could eventually be arrested—thrown into a filthy cell to starve and rot because he hadn't cut off all the loose ends.

If only the loose end in this case were not his own flesh and blood. Then again, he reasoned, that was all the more reason why it needed to be done.

Antonia Mesa had fallen asleep on her knees—again. Even with her worsening arthritis, she was spending so much time in prayer these days that her eyes would grow weary and the next thing she knew she would awaken with her head on the bed, her back, legs, and feet screaming in pain.

It was no different tonight. As her *nieto* lay in the next room, *la abuela* opened her eyes to find that once again she had nodded off. Her body was so stiff that it took nearly five minutes to move herself from the floor to the comfort and warmth of her bed. But even then, as she pulled the covers up and sighed with relief at the feel of the familiar resting place beneath her, she continued to pray, determined that even if Roberto killed her, as she knew he planned to do, he would eventually repent and turn his heart and life over to the God who so relentlessly pursued him.

Gracias, Padre querido, she prayed silently. *Thank You, dear Father, that You love my Roberto so much more than I do. Thank You that You have forgiven me, and therefore I know You will also forgive my foolish* nieto —*and his parents as well. Mercy, Father, to Roberto, to me —to us all! Without You, we have no hope. But You, Lord— You can do anything!*

Virginia hummed as she prepared for bed. The Campos family had all turned in for the night, though she could still hear an occasional muffled giggle coming from the children's room, followed quickly by a reprimand from one of their parents. Each instance brought a smile to Virginia's lips, as she remembered the many back-and-forth exchanges between herself and her own large clan when they were still young.

It all passed so quickly, she thought, braiding her long, silver-streaked hair as she sat on the side of her bed. *One day it seemed there were children everywhere —running, laughing, playing —and then they were gone, living their own lives, raising their own children, maintaining their own households.* The thought brought a nostalgic twinge to her heart, but she continued plaiting her hair. *How useless I felt when I looked around and found myself alone —and then You brought me here, Lord. Here to live with this beautiful familia and pray for these beloved people of San Juan Chamula, who are so lost in spiritual darkness.* She shook her head in awe as she finished her task and rubber-banded the braid in place. *How is it that I should be so blessed to be entrusted with such an important mission? I always imagined myself growing old in Tijuana, sitting side by side with Alberto . . .*

At the thought of her estranged husband, Virginia closed her eyes, picturing him as she had last seen him—young and handsome, yet determined to go his own way and leave her to raise their children all alone. She had been angry at him for a very long time—hated him, even—but the love of Jesus had massaged her heart until the hardness had melted away and only the bittersweet memories remained. Now she prayed for him daily, especially as he approached the end of his days on earth. Virginia could not bear to think that the man who had once shared her life and her love would spend eternity in hell.

But tonight, she realized, God was calling her to do something besides pray. Suddenly and clearly, she recognized that God wanted her to write a letter to Alberto—a letter of love and forgiveness, before it was too late for him to receive or read it.

Virginia got up from her bed and went to the rickety three-drawer dresser that sat in the corner and held all her belongings. She opened the second drawer and pulled out a pad of paper and a pen, then returned to her bed, sat down, whispered a quick prayer, and began to write.

Suddenly a picture of Susana popped into his mind,
and he smiled.

Chapter 13

WITH HECTOR GONE TO SAN DIEGO TO VISIT HIS
father, Marty considered how best to spend his day.
The beach always beckoned, and there seemed nowhere
better to commune with God. The sun had risen clear and
warm, with no sign of clouds on the horizon. He would be
foolish not to take advantage of the perfect weather and drive
south to stroll along one of the many stretches of sand that
beckoned him.

And yet...what was it that held him back? The two older
children were in school, and Lupita had gone with Mariana
to visit a neighbor. That left Marty to enjoy the rare quiet and
solitude of the Rodriguez home. Maybe he should just remain
there, rather than drive to the beach. After all, his objective
was to hear from God, and he could do that anywhere.

Sitting at the kitchen table and sipping a cup of the strong
coffee Mariana had made for him before leaving, he wondered
if Hector had arrived at his father's bedside, and if so, how the
visit was progressing. Setting down his cup, he closed his eyes

and began to pray for a breakthrough. "Soften Mr. Rodriguez's heart, Father," he mumbled softly, "and give Hector wisdom as he speaks with him."

He continued to pray, as his mind took him from one need to another. In between, he read from the open Bible that sat on the table beside his coffee cup. By the time he realized he needed a refill to warm what was left of his morning drink, he had decided he would get in his car and drive to the beach after all.

"We can continue our conversation there, Lord," he said, rising from the table and taking the nearly empty cup to the counter for one last warm-up. "I really need to hear from You, Father. You know I've wanted to serve You in full-time ministry for years—and I believe that's what You've called me to do—but I need more direction. Where do I go, Lord? And do I go on my own, or through an organization?" He poured the coffee, unplugged the pot, and shook his head. "I just don't know, Father. You'd think after all that time in Bible college that I'd have it mapped out in front of me, but I don't. Is it because I'm not listening, not understanding? Help me to know, Lord. Please."

Drinking from his cup while he walked, he went to the bedroom he shared with Hector Jr. and Manolo and gathered up his wallet, keys, and sunglasses. He took one last swig from his cup, and then set it in the sink before snatching up his Bible and carrying it with him to the front door.

A walk on the beach, he thought, *and then a nice lunch somewhere. What a perfect day that would be!* Suddenly a picture of Susana popped into his mind, and he smiled. *The only thing that would make it better would be if she were coming with me.*

Shaking his head, he stepped out onto the rickety porch, pulling the front door shut behind him. *Forget it,* he told himself. *This is no time to get caught up in thinking about Susana—or any other woman, for that matter. I came here to spend time with God, to receive godly counsel, to get some direction for my life. How can I do that if I get sidetracked by those beautiful dark eyes and—*

His thoughts were interrupted as he walked toward his car and spotted Susana coming down the street, straight toward him. Despite his self-admonitions of a moment earlier, his heart danced as he imagined the two of them sharing lunch at some quaint seaside café. Stopping beside his car, he waited, watching her as she approached.

It was obvious to him when she spotted him, as her step faltered slightly before she resumed her trek, her head now bowed and eyes seemingly fixed on her feet. It seemed she was about to pass him by and head straight for the front door when Marty stepped toward her.

"Good morning," he said, watching closely for any reaction on her part.

Susana stopped, lifted her head, and turned slowly in his direction. Marty was certain the look of surprise on her face was carefully planned. He smiled and waited.

"Good...morning," she answered, her cheeks coloring slightly. "I...didn't see you there."

Not really a lie, Marty reasoned, *since you made it a point to stare at the ground as you walked by me.*

"If you came looking for Mariana," he said, "she and Lupita have gone to visit a neighbor. She didn't say which one."

Susana's look of surprise took on a much more genuine tone as she assimilated the news. "Oh." She nodded. "I...didn't know." Her eyes—as dark and lovely as Marty had been imagining them all morning—darted nervously from the house, to Marty, and then in the direction from which she had come. "I'd...better go back home then. Please tell her I was here." She dropped her eyes and then her head, as she took a step as if to return home.

"Wait," Marty said, reaching toward her, though she wasn't close enough for him to touch. "I..." He paused. Was it even proper to invite her to go with him? As much as he wanted to do so, he knew things weren't the same here as back in the States. Susana came from an old-fashioned family, and though Hector and Mariana had allowed him to walk Susana home the other night, he doubted they'd be too pleased if he began taking her out on dates without someone to chaperone.

Susana raised her head once again, and their eyes locked. Marty felt his knees go weak. What was it about this young woman that affected him so differently from the myriad other girls he had met at school or church? Though many of them were attractive, he was easily able to ignore their charms and keep his mind focused on his immediate concerns. When he looked at Susana, everything except gazing into her eyes and hearing the sound of her voice seemed to vanish from his thoughts.

She raised her eyebrows questioningly. "Did you wish to ask me something?"

I sure do, he thought, his lips clamped together so the words would not escape. What was he to do? Should he take a chance and invite her?

Before he could answer, he heard Lupita's voice, chattering in the distance. Looking toward the sound, he saw the answer to his predicament. Mariana and Lupita were nearly home, and he had no doubt that the little girl would be thrilled to accompany her *Tía* Susana and *Tío* Marty on a day at the beach. Now if only Mariana would agree…

Hector was stunned at how quickly his father had deteriorated since he last saw him. His heart contracted with a twinge of guilt that he hadn't come sooner, but there were so many other duties to attend to and people to pastor and shepherd. If only his father hadn't run off those many years before! If only he had stayed home where he belonged, with his wife and children! How different their lives would all have been — including Virginia's. Though Hector had resigned himself to the fact that his mother would undoubtedly live out the remainder of her life ministering to what she called her "little flock" near the Mayan village of San Juan Chamula, Hector would never stop wishing that she were still living near her family in Tijuana, where life was at least somewhat predictable and safe.

His father's eyes had been closed when he arrived, and Hector wondered if he should try to wake him. He knew the man was no doubt in pain much of the time, and sleep was his only means of escape. And yet, wasn't his eternal salvation more important than a temporary respite from physical torment?

Pulling the metal folding chair to the side of the bed, Hector sat down and took his father's hand, which lay limp and lifeless against the white sheet. The veins stood out under his dry, mottled skin. Hector's mind flashed back to his childhood, before Alberto deserted them, to the memory of the father who had seemed the handsomest and strongest man in the world, the man Hector had hoped to be like one day. The thought nearly tore the sob from his throat, but he swallowed it again, determined to maintain his composure.

"Papa?" Despite his best efforts, his voice cracked, but he tried again. "Papa, it is me, Hector, your son. I have come to visit you. *Por favor*, please, Papa, open your eyes."

He waited, watching Alberto's eyelids roll slightly. He had heard him, he was sure of it.

"Papa?" Hector's voice was louder this time, more even and authoritative, though he always maintained a tone of respect. "Papa, wake up. It's me, Hector."

Alberto's eyes opened slowly, as if they were weighted down with the pain that no doubt penetrated every pore of his body. After a moment they focused on Hector, and recognition brought a spark of life to the rheumy orbs.

Alberto's mouth opened and his lips moved, but no sound came forth. Again Hector waited. At last the old man tried again. "Hector," he croaked. "My son."

"Yes, Papa," Hector said, once again choking back a sob. "I came to see you—to tell you how much I love you, and...how much Jesus loves you."

The light in Alberto's eyes flickered and died, though he continued to stare at his son. Hector hadn't meant to jump in so quickly, but from the look of things, there was no time to waste.

"He wants to forgive you for your sins," Hector said, determined now to plunge ahead before his father drifted back to sleep. It was obvious the morphine dosages had been increased, but God was greater than morphine. His Spirit could reach anywhere. "All you have to do is ask Him," Hector said, the sob escaping at last. "I'll pray with you. I know it's hard for you to talk, but I can pray and you can listen. When you agree, you can squeeze my hand. Papa, *por favor*, will you pray with me...while there's time?"

Alberto's eyes turned to ice, and to Hector's surprise, he somehow managed to find the strength to withdraw his hand. Without a word, the hardened old man closed his eyes and turned his head to the wall, signaling an end to the visit.

With a heart of lead, Hector continued to sit beside the bed and pray, but his father didn't move for nearly an hour. At last Hector rose from his seat and shuffled from the room, fighting despair as he searched for the hope that he knew was just a breath away.

The tide was low when the three of them arrived at their destination. Marty's heart soared with gratitude over the fact that Mariana had agreed to allow Lupita to join him and Susana for a trip to the beach. She had even insisted on packing a lunch for them, ending Marty's dreams of sharing a romantic lunch at a seaside café with Susana. But then, it would have been a bit less than romantic with Lupita sitting between them.

Even now, as they made their way down the beach in search of a perfect picnic spot, the little girl skipped and frolicked on the packed, wet sand. They had all opted to leave their shoes in the car, and Lupita thought it delightful that they were leaving three trails of footprints behind them as they walked. Her nonstop chatter made it difficult to sustain any sort of conversation with Susana, but Marty also thought it helped relieve the tension that otherwise might have put a strain on the event.

Once they had settled on a spot, Susana and Lupita immediately spread the blanket and laid out the food. Marty was amazed at how quickly Mariana had assembled such a delicious spread—warm flour tortillas wrapped tightly in foil, tender chunks of *carnitas* from yesterday's dinner, freshly grated cheese, and homemade salsa. He hadn't realized how hungry he was until the food was dished out and offered to him on a paper plate. After offering a brief but heartfelt prayer of thanksgiving, Marty was the first to take a bite of the delicious pork, sprinkled with cheese and salsa, and wrapped in tortillas. His companions quickly followed suit, and Marty realized it was the only time since they left the house that Lupita had stopped talking.

With the warm sunshine almost directly overhead and shining off the nearly quiet sea waters, Marty wondered if life could possibly get any better than it was at that moment. A stab of guilt reminded him that he had planned to come here today to spend time alone with God. Instead he was eating and enjoying the company of two very special young ladies. And his heart was more content than it had been in a long, long time.

Smiling, she neared the cottage,
unaware that she was being watched.

Chapter 14

VIRGINIA WAS RELIEVED THAT THE LETTER WAS written and mailed. She had personally taken it into town early that morning to be sure it would go out soon. Mail delivery took a bit longer from their remote little village, but she was confident God would get it to Alberto on time.

On time, she thought, as she returned from posting the letter, basking in the midmorning sun that warmed her aging bones. *How much time does dear Alberto have left? Not much, I imagine—at least from what Hector tells me. But then, how much time do any of us have? Only You know, Lord. Only You...*

She picked up her pace just a bit as she considered that today was the day her little flock would come for their reading lesson. Smiling at the thought, she was confident that all but Imix and Kawak knew it was much more than that, but God would reveal that to the two Mayan women in His time.

And that's the key, isn't it, Father? Your time—and Your purposes. Above all, Your glory. May it always be so in my life, dear

Lord. And when my time here is over, I will rejoice in Your faithfulness to carry me home at last.

With a joyous peace in her heart, Virginia continued on her way out of town until she rounded a bend and came in sight of the Camposes' home. No matter how many times she gazed upon it, she never saw the poverty, but rather the love that radiated from it. And she was always grateful that God had placed her there.

Smiling, she neared the cottage, unaware that she was being watched—and that the eyes set upon her were for evil, not for good.

The spirits were angry today; Evita could feel it. And that made her angry as well. She had been patient, waiting to see if Kawak would succeed in convincing Imix to stop attending the studies with the foreigner. But so far the girl had been unable to dissuade her friend from continuing the weekly meetings. As a result, it was obvious that it was time for Evita to take action.

She had watched the old woman set out from the Campos home this morning and walk into town, no doubt posting a letter to her family back in Tijuana. Why hadn't the old woman stayed there where she belonged? Why couldn't she understand that she wasn't welcome here, with her blasphemous ideas and troublesome teachings? San Juan Chamula was an entity unto itself, a monument to the Mayans who dwelled there—and who had done so long before *los conquistadores* or the Aztecs had invaded their land and disrupted their way of life. True, some of the *Mexicanos* had adapted, blending beliefs and superstitions with the land's rightful owners—but others had not. The *evangelicos* had come in with their own version of the Bible and even implied that the Mayans who had adopted some of the Catholic traditions, blending and mixing them with their own Mayan faith, were not true Christians. The woman called Virginia was one of the worst. Not only did she refuse to accept the practices of the Mayans who were there before her, but she also dared to teach them another way. And that could not be tolerated.

If the spirits were indeed angry—and the level of darkness seemed to indicate that was the case—then it was time for Evita to take action, even as she had sensed when she lurked outside the Camposes' home the night before. She would seek for wisdom beyond her own to put a plan into place, and then she would do what she must to carry it out.

Roberto was furious and frustrated—with his *abuela*, with the entire situation, but mostly with himself. He had allowed himself to pass up several chances to take care of his problem, and he knew it was a sign of weakness that would eventually get him into trouble. And trouble in his world could be deadly.

At least he could be thankful that Paco was no longer around to call him on it. If he were, Roberto would have had to "eliminate" his *abuela* long before this or face the certainty that Paco would alert the gang to Roberto's betrayal—in which case his *abuela* wouldn't be the only one on the wrong side of the grass right now. The only difference was that the old woman believed she was going to heaven when she died—and no doubt would if there were such a place. Roberto, however, doubted there was. If he was wrong, that meant there was also a hell, and it was certain he would one day set up permanent residency there.

Maybe today would be the day to set things right. Roberto's parents would be gone, and his *abuela* would no doubt be home alone. He had not slept at home the last couple of nights, thinking it might be easier to do what he must if he weren't spending quite so much time in the room next to hers. Perhaps, too, she would become complacent and think he had decided to let her live. Catching her by surprise, possibly even from behind so she wouldn't know what hit her, would be the simplest and cleanest way.

Yes, today he would follow through on what he should have done the moment his *abuela* stuck her nose where it did not belong. After all, she was just an old woman whose life was behind her. What difference did it make if he took her out today or allowed her to survive a few more years? It wasn't as if her life mattered to anyone else.

As he checked his ammunition, he determined to get through the day without flinching—and without giving in to the ache that chewed at the edges of his heart. There was no room in his life for sentimentality. It was kill or be killed—and he wasn't about to offer his life in exchange for hers.

Señora Antonia Mesa had been up since long before daylight, once again wearing out her knees on behalf of her rebellious *nieto*. But now her daughter and son-in-law had left for the day, and her stomach was beginning to call for nourishment. Rising painfully from her spot beside the bed, she hobbled to the kitchen, where she turned on the fire under the teapot. Perhaps something hot would help her move a little easier.

While the water heated, she warmed a tortilla and a bit of rice from the night before. It didn't take much to fill her up these days, and she couldn't help but remember that it had been the same with her own grandmother in the last days of her life.

Her heart squeezed at the memory. It had been so long ago, and yet Antonia would never forget the beloved woman who had raised her when her parents were killed by two *bandidos* who had come to rob them and then became angry because the poverty-stricken couple had nothing worth taking. When the intruders had spied little Antonia hiding under the table, they had threatened to take her and sell her, but Antonia's parents had literally fought them to the death in an effort to protect their only child.

Wide-eyed, four-year-old Antonia had watched the entire event, including the murders of her mother and father. But the valiant couple had not died alone. Antonia's father managed to kill one of the *bandidos* and wound the other before he and his wife succumbed to their wounds. By the time the *policia* arrived, the second *bandido* was dead as well, and Antonia was still hiding under the table, crying and waiting for someone to come and rescue her. At last her *abuela* had come, summoned by the *policia*, and Antonia had gone home to live with her and to share with her in their common grief.

Now grief had found her once again, and this time she was the *abuela*, longing to rescue her *nieto*, who seemingly was determined not to be rescued. But during those many years since Antonia had sat under the table and watched her parents murdered and this morning as she sat at another table, eating tortillas and rice and drinking hot tea, she had come to know the One who was greater than any *bandido* or evil way of life. And she was determined to continue beseeching that One until her beloved Roberto was rescued at last.

She smiled at the thought. Her pastor, Hector Rodriguez, had assured her that he, too, was praying for Roberto, and she didn't doubt for a moment that he was. Antonia loved the little *Casa de Dios* congregation led by Pastor Rodriguez, and she was so grateful that their meeting place was only blocks away. As she sipped the last of her hot drink, she decided she would go there today to pray. She knew the front door was always open, and sometimes another parishioner was also there, praying and seeking God. Perhaps, if she found someone else there when she arrived, they could join together in prayer, for the Scriptures assured them that if two or more would agree together in prayer in the mighty name of Jesus, their prayers would be answered.

Rising from the table, she reached out to gather her cup and plate to take them to the sink, but stopped, sensing that she was no longer alone. Who could it be? Had her daughter and son-in-law returned early? But even before she turned to face the intruder, she knew the answer to her question.

For the first time since Hector could remember,
he doubted the faith he preached to others.

Chapter 15

THE VISIT TO HIS FATHER THE PREVIOUS DAY STILL haunted Hector. That wasn't unusual, of course, but to see him deteriorating so quickly and to know his time was nearly gone, yet still have him refuse to hear the truth, tore at his heart. How many times had one of his parishioners come to him and asked him to pray for a lost loved one? And how many times had he answered with confidence that God was faithful and would bring the lost sheep home? So why was it so difficult to believe when that lost sheep was his own flesh and blood, the man who had given him physical life, even if he had ultimately opted out of being his father?

For the first time since Hector could remember, he doubted the faith he preached to others. He needed to talk with someone about it, ask for prayer and an encouraging word, but to whom did a pastor go in order to confess his lack of faith?

Mariana no doubt already knew, though he had not said a word and had tried to maintain a strong façade. But he sometimes thought she knew him better than he knew himself.

However hard he tried to hide something from her, she always seemed to see right through his cover-up and call him on it. He imagined it was only a matter of time until she did so regarding Alberto.

Hector sighed, as he sat in the tiny room where he used to sleep as a boy and which now served as his pastor's office in the old house-turned-church, where he knew every splinter and creak. He often came here on Saturday to read his Bible and pray, and to receive direction from the Lord for his Sunday sermon. Sometimes he made notes; sometimes he didn't. Today he tried, but nothing came. But it was still early; perhaps the Lord just wanted him to be still and wait for a while.

He had risen while the house was quiet and walked in the early morning fog for this weekly meeting with God, marveling at how different his home was when everyone was still asleep. Though he appreciated the rare moments of silence, he much preferred the more normal noise level of a family that enjoyed life—and one another.

Inexplicably, the image of *la abuela* swam before his eyes, and he considered what it would be like to know that your own child or grandchild was a criminal. It was almost beyond comprehension, and yet *Señora* Mesa lived with that truth every day of her life.

She also lived with the truth that God loved her wayward Roberto more than any of them could ever imagine, and so the faithful saint devoted much of whatever was left of her life here on earth to praying for his salvation. Surely God would answer and bring the lost sheep home.

At the thought, Hector realized how ridiculous it was for him to believe God could rescue a thief and a murderer but not an old man who had deserted his family. How small he sometimes made the God of the universe!

Slipping from his chair to his knees, he began to petition that great God for the redemption of a young man named Roberto and a very old one named Alberto. He also prayed for *la abuela's* strength and protection in the midst of what he sensed was an intense spiritual battle.

It seemed Lupita had not stopped chattering since Marty and Susana took her to the beach the day before. But Mariana didn't mind. She was pleased to see her daughter so full of life and laughter—and her sister and Marty so obviously in the early stages of what could turn into a long and permanent relationship. At least, Mariana certainly hoped so.

And it wasn't just because she thought they made a cute couple, though they certainly did. No, it was much more than that. Mariana was very protective of her younger sister, and she knew how innocent and naïve the girl was. She'd scarcely looked at a boy in her life, let alone expressed an interest in or dated one. But over the last years, since Marty had been coming to spend his summers with the Rodriguez family, Mariana couldn't help but notice what she was certain was Susana's growing attraction and admiration of the handsome *gringo* with a heart to serve God's people.

That, of course, was the real issue, for Mariana knew that her sister shared that passion for winning the lost and building disciples. For some time now Mariana had nursed a hope that God might be bringing the two young people together to minister as a couple. If so, she hoped it would be nearby, as she couldn't imagine her sister going off to serve on the missions field where Mariana might not ever see her again.

That was her only reservation about this budding romance. It would be so much easier if Susana would settle down with someone who owned a nice little shop somewhere in Tijuana, where Mariana wouldn't have to worry about her. Of course, it would be wonderful if Marty decided to stay and minister right there in the neighborhood, with Susana at his side, but that was almost too much to hope for, and so Mariana dismissed it and left the situation in God's hands. After all, it wasn't up to her to try to run her sister's life—or her own, for that matter.

With that in mind, Mariana interrupted Lupita, who was still regaling Manolo with tales of her adventures at *la playa* with *Tío* Marty and *Tía* Susana.

"Come, *mija*," she ordered. "You can tell your *hermano* more about your trip to the beach later. For now you can accompany me to *la tienda* while Manolo finishes his chores."

A glance at her middle child told her that he had mixed emotions about her rescuing him from Lupita's endless chatter. There was a hint of relief in his expression, undoubtedly due to the fact that he was a bit envious at having missed the beach excursion and was tired of hearing about it, but he also appeared less than thrilled at the tasks ahead of him.

Of all Mariana's children, Manolo was the most difficult to motivate. He had an amazing ability to take what should be a ten-minute job and turn it into a three-day ordeal. *All the more reason to see that he gets it done*, Mariana reminded herself.

"Let's go," she said, looking from Manolo to Lupita and back again. "I need to get some fresh vegetables for dinner, and I want everything picked up from the floor when Lupita and I return. Is that clear?"

She waited while Manolo hung his head, then shrugged his shoulders resignedly. "*Sí*, Mama," he answered, sounding as if he had just agreed to receive forty lashes.

Smiling, she took Lupita's hand and headed for the front door. Marty and Hector Jr. were in the boys' room, having a "men's" Bible study, so Mariana had postponed little Hector's chores until later in the day. Besides, she didn't have to worry that he wouldn't do them. Her older son was a responsible child who willingly did as he was told.

How different they all are, Mariana reflected as she and her daughter began their short walk into town. *You have made each of us unique for a purpose, haven't You, Father?*

And then she thought of Roberto, *Señora* Mesa's *nieto*, who had practically grown up in the church, attending faithfully with his *abuela* for years, even after his parents stopped coming. *What happens to turn a child away, Lord?* she asked silently, Lupita's tiny hand clamped tightly in her own. Mariana slowed her steps slightly so the child wouldn't have so much trouble keeping up. *How grateful I am that my parents taught us of Your love and led us to You when we were young! And yet,* la abuela *tried to do the same for Roberto.*

She sighed. *Ah, perhaps I do not have the answer as to why some stray away, but I know the One who brings the strays home. Please do that for Roberto, dear Lord... before it is too late for him.*

Squeezing Lupita's hand, Mariana found herself fighting tears. "Come," she said. "Hurry a little, *mija*. I want to have time to stop at *la iglesia*, the church, and see your papa before we go back home. He should still be there, preparing for the service tomorrow."

Marty couldn't get Susana off his mind. Even his Bible study with young Hector, during which he marveled at the boy's depth of spiritual understanding, had not diminished his desire to see her again. He didn't want to risk scaring her off by overwhelming her, so he resisted the urge to invite her to accompany him to a nearby park for the day. But that didn't stop him from praying and hoping that the gentle, lovely young woman would once again come to the Rodriguez home for dinner.

You're getting too serious, he scolded himself as he paged through his Bible, determined to spend some time alone with the Lord and not get sidetracked again. That's what he had come here for, wasn't it—to hear from God? Yet it seemed he was no closer to discovering God's immediate direction for his life than when he was still sitting in the classroom in San Diego.

Settling in to read the early chapters of the prophet Isaiah, Marty at last was able to shut out the distracting images and thoughts of Susana and to concentrate on God's Word. As he did, his peace returned, and though he heard no booming voice or even a whisper telling him which way to go, Marty sensed that God was telling him to relax and trust Him—to focus on being faithful today, and tomorrow would take care of itself.

He smiled. How was it he could so easily lose sight of that simple truth? How many times would his heavenly Father have to remind him of it before it finally worked its way down into his heart and rooted out the doubt and confusion? For that really was all that God required of him—to be faithful today and to trust God for the details.

Closing his eyes, Marty sighed. Life was so easy and good when he kept it in perspective. He knew God's plans for him were good—whatever they were—so all he had to do was love God with all his heart and be obedient to Him today, knowing that God would then escort him right into the future He had planned for him before the foundation of the world.

Smiling, Marty opened his eyes, set down his Bible, and went off in search of two boys who might want to play Frisbee with him.

But now, there he was,

his dark eyes wet and his face blotchy.

Chapter 16

HECTOR WAS STILL ON HIS KNEES PRAYING WHEN he heard the hesitant rap on his office door. Opening his eyes and looking toward the doorway, he was mildly surprised to see *la abuela* standing there—stunned to see her *nieto* standing beside her.

When was the last time Roberto had been to church? Hector couldn't remember, but he knew it had been a few years. But now, there he was, his dark eyes wet and his face blotchy. *Señora* Mesa, on the other hand, was absolutely beaming.

So, he thought, smiling as he rose from his kneeling position, *the Good Shepherd has brought another lost sheep home.*

The thought sent a rush of warmth through his chest, and for a moment he thought he would join Roberto in tears of joy. He opened his arms as he stepped forward and enveloped them both in a welcoming hug, starting a flow of tears from all of them. Recognizing the sacredness of the moment, as well as Roberto's obvious need of privacy in the midst of it, Hector reached out and pushed the door shut, then opened a couple of folding chairs in front of his desk. Roberto sank down on one of them even faster than his elderly *abuela*.

Hector pulled his own chair around to the front of the desk, forming a small circle of three. There were so many things he wanted to say, but wisdom and experience cautioned him to wait, to give the young man an opportunity to speak first. At last he did.

"I... I was going to... kill my..." His voice trailed off, and he dropped his head as tears dripped from his down-turned face. "My... *abuela*," he finished, as sobs shook his shoulders. "I went to the house to kill her, but... I couldn't do it."

Hot lightning sliced through Hector's heart at the young man's revelation. No wonder God had called him to intercede! His hand trembled as he reached out and laid it on Roberto's tattooed arm. "But you didn't," he said, his voice just above a whisper. "*Gracias a Dios!*"

Roberto nodded, his head still bowed as tears dripped onto his clasped hands, resting between his knees. "*Sí*," he agreed. "Thank God."

Hector raised his eyes and caught the grateful gaze of *Señora* Mesa. Her eyes, too, were wet, as tears trickled down the deep ravines of her weathered face. Hector thought he had never seen such a beautiful woman.

"God has answered our prayers," she said, and Hector nodded in agreement.

And then, like a dam unleashing tons of pent-up water, Roberto opened his mouth and let his story pour out—from his first ventures into gang involvement, through the months and years of ever-deepening sin and criminal activity, to the murder and subsequent death of Paco, and finally to his decision to silence his beloved *abuela*.

"But I couldn't do it," he said again, raising his head at last and fixing his eyes on Hector. "I tried, but..." He shook his head. "I just couldn't. When I looked at her, all I could think of were the times she held me in her arms and comforted me when no one else had time for me. How she was always there to fix me my favorite foods and tell me stories about... Jesus."

He dropped his head again for a moment, then quickly looked back at Hector. "That's what got me—those stories about Jesus. While I stood there in the kitchen with my gun aimed at my *abuela*'s head, it was like every story she ever told me about Jesus and how much He loved me came rushing back, and...and all of a sudden, I knew it was true. The next thing I knew I was on the floor, crying, and *Abuela* was beside me, weeping and praying. And I started praying too." He shook his head in apparent wonder. "God answered, Pastor. He forgave me and changed me. It was like He took out the rock that had been in my chest and gave me a new heart, you know?"

Hector nodded. Yes, he knew very well. He had seen it happen many times. It had happened to him years ago when he was still a child, and now he was once again witnessing the greatest miracle that could ever happen to anyone. Smiling, he said, "That is exactly what happened, Roberto. The Scriptures tell us that when we turn to God, He takes away our heart of stone and gives us a heart of flesh—tender and loving and kind, a heart that seeks to serve God and others, rather than ourselves. You are no longer an enemy of God, Roberto, but a friend, a son. Do you understand?"

Roberto's eyes glistened as he nodded in response. "I don't understand much," he admitted. "But I understand that He loves me and forgives me, and that I belong to Him now. Is that enough, Pastor?"

Once again hot tears of joy stung Hector's eyelids, as he answered, "*Sí*, Roberto. It is enough. For now, it is most certainly enough."

Virginia had enjoyed an especially joyous and extended time of fellowship with her Lord that morning, and now that peaceful time had been extended as she found herself alone in the Campos house—a rare occurrence, indeed. Diego and Eldora

Campos had invited her to join them on their excursion into the village, but she had declined, anticipating the solitude and sensing that God had purposed for her to stay behind. As she cleaned the little shack that had become such a place of joy to her, despite missing her family back in Tijuana, she spent the time singing hymns of praise and gratitude. Though Virginia loved music, she seldom sang aloud unless she was alone, as she knew God had not blessed her with the voice of a songbird.

I sound more like an old crow than a canary, don't I, Lord? she observed, even as she continued to hum. *But something tells me You get great joy from hearing me sing praises to You. And so, my Father, I will continue to offer my voice to You—along with my entire life. I am Yours, dear Lord, to do with as You wish, for as long as You wish. You have seen fit in my old age to send me here to the people of San Juan Chamula, who so desperately need You, and I thank You for the opportunity. How easy it would be to sit with* mi familia *in Tijuana and rock away my final days on earth, with my children and grandchildren surrounding me! But You, Lord, have called me here, and I want only to fulfill Your purpose for me.* She sighed, smiling as she switched from one hymn to another and kept right on humming. *And when that purpose is done—oh, Father, how happy I will be to cut the final strings that hold me here and soar upward into Your presence!*

With a smile on her lips, Virginia took the broom and opened the door to the children's room. The scene that greeted her brought a smile to her lips. How many times had she walked into her own children's rooms and been greeted by such an explosion of clutter! The Campos children, of course, didn't have nearly as many belongings as her children had enjoyed in what Virginia then thought were near-poverty conditions. But even with so little, the four children who inhabited this tiny room had managed to leave behind a sense of joy and innocence, of love and caring and belonging.

How awful it would be to grow up any other way, she thought, *no matter how many toys or clothes a child might have!* She shook her head. *No. It is the love of God and one another that makes the Campos* familia *so rich. And it is that same love that You blessed me and my own* familia *with that made us rich as well, Father. Thank You, Lord, for giving me a life that taught me what really mattered.*

She smiled, a sense of contentment flooding her and bringing tears to her eyes, as she sensed that she had done all that God had called her to do. Her mission was complete—though she couldn't imagine why she would be so sure of that fact at that very moment.

Shrugging, she returned to sweeping and singing, until she heard the step behind her and turned to greet what she imagined was the Campos family, who had apparently returned much earlier than planned.

It was the first day in what seemed a very long time that Rosa had felt comfortable coming outside to play. Carefully she ventured into the front yard, only to be confronted by the tree she had been sitting under on that horrible night. And then there had been that terrible sound on another night, when she had dared to peer out her window and see the car that had crashed into the very same tree. Though Rosa's sense of fear had dissipated enough for her to once again play outside in the warm Mexican sunshine, she would keep her distance from that tree and all its terrible memories.

If only it were that easy! It seemed no matter how hard she tried to shove them from her mind, the scenes remained: the image of the two men, chasing the one who was fleeing and finally gunning him down, and what she had witnessed after the car crash when the driver stumbled from the car and hurried down the street, leaving his passenger to die alone.

Death frightened Rosa. She was only a little girl, but already she had seen the horror of it up close—and there was no one she could tell about it, no one to hold her while she cried or to tell her that death would not stalk her until she, too, was snuffed out in a moment of time.

Despite the warm sunshine, she shuddered. Though her fear wasn't as great as it had been the previous few days, it was not gone altogether. Sooner or later it would return for her, and she could only hope and pray that she was fast enough to outrun it.

At the hesitant knock on the door, Hector called, "Come in."

Chapter 17

HECTOR HEARD HIS DAUGHTER BEFORE HE SAW
her. He also heard his wife softly but sternly reprimand
Lupita and call her to her side as they approached
Hector's office. Roberto's eyes grew wide at the realization
that the privacy of the pastor's office was about to be invaded,
but Hector held up his hand to reassure him.

"It is *mi familia*," he said. "You have nothing to fear."

At the hesitant knock on the door, Hector called, "Come
in," and then watched Roberto's face soften at the sight of
Lupita, entering just ahead of her mother.

"Papa!" The little girl appeared to explode with excitement
at the sight of her father, as if it had been weeks or months
since she had seen him, rather than hours.

Hector smiled and held out his arms. "Is this the most
beautiful little girl in all of Tijuana?" he asked, enveloping his
delighted daughter in his arms.

Lupita giggled. "*Sí*, Papa," she said, burying her face in his
shoulder. "Mama and I came to visit you."

"So I see." Hector chuckled, pulling Lupita from his chest and turning her to face the others. "But we must not forget our manners, *verdad*? We have other visitors as well, and it is polite to greet them. You remember *Señora* Mesa, don't you? And this is her *nieto*, Roberto. Say hello to them, Lupita."

Shyly the child said, *"Buenos días,"* and then dropped her eyes, as the others exchanged greetings as well. Hector had not missed the surprise on Mariana's face when she spotted Roberto sitting beside his *abuela*, but she had recovered quickly, an expression of joy replacing her momentary shock as she embraced the repentant young man.

"Welcome," Mariana said. "It is so good to see you again, Roberto. We've missed you! You and your *abuela* must come to our home for dinner one day soon."

Roberto's surprise at the invitation appeared greater than Mariana's just moments before, but he nodded and graciously accepted.

And then, Mariana, ever the gracious pastor's wife, took Lupita from her papa's arms. "We must be going," she said, despite her daughter's protests. "We were on our way to *la tienda* to buy some vegetables. Please excuse the interruption. I am sure you have things to discuss."

Hector smiled, even as he kissed his wife and daughter good-bye. What a miracle that God had blessed him with such an amazing partner! She always seemed to know exactly what to say and do, for which Hector was extremely grateful.

He closed his office door behind them and turned back to *la abuela* and her *nieto*. It was always a joyous time when a lost sheep returned to the fold, but there were practical issues to deal with as well. The prospect of what to do about Roberto's criminal past and the fact that he was no doubt wanted for multiple crimes loomed large, and there seemed to be little point in postponing the discussion. Would the young man be receptive to the suggestion to turn himself in, knowing what that would most likely mean for his future?

Hector took a deep breath and sat down behind his desk, ready to broach the subject, when a loud popping sound interrupted his thoughts. The sound was quickly followed by more pops, loud and repetitive, and it was obvious then that the original sound had not been something as harmless as a car backfiring. Someone was shooting, and that someone was very close by.

Mariana and Lupita!

The thought flashed in Hector's mind, even as he catapulted from his chair and bolted toward the office door. But Roberto got there first, nearly ripping the door from its hinges as he raced to the front of the little church. Just steps behind the larger, younger man, Hector saw that the door was already open, and he realized his wife and daughter must have stepped outside just before the firing began.

"*Ay, Dios mio!*" he cried, his heart breaking at the thought. "Protect them, Lord! Cover them, Father!"

The shooting stopped, replaced by the sound of squealing tires, just as Hector burst through the door into the sunlight that had begun to burn through the morning fog. He scarcely caught himself before tripping over Roberto, who had exited the door only seconds ahead of him and now lay sprawled across the stoop, covering two unmoving bodies beneath him.

With a strength he had no idea he possessed, Hector moved Roberto's already lifeless body, exposing Mariana and Lupita, who lay facedown, Mariana's arm stretched protectively across her child.

Mariana moved first, groaning as she lifted her eyes to gaze toward Hector. Before the grateful man could respond to the knowledge that at least his wife was still alive, little Lupita pushed herself up into a sitting position and whined, "Roberto almost squished me, Papa!"

Nearly giddy with relief, Hector pulled the child to his chest, covering her with kisses until he realized his wife had not yet joined them. Transferring his attention back to Mariana, he saw that she still lay where she had fallen, and that a small pool of blood was beginning to spread from beneath her. Her eyes fluttered as she gazed at him.

"Lupita is...all right?" she whispered.

Hot tears stung Hector's eyes as he nodded. "She is fine, *preciosa*. She is fine. Don't worry...and don't move. I'll call an ambulance. Just be still. You're going to be all right, *mi amor*. I promise."

With Lupita still in his arms, Hector jumped to his feet and spotted *la abuela*, who stood weeping in the doorway. A black shawl covered her shoulders.

"Use your shawl to stop Mariana's bleeding," he ordered.

Understanding invaded her tear-filled eyes and she nodded in response, as Hector raced to his office to call for help.

Imix was nervous. When she and Kawak had attended the study at the Campos home earlier in the week, Imix was certain her friend was up to something, though she couldn't pinpoint why she felt that way. Perhaps it was the spirits speaking to her, warning of impending trouble. Kawak insisted *la curandera* had told her they could hear from the spirits if they practiced listening, but Imix wasn't so sure she wanted to hear from them. The few times she had ventured anywhere near *la curandera*'s dwelling place, the darkness had nearly smothered her, and she had since taken to staying at least a block away from the obviously powerful woman's home each time she set foot on the streets of San Juan Chamula.

It was different when she visited the Camposes' home and listened to the outsider named Virginia. Though Imix didn't always understand everything the woman said, she was drawn to the light she sensed each time she was near her. Now something was wrong; she was sure of it. Kawak was more secretive than ever, and the skies over their little town seemed heavy with darkness, despite the warm sunshine. But it was the smile she had seen on *la curandera*'s face as the woman passed Imix on the street, coming from the direction of the Camposes' home earlier that morning, that sent a chill slithering up Imix's spine. Surely the shaman's apparent pleasure could not bode well for the woman named Virginia.

Celeste Johnson was not happy with what she saw in her full-length mirror. Why couldn't she rid herself of those extra ten pounds? She had always been able to lose weight easily before, but now, in her early fifties, the bulges refused to disappear. And the lines around her eyes and in her neck were becoming more pronounced as well. Though people told her she looked great "for her age," she didn't want to be a good-looking, fifty-ish woman; she wanted to be young again—young and beautiful and desirable. Oh, men were still attracted to her, but she could no longer convince herself it was because of her beauty; rather, she knew it was for the money her husband had left her twenty years earlier, money that had been invested wisely and produced a generous return. But what good was all of that money if there was no one to enjoy spending it with her?

She had even thought about jumping into her Mercedes and driving down the coast to visit Marty in San Diego, but then she remembered he had called to say he was going down to Tijuana to visit those dreadful friends of his, some family he had met while spending his summers down there trying to help the poor.

Celeste sighed and shook her head. Where had she gone wrong? She had given Marty the best of everything—the best schools, the best nannies, the best clothes and food and medical care—and yet he chose to throw his life away on people who were so obviously beneath him. What was he trying to prove anyway?

With one last disgusted glance, she turned from the mirror and made her way to the wall-to-wall walk-in closet that housed her collection of clothes for every possible occasion. Perhaps she could find something that would hide those extra ten pounds. With the right combination of makeup, she might even be able to camouflage the wrinkles as well, opening up all sorts of opportunities at the evening's charity dinner.

Hector paced the small waiting room floor, praying for the woman who shared his life and his heart. How many times had he prayed for others in this very room, as they awaited word of their own loved ones? How many times had he assured them that God held their loved ones in His hand and they could trust Him with the outcome? Where was his faith now—now that the loved one whose fate lay in God's hands was his own beloved *esposa*?

"Any news?"

The voice interrupted his thoughts, pulling him back to the reality that others, too, awaited word of Mariana's condition. Hector turned to see Marty standing at his side, his blue eyes full of concern. "Susana is with the children," he said quickly, answering the question in Hector's heart before he could even formulate it in his mind, let alone speak it.

Hector nodded. "*Gracias, amigo*. And thank God that Lupita wasn't harmed in any way. I asked the Lord to protect them, to cover them, and He did—first with Mariana covering Lupita, and then...Roberto, covering them both." His voice cracked, and he closed his eyes, fighting a fresh onslaught of tears at the reminder that the one who had so recently turned from his life of crime to receive the forgiveness that only the Savior Himself could give was now in that very Savior's presence. Perhaps it was just as well, considering what his fate would likely have been were he still alive to face the legal system. But oh, how this must have devastated the young man's beloved *abuela*! Even with forgiveness, there was a price to pay when—

"Hector?"

He shook his head, clearing his thoughts. "No," he said, his voice cracking again. "No word yet on Mariana. She is still in surgery."

Marty's smile was tentative. "She's going to be all right," he said, his words sounding more like a question than a statement.

Hector could only nod in agreement, praying the young man's assessment would prove true. What would he do if it didn't? How would he go on if Mariana...?

No. He could not allow himself to complete the thought. Mariana had to be all right. There simply was no other acceptable outcome. And for the first time since becoming a pastor, he understood the denial he had seen in so many of his parishioners as he had counseled them in similar situations.

"Oh God," he prayed, as he returned yet again from checking his empty mailbox, "what should I do?

Chapter 18

MARTY FOUGHT TEARS AS HE STEERED HIS FAITHFUL El Camino toward the Rodriguez home, wishing he had some good news to deliver to those who waited for him there. Though he and Hector had not revealed to the children how serious they suspected their mother's injury to be, Marty imagined the boys at least were aware that their mother's condition could be grave. Lupita knew only that her mother and Roberto had protected her from "*los malos,*" the bad men with the guns, but she still wasn't quite sure why the two had nearly "squished" her, as she described it.

And, of course, the little girl had no idea that the tattooed man named Roberto had died, only hours after crying out to the Lord for forgiveness. Marty was overwhelmed at the mercy and faithfulness of a sovereign God who would allow this thing to happen in His perfect timing, but he was also grieved that such a young life had been wasted in sin.

But Mariana, the humble, faithful pastor's wife and devoted mother of three? Surely God did not intend to take her so soon from all those who loved and needed her! How would anyone explain such a thing to her children—to her sister Susana?

The thought of Susana ignited a lightbulb in Marty's mind. Neither Mariana's family members nor Hector's siblings had been at the hospital. That must mean that no one had yet had a chance to notify them, not even Susana, who was busy with Hector and Mariana's three children. It was up to him to contact the families immediately. He would start with Hector's brother Jorge. Marty knew where Jorge's shoe repair shop was located, and then Jorge would be able to get hold of everyone else.

With a clear direction on what to do next, Marty turned the corner toward the shop, ready to deliver the news.

Within moments after the families were notified and had gathered in the small waiting room to support Hector and to pray for Mariana, the doctor emerged from the operating room, a tentative smile igniting hope in Hector's heart. She was going to be all right! His beloved Mariana was going to make it!

"She came through the surgery fine," the doctor said, confirming Hector's fragile hope. "Thank God the bullet missed her heart by inches!"

Tears blurred Hector's vision. "*Sí, gracias a Dios,*" he murmured, as did the cluster of relatives huddled around them.

"If all goes well," the doctor continued, "she should be able to go home in a couple of days, and I see no reason that she won't have a full recovery, though she will need to rest and regain her strength."

A chorus of "I'll be there to help" and "We'll take good care of her" comments quickly followed, as the group emitted a collective sigh of relief, and tears of gratitude flowed freely. What a faithful God they served! Mariana had been spared.

Under any other circumstances, Susana knew that she and Marty would never have been left alone in Hector and Mariana's living room, sitting next to one another on the couch and talking of the events of the day. But the family members had all gone home, and even Hector had fallen into bed, exhausted and relieved now that he knew his wife was going to make it. The fact that Susana's parents and siblings had allowed her to stay at Mariana's home with Marty, even for a short time, was nothing short of a miracle.

"Have you heard anything more from *la abuela* today?" Marty asked, jarring Susana's thoughts.

La abuela? Susana felt her eyes open wide. Oh, *Señora* Mesa, of course! The poor lady had lost her *nieto*, and they had nearly forgotten her in the concern for Mariana. How the dear woman must be grieving, and how like Marty to be the one to think of her.

"I'm afraid I haven't," Susana admitted, feeling convicted of her selfishness. "Do you suppose it's too late to call and check on her now?"

Marty paused before answering, his blue eyes pensive, warming Susana's heart. "More than likely," he admitted. "But first thing tomorrow, I think we should go over there, don't you?"

Susana nodded. *We?* Did he mean that he wanted her to accompany him to visit *la abuela* and her family? Apparently he did, and Susana liked the idea very much.

"*Sí*," she said. "I believe you're right. Tomorrow morning would be best. This must be a terrible night for their entire family. And it would be better to go in person than to call."

She watched Marty's Adam's apple bob as he swallowed before answering. "This must be especially hard for *Señora* Mesa's daughter and son-in-law, who aren't believers. At least *la abuela* has the assurance that her grandson is with the Lord and she will see him again one day soon. Her family doesn't have that same peace or joy."

"Then we must pray that they will," Susana said, impulsively reaching out to take Marty's hands in her own and then feeling the heat of embarrassment creep up her neck and into her cheeks at the realization of her actions.

Marty's smile put her at ease, as he nodded. "You are so right, dear Susana," he said, his words a caress that sent an easy chill down her spine. "Let's pray for them—and for everyone involved in this situation. It has been an amazing day, hasn't it?"

Susana nodded, scarcely trusting herself to speak. It had been an amazing day, indeed. And they would make a point to pray for the shooters as well, since it was quite obvious that they, too, needed the Lord, whatever their reason for shadowing and murdering the so-recently converted young man.

The Camposes' home seemed shrouded in the darkness of grief, though Imix imagined that she still saw a light shining through, calling her to come closer. Yet how could she? The rumors of the disappearance had already spread through the town, and though no one had spoken the words, it was obvious that everyone believed the stranger named Virginia might never be found—certainly not alive. She was gone, vanished, as other intruders before her, and Imix was surprised at the depth of loss she felt—not only because she would no longer be able to go to the Camposes' home to learn about the signs on paper that spoke words to those who knew their meaning, but also because she would no longer be able to see the joy that always seemed to shine from Virginia's eyes and that even now seemed stronger than the darkness surrounding the little house.

Hector was concerned. Though Mariana was home from the hospital and seemingly growing stronger by the minute, he had not received his weekly letter from his mother. Virginia Correo Rodriguez never missed writing to her children and their families, and her letters had never been more than a day or two late before. Hector hadn't noticed the letter's absence at first, as he had been too busy with getting Mariana home and also performing the quiet, simple funeral for Roberto—a private service with no publicity, as the police had advised that it could become a gang affair if word got out. But they had buried Roberto without incident, and Hector could only pray that there would be no retaliation for Roberto's death. Since he'd been unable to discover whether Roberto had been shot by rival gang members who just happened to see him enter the church with his *abuela* or whether members of his own gang had suspected him of "ratting them out," he had given the problem to God and left it in His capable hands.

Soon after the service, however, Hector realized he had not heard from his mother. When he checked with his siblings and learned none of them had received letters either, his alarm bells wouldn't stop ringing. With no phone at the Camposes' home and much of San Juan Chamula virtually unreachable by cell phone, he was having a difficult time restraining himself from jumping on a bus to go check on her. But how could he? He had a recovering wife to care for, as well as three children and a congregation that needed him, and his siblings were in similar situations.

"Oh God," he prayed, as he returned yet again from checking his empty mailbox, "what should I do? Do I stay here with my wife, or go to check on my mother? Show me, Father. Give me an answer, Lord. Please...let me know if my mother is all right."

A woman's voice penetrated his pain.

Chapter 19

WHEN MARTY AWOKE, THE ROOM WAS DARK. The soft, even breathing of little Hector and Manolo assured him that his roommates were asleep, but someone had awakened him.

Was it You, Lord? he asked silently. And immediately he knew. God had called him to prayer.

What is it, Father? What am I to pray about?

Lying on the floor on his bedroll, Marty waited and listened. As his mind began to focus on Hector's mother near San Juan Chamula, he found himself praying for her safety. Hector had told him earlier that day that he was very concerned for her, as neither he nor his siblings had heard from her as they always did each week like clockwork. Though Hector had downplayed the situation, Marty knew his friend was deeply troubled. He also knew there was no way for Hector to contact his mother except to go to Chamula, and he certainly couldn't do that with Mariana still recovering from her gunshot wound.

Is that it? Marty asked. *Do You want me to go and check on Hector's mother for him? Is that why You awakened me?*

The peace that flowed into his heart at that moment was all the answer he needed. He would tell Hector of his decision in the morning.

Hector's relief was immediate, and his gratitude overflowing. *Thank You, Lord*, he prayed silently, even as he hugged his friend and clapped him on the back. "*Gracias, amigo*," he said. "I can't tell you what this means to me!"

"I'm glad to help. We're family, remember?" Marty smiled, first with his lips and then with his eyes. "*Familia*."

Hector laughed. "*Familia. Sí!* You are so right, *hermano*. We are truly brothers, you and I. But *mañana*? You want to leave tomorrow—so soon?"

Marty shrugged. "Why not? The sooner I leave, the sooner I can return with good news to put your heart at ease."

"Good news. *Sí*." Hector felt his chest contract with worry, though he tried to dismiss it. "I'm sure there's nothing to be concerned about. The letter was probably just lost in the mail, or..." He took a deep breath, ignoring the thought that though one letter might have gotten lost in the mail, it was nearly impossible to imagine that all nine of them would have vanished. "So, I will write down the directions for you, once you get off the bus in San Juan Chamula. You will like the Campos *familia*. They are wonderful people." He stopped. "Unless you're planning to drive there. Are you?"

Marty's eyebrows shot up. "In my El Camino? You're kidding, right?" He laughed. "No way. I'll leave the beast here in your care. The bus will work just fine for me."

Hector laughed. "I hope you don't regret it halfway there. Riding the bus to Chiapas isn't exactly like riding a tour bus in the States, you know."

Marty smiled. "I'll be fine," he assured him.

Hector imagined his friend was right...but he also imagined he was in for a few surprises along the way.

Alberto Javier Rodriguez knew his time was nearly spent. He sensed it as surely as he sensed the demons dancing nearby, salivating with anticipation. And yet he felt powerless to stop the inevitable.

Where was his son, Hector, the preacher who not only prayed for him and told him about Jesus but also sent others to do the same? Why wasn't he here now, when he needed him?

But would it make any difference? he wondered. *Would I listen to him any more now than when he was here last time?* He groaned, the ever-present pain melding with the fear of losing his mind—and his soul. Why were his thoughts so muddled? Was it just the drugs, or was he already passing over to the other side, wherever that might be?

It occurred to him then that though he and Virginia had produced nine offspring, only Hector had come to see him. Where were the others? Were they so busy with their own lives that they had no time for him? Were they unaware of the few miles that separated them on each side of the border? Or was it possible that they simply didn't care?

Whatever the reason, the miserable old man had never felt more lonely or frightened in his entire life. It was as if he, the one who had abandoned his family, had now himself been abandoned.

I will never leave or forsake you.

The somehow-familiar words drifted silently through his mind, haunting him with a memory never fully experienced, a promise as yet unfulfilled. Where had he heard the achingly sweet words before?

He listened, and this time it was Hector's voice that repeated the words: *I will never leave or forsake you.* Yes, of course, that was it! Alberto's pastor-son had been sitting beside his bed, reading to him from the Bible.

Is it true? he wondered. *Is it possible those words were spoken by God…for me?*

Before he could dismiss the dim flicker of hope that dared to flutter in his broken heart, a woman's voice penetrated his pain. "You have a letter, Mr. Rodriguez. Would you like me to read it for you? It's postmarked from San Juan Chamula, Chiapas State."

As the ancient bus groaned and rumbled toward San Juan Chamula, Marty smiled at the realization that he was very near to his final destination. He had never imagined himself a wimp, but he knew now that some of his privileged past had clung to him, despite his attempts to free himself from it. Now he knew that he was not only a wimp but a whiner as well. For the past few hours he had done little but silently complain to God about every bone-jarring bump, every tooth-rattling pothole, every delay-causing detour along the way. True, he'd spent several summers in Tijuana and should be used to roads like this, but he'd never traveled this far on them before.

Others around him had scarcely seemed to notice, as they chattered among themselves or dozed peacefully in their uncomfortable seats. Even the half-dozen chickens seemed undisturbed by the trip, clucking and scratching as if they were still at home in their familiar coop.

I'm going to have to toughen up a bit, aren't I, Lord? Marty mused. *I can't very well go out onto the mission field with expectations of comfort and ease. If I wanted that, I should have stayed home with my mother, where the greatest inconvenience I ever experienced was when the pool heater wasn't working properly and I had to swim in cold water.*

Marty stared out the window at the thickening vegetation as the bus jolted them along an ever-worsening road toward the Mayan town hidden away in the midst of the rain forest. He knew the altitude in Chamula would test his lungs' ability to adjust, just as the primitive living conditions would challenge his commitment to serve God wherever he was sent.

At the thought, Marty shook his head. No. He would not give in to the siren call of an easy life if God indeed had something else planned for him. He had come to Mexico to discover the Lord's plan and purpose for his life, not to find a way to avoid it. Whatever else happened during his stay in San Juan Chamula, Marty was determined to keep his heart open and listen for God's direction.

Imix's heart beat a tattoo of terror against her rib cage, as Kawak pulled her inside the shaman's abode. Imix had not wanted to come anywhere near the place, but since the stranger named Virginia had disappeared, Imix knew that she, too, was in danger for having willingly spent so much time receiving instruction from the despised stranger. Kawak had convinced her that a visit to *la curandera* would dispel the rumors that Imix had been converted to the outsider's beliefs.

The oppressive darkness and sickeningly sweet scent of incense only added to Imix's unease. If this were truly the place where the ancient spirits communed with the woman named Evita, why did it feel so evil? Shouldn't it be a place of joy, a place where believers in the ancient ways could come with confidence and be welcomed with peace?

When the healer laid her cold hand on Imix's bare arm, the girl nearly fainted. Somehow she managed to stay on her feet, though she hadn't been able to contain the cry that had escaped her lips. Even now, as *la curandera* led Imix and Kawak to the center of the room, where they eased themselves down onto the blanket of branches and pine needles that covered the floor, Imix wanted nothing more than to break free of the woman's grasp and run screaming from the room, never to return again.

But she sensed that for her own safety and that of her family, she must stay and hear what the healer had to stay. And so she sat, breathing as slowly and deeply as she was able and praying to whatever invisible spirits might be lurking around that she would somehow escape this horrible place alive.

Denying a sob, she sighed instead,
eyeing a few stray age spots on her hands.

Chapter 20

CELESTE WAS BORED—OR WAS SHE JUST LONELY? Sometimes she had difficulty discerning between the two. As a result she had spent much of the previous two decades of her life "entertaining" men in an effort to quell the unnamed emotion.

Now, as she lay in the lounge chair beside the pool, a large beach umbrella shading her delicate skin from the sun's damaging rays, she sipped the icy lemonade prepared for her by her housekeeper only moments earlier.

Sylvia. She had been in Celeste's employ for nearly fifteen years, faithfully waiting on her employer's every need or whim throughout that time. Of course, Celeste paid her handsomely for her duties and therefore felt no guilt over the many demands she put on the middle-aged woman. However, though Sylvia was actually three years younger than Celeste, the pampered diva always thought of her employee as being older than she. At least, she certainly looked that way, with her ample waistline and graying hair, pulled back in a bun at the nape of her neck, not to mention the frumpy housedresses and sturdy, platform shoes that were her trademark. Celeste didn't insist that Sylvia dress differently, since she was at least neat and clean and always prompt and efficient, but she couldn't imagine how a woman looking fifty in the eyeball could help but be consumed with her looks.

Perhaps it's because she never cared before, Celeste reasoned. *I suppose if you've never been considered a beauty, it doesn't bother you when you reach the age where beauty fades and there's nothing left but memories. But I was always beautiful. Everyone told me so—my father when I was little; Martin, before he died; and all the others since. But now?* She sighed, and for a moment her mind flashed back to the charity dinner a few nights earlier and the way the younger women in attendance had quickly garnered the male attention, leaving her to wonder why she'd bothered to come. The slight still ran deep, as she glanced down at her still mostly toned legs, marred only slightly by encroaching spots of cellulite. *What am I supposed to do now?* she cried silently. *Start spouting the phrase that "beauty is only skin deep"? Ha! You either have it or you don't.*

Denying a sob, she sighed instead, eyeing a few stray age spots on her hands. *And it seems it's time I admitted that I no longer have it—whatever "it" may be. So what, then, is left for me? Is there nothing to look forward to, nothing to anticipate... or is it truly all behind me now?*

Marty was glad Hector had taken the time to meticulously write down the directions from the bus stop in San Juan Chamula to the Campos home, as it was apparent that none of the town's residents was anxious to talk to him. From the moment he exited the belching, smoking vehicle, he had felt as if he were in enemy territory. Not only did the citizens of Chamula eye him with what appeared to be antagonistic suspicion, but it seemed to him that the atmosphere of the entire area was so choked with evil that Marty could scarcely breathe.

Of course, as he trudged toward the Campos home, carefully following Hector's instructions, he recognized that some of his shortness of breath was due to the 7,200-foot elevation, which was a far cry from his San Diego/Tijuana digs. But the heaviness that weighed him down in this throwback to Mayan history was more than altitude.

By the time he reached what appeared to be the home Hector had described to him, Marty was beginning to get the hang of breathing deeply as he walked, something he never even considered at home. He hoped he could even his respiration completely by the time he spoke to the Campos family, as he didn't want to appear any more of an outsider than absolutely necessary—though he had little doubt that his appearance in town was already making the rounds of the local gossip circuit.

Taking one more deep breath, Marty began the final approach to the humble abode, noticing a struggling garden at the side and remembering that Hector had mentioned how Virginia enjoyed tending it. Yes, everything about this home affirmed that he was at the right place.

When he reached the door, he raised his hand to knock, and then stopped. Someone was watching him. He turned to look behind him, just as an indiscernible flash disappeared behind the trees. Obviously his presence in this little out-of-the-way town had made more of an impact than he had realized.

Refocusing his attention on the task at hand, he turned back to the door and completed his interrupted knock. He only prayed that Virginia Correo Rodriguez herself would answer, dispelling the doubts and concerns that plagued her family back in Tijuana.

La abuela awoke from a troubled nap, having dozed only fitfully during the past couple of hours. Lately it seemed that no matter how tired she felt, she seldom slept soundly. She wondered if it was because, even as her consciousness drifted away, she heard the call to come home growing ever louder. And oh, how she wanted to answer! Her homesick heart was so restless...and tired. But each time she prayed and asked *El Señor* to take her to Himself, the whisper to her heart was the same: "Not yet, *mija*. Not yet."

This afternoon her jumbled thoughts were of more than just her sweet Roberto, gone from her but safe now with the Lord. Of course, each bittersweet thought of her *nieto* led her to the need for her daughter and son-in-law to make the same decision Roberto had made before he died: to stop living their own lives, going their own ways, and turn around and begin the trek back to the Father. If the old woman had nothing more than the promise of her family's salvation, it would be enough; she could die in peace.

But today she thought of the young *gringo*, the boy named Marty who had come to stay with the Rodriguez family — the one *Señora* Mesa was certain had his heart set on young Susana Lopez. It was his face that swam before her thoughts at this moment of waking, and she sensed the need to pray for him — for wisdom, for discernment, for protection.

And so she did.

Mariana felt woozy, but it was so good to be out of bed, even if only for a little while. Sitting outside on a kitchen chair that had been moved from inside the house to the front yard, she basked in the late afternoon sunshine, her heart bursting with gratitude and joy. What a wonderful caregiver Hector had been, and how glorious to see her children playing together under his watchful eye.

When the partially rounded soccer ball suddenly took a detour and flew in her direction, Mariana flinched and squealed, but Hector was there to deflect the black and white orb before it made contact.

"*Lo siento, Mama*," Manolo cried, rushing to her side. "I'm sorry! I didn't mean to kick it toward you. Are you all right?"

The entire *familia* was gathered around her now, *oohing* and *aahing* with joy and relief that she wasn't hurt, and clucking their tongue at Manolo for not being more careful.

"I'm sure he didn't mean to kick it in my direction," Mariana assured them, stroking Manolo's hair in an effort to comfort him. "Besides, your brave papa has protected me."

Hector laughed. "I'm not sure about the brave part; I just have good reflexes." He bent down and kissed the top of Mariana's head, and the slight smell of sweat made her smile. How her husband loved to play with his children—and how she loved him for being such a good papa to them.

God had spared her life, and she was so grateful for the chance to be with her precious *familia* and watch them interact together. But what of Virginia? Mariana knew that her welfare was continually on Hector's mind, as it was on hers. How she prayed that Marty would return soon with good news and a simple explanation of what had happened to the missing letters.

Spotting a forlorn Susana, sitting alone on the stoop, Mariana knew she wasn't the only one anticipating Marty's return. Something was brewing between those two, and Mariana smiled at the thought of what it might be.

Marty heard a sound—a whisper, a whistle—

he wasn't sure.

Chapter 21

ARTY'S HEART WAS HEAVY AS HE THREW HIS knapsack full of the meager belongings he had brought with him over his shoulder and shut the door to the Campos home, heading for town to catch the bus that would carry him back across Mexico and eventually deposit him in Tijuana, where he would deliver the news that no one wanted to hear.

Though he had arrived in San Juan Chamula with at least a shred of hope for Virginia's safety still intact, even that had now been lost, as the family told him how just two days before his arrival Virginia's body had been found. They had even taken him to the freshly dug gravesite, where they told him of the simple ceremony they had offered for their beloved friend and where Marty had then prayed and said good-bye to the woman who had given her life to help spread the gospel any way she could.

As he trudged toward town, Marty reviewed his brief visit. Surprised to see him standing at their front door, the Campos family had welcomed him with open arms, quickly preparing him the finest meal they were able to muster from their sparse supplies, and giving him Virginia's bed to sleep on. As he lay there at night after the family had gone to bed, he had wondered about the many nights Virginia had lain in the same bed, thinking and praying and thanking God for His goodness, even as Marty did before drifting off to sleep.

The family had also told him the sad and disturbing story of how they had come home from town one day the previous week, only to find Virginia gone. Her few belongings were exactly as she'd left them, but there was no sign of her anywhere. And then word had come that her body had been found, and that it was likely she had not died of natural causes, though it was also likely that no one would ever be prosecuted for her murder.

And now he was leaving. After two nights in Chamula, talking with the Campos family and listening to their many memories of Virginia Correo Rodriguez, there seemed to be no reason to stay longer. He dreaded returning with such a grim report, but he knew Hector and the entire Rodriguez family were waiting for him, and the news wasn't going to get any better if he put it off. At least he could return Virginia's meager belongings to her family and end their agonizing distress about her condition.

Midway between the Campos home and the entrance to town, Marty heard a sound—a whisper, a whistle—he wasn't sure. Turning toward the direction where the noise had originated, he scanned the area but saw no one, though he realized someone could easily be hiding behind one of the many trees along the way.

Determined to get to the bus stop without further interruption, he set out at a quicker pace, only to hear the sound again. This time he stopped in the middle of the road and hollered in Spanish, "Who's there, and what do you want? Come out so we can talk."

Within seconds a young Mayan woman stepped hesitantly from behind a tree, her eyes downcast and her black hair hanging straight down her back, a few wisps spilling over onto the front of her shoulders. Though the Campos family had introduced him to the handful of other *evangelicos* in the area, Marty did not remember this one being among them. And apart from that tiny band of believers, no one in San Juan Chamula had made any effort at all to welcome or even speak to him.

"Can I help you?" Marty asked, hoping to coax the girl the rest of the way into the road so they could speak face-to-face. When she didn't move or respond in any way, he changed his tactics and walked slowly toward her.

"I'm Marty Johnson," he said. "What's your name?"

Still she didn't speak, but by now Marty was close enough to hear the short, obviously frightened pants of her breathing. Did he dare reach out to touch her?

Feeling constrained, he waited. At last she lifted her head, though her eyes were still downcast.

"I am Imix," she said, her voice as soft as rippling water. "I...knew the woman named Virginia."

Marty's heart leaped. If Imix knew Virginia, perhaps she also knew who was responsible for her death.

"How...did you know her?" Marty asked, keeping his voice low and nonthreatening.

At last she lifted her lids to gaze upon him with eyes so dark and large they appeared to be deep pools of velvet. "She was my...teacher. I went to her class to learn of the marks on the paper."

Part of Virginia's "little flock," Marty thought, remembering that Diego Campos had told him about two Mayan women who had recently started attending the weekly meetings. He waited again.

"She...disappeared," Imix offered, watching Marty's face as she spoke. "She is...dead."

He offered her a sad smile. "I know," he said, still careful to speak softly and evenly. "The Campos family told me. They came home from town one day and she was gone. And now they have buried her. They took me to her grave."

Imix ducked her head. "It is very sad," she whispered.

Marty hesitated, then asked, "Do you know what happened...how she died?"

The girl's head snapped up, her dark eyes wide. "No!" She shook her head. "I do not know...and I cannot say. Now you must go. Do not stay here. It is dangerous for everyone—you too." Her eyes darted from side to side then, and the rise and fall of her chest seemed to have quickened. "I must go. If they see me..."

Marty frowned. "Who? If who sees you? The people in town? The shamans? I've heard of them, and I know they don't appreciate outsiders coming around."

Imix's eyes grew even wider. "Do not speak of *la curandera*. The spirits will hear you." She glanced up into the sky. "They are always near...listening. Watching." Looking back at Marty, she said, "You must go now. Now! Do you understand? Go!"

And then she disappeared, racing back into the trees where she'd first hidden and called to him, running as fast as she could from the stranger who had come to check on Virginia—and from the spirits, who watched and listened.

Nothing had been the same for Alberto since he'd heard the letter—the words from his wife who spoke to him from so very far away. She had forgiven him...and she still loved him. How was that possible, after all these years and after all he had done?

More amazingly, she had spoken of God's love and forgiveness, even as Hector did each time he came, telling the hardened old man that there was still hope for him, even now.

No. It could not be. Perhaps his wife could forgive him, even love him...but God? Never. God was perfect. He was just and righteous and holy. Alberto was none of these. If

Alberto had learned anything in his sixty-five years of life, it was what he was . . . and what he was not. He knew he was selfish, pitiful, mean, and spiteful—definitely not qualifications for getting into heaven. And he was not good or pure or kind, or even friendly for that matter. Few people liked Alberto, and for good reason, though he had once been an outgoing, fun-loving man who enjoyed his children and cared for his wife.

How had he lost those good traits along the way? How had they been so overshadowed by the bad? And how could there be hope for someone who had so little to offer?

Perhaps it was better before he heard from Virginia. Her words had rekindled a flicker of hope in his heart that could only lead to devastating disappointment. Better to accept the terrifying truth than to cling to what could never be.

Alberto squeezed his eyes shut and groaned. Could there be a more wretched soul on earth than he? No, he decided. He was the lowest of the low, and even now the demons danced with anticipation.

Celeste had not cried herself to sleep in years. She had either made sure there was someone beside her to warm her bed if not her heart, or she had drunk herself into unconsciousness. Tonight she had neither, her stomach too queasy to accept liquor and her appearance too ghastly to hunt for a male companion.

And so she cried—quietly at first, gaining strength as she went along. Soon she was screaming and pounding the pillow, glad Sylvia's room was at the opposite end of the spacious house that echoed Celeste's emptiness. Why had Martin died so young and left her alone to raise their son? They had planned to be a lifelong couple, raising several children and growing old together. Instead, Martin—who never met a challenge he didn't accept and who thrived on adventure—had insisted on learning to skydive. It was little solace when the instructor told Celeste that Martin was the only student he'd ever lost on the first jump. Should Celeste have been honored to be the first such widow? Should she have been grateful that her husband was an only son, the heir to a substantial sum of money, which, along with a large life insurance settlement, had all passed to her, so at the very least she didn't have to worry about money while she spent the remainder of her life alone?

Alone. Shame on her. She knew she shouldn't think that way. After all, she'd had Marty to keep her company. But every time she'd looked at him, she'd seen her dead husband— in his features, his mannerisms, his readiness to try anything, regardless of the danger involved. And her heart had broken again…and again…believing that one day her son, too, would attempt one challenge too many, and she would stand alone over his grave, saying good-bye.

It was more than she could bear. If only she weren't such a coward herself, she would take her own life and be done with it. But though she'd considered it countless times, she'd never been able to move past thinking about it to actually doing it.

Perhaps being a coward had its advantages after all.

And then she saw it. On a little table behind and to the side of the desk sat a framed picture.

Chapter 22

ROSA'S BIRTHDAY WAS THE NEXT DAY. SHE WOULD be ten years old. She had to survive only one more day and she would be able to celebrate her *cumpleaños*. Since witnessing the murder from her front yard, the little girl had taken to looking over her shoulder, imagining that someone was following her. But with each passing day, her fear lessened and she ventured out a little farther from her home.

Today was an especially exciting day, as she was going to town with her mother to buy the candy for her *piñata*. All her cousins were coming to the party, and Rosa somehow sensed that the celebration would mean more even than simply the passing of another year on her way to adulthood. It was as if she would be receiving a completely unexpected but life-changing gift.

Nearly dancing as she and her mother left the house, she scarcely noticed when her mother took a detour on their way to town. "I want to stop by that little church a few blocks from here—*Casa de Dios*. *Mi amiga* Filimina has been inviting me to go, but I want to take a look at it first."

Rosa nodded absently, absorbed now with counting cracks in the sidewalk—and pebbles in the dirt where there was no sidewalk. What sort of *piñata* would her parents choose for her party? She could hardly wait to find out.

Marty's heart cried all the way back to Tijuana. He scarcely noticed the bumpy bus ride, the odors of too many unwashed human and animal bodies in too close quarters. His dread of having to report back to Hector that his mother was truly gone—most likely murdered—made the trip pass far too quickly.

Before he knew it, the bleary-eyed *gringo* flowed from the bus doors in a flood of humanity that spilled out onto the streets of Tijuana. His clothes felt glued to him, his hair a mop of grease, his eyes sandpaper. What did it matter? His mission had been a failure. He had expected to return with good news that would put the Rodriguez family at ease. Instead, he had to tell them that they would never again see their beloved mother and grandmother this side of heaven.

Why did she go there, Lord? Why did You send her? From what the Campos family told me, she had not one convert to show for her time. Sure, she taught a handful of people to read a few words, but did that really make a difference? Shouldn't her life count for something? He shuddered at his next thought: *Shouldn't her death have some sort of lasting meaning?*

The Rodriguez house was in sight now, and his heart grew heavier with each step, as Virginia's sacrifice began to become personal. *What does this mean to me, Father? Here I am, supposedly seeking You for clear direction on what to do with my life, how best to serve You. Am I to end up like Virginia? Will my life just one day end, with nothing on this earth to show for it?*

He shook his head, forcing one dragging foot in front of the other as he turned into the fenced yard of the Rodriguez home. *Help me, Lord. Help me know what to say, how to—*

His thoughts were interrupted by a four-year-old whirlwind, who exploded through the front door and immediately wrapped her arms around his leg.

"*Tio* Marty!" she cried. "You're back! Mama, Papa, *Tio* Marty is here!"

Marty took a deep breath and ruffled Lupita's hair. He forced a smile. "Yes, I'm back, *mija*. And *gracias* for the warm welcome."

Rosa felt her eyes widen when they walked into the church and she saw the large wooden cross on the front wall. Irregular rows of metal chairs filled the room, but nothing else indicated that this small building in a run-down neighborhood was in actuality a church. Perhaps her mother was wrong. After all, Rosa had been to church before—not often or regularly, but occasionally—and the big buildings with the statues hanging on the walls and the candles burning in front of the altar looked nothing like this place. Still, until she knew otherwise, she would treat it as a church and remain silent.

Walking just behind her mother, they approached a door marked *Oficina*. Rosa wondered if they would find anyone inside.

Her mother knocked, and in less than a minute the door was opened by a nice-looking man with dark hair and a mustache. Rosa knew he couldn't be a priest, or he would be wearing some sort of long, dark robe. Instead he stood in the doorway, dressed as if he were about to go outside and work in the garden.

The man smiled. "May I help you?"

For the first time since they'd come into the little building, Rosa's mother appeared uneasy. *"Buenos días, señor,"* she said, her voice hesitant. "I'm looking for...*el pastor*. Is he here?"

The man's smile widened. "I am Pastor Hector Rodriguez. And you are...?"

Rosa thought for a moment that her mother had forgotten her name, but at last she said, "I am... Teresa Diaz. *Mi amiga* Filimina Vega has been inviting me to come to church with her, but I wanted to...to..."

Teresa's voice trailed off, and now Rosa wondered if her mother had forgotten why they came. Rosa frowned. Why had they come, anyway? She had no idea, but she waited patiently to see if her mother would remember.

Pastor Rodriguez chuckled. "Perhaps you came to check us out," he suggested. "To see what we are about before you come to a service." He nodded his head and gestured for them to come into his office. "That is a wise thing to do, *Señora* Diaz. The Holy Scriptures tell us to be wise as serpents but gentle as doves. You have come with the right attitude. Please, come in. You are welcome here."

He stood back so they could enter, smiling down at Rosa, who ducked her head but not before recognizing the warmth in his eyes. She felt herself relax as he asked, "And who is this lovely young lady?"

"I am Rosa," she answered before her mother could speak for her. "I'm nine, but tomorrow is *mi cumpleaños*. I'll be ten!"

The man named Hector raised his eyebrows, looking quite surprised. "Ten years old tomorrow? You really are a young lady then, aren't you?"

Rosa caught her mother's smile and she knew the pastor was teasing her, but she didn't mind. She had already decided she liked him, though she couldn't imagine why anyone would want to be a pastor in such a small, simple church.

She spotted the two folding chairs in front of his desk at the very moment the pastor indicated them, and she plunked down in one as her mother settled into the other. Hector then took a seat behind the desk and continued to smile at them.

"So," he said, "what would you like to know?"

Hesitantly Rosa's mother began to voice her concerns and questions, and though Rosa tuned out much of what was said, she sensed that her mother was pleased with the pastor's answers. As discreetly as possible, the almost ten-year-old girl let her eyes wander around the room, landing first on the pictures that hung on the wall—pictures of Hector and what was no doubt his wife and children. Rosa thought she recognized one of the boys from school.

The man's desk, though dusted, appeared very old and very used. Several books, including two that Rosa was fairly certain were Bibles, were spread across its surface.

And then she saw it. On a little table behind and to the side of the desk sat a framed picture of a tattooed man. He wasn't smiling, nor was Rosa. In fact, it was all she could do not to jump up and run screaming from the room. The pastor knew one of the men who had killed the other man in front of her house the night she watched from under the tree! Possibly the man in the picture was even related to Hector Rodriguez, who called himself a pastor and smiled at little girls, making them feel welcome. Did he know what sort of person he had on display in his office?

The voices of her mother and the pastor began to fade to a dull buzz in her head, as the room grew warmer and Rosa's ears started to ring. She felt light, dizzy, airy, as if she were floating above the chair where she still sat, frozen at the sudden realization that she probably wasn't going to live until her tenth birthday after all. If the man in the picture, who was undoubtedly one of the pastor's friends or relatives, came into the room while she was still there, she wouldn't live until nightfall.

Summoning what little strength she had, she pushed herself to her feet, determined to escape and explain to her mother later, but the room began to spin and blackness closed in before she could make it to the door.

By the time Hector got home for lunch, his heart was singing. What a blessing that God had used him to dispel the fear of a little girl who had witnessed a terrible act. She now understood that the man she saw in the picture was dead and could no longer hurt her. He had also been able to assure Rosa that the other man couldn't hurt her either, since Roberto had confessed to the pastor in their sole meeting together that Paco had died in the car accident in front of the very home where the two former gangbangers had committed the crime. The little girl had cried with relief, saying it was the best present anyone could ever receive on the day before their tenth *cumpleaños*, even though she was sorry for *la abuela* who had lost her *nieto*.

Of course, the story had led to obvious questions from both mother and daughter about the eternal fate of those who had lived such a terrible life. Hector had carefully explained that though they had each paid the ultimate price for their sins, Roberto had repented and turned to Christ before breathing his last, and he was now in heaven with his Savior. Sadly, Hector could not offer them the same assurance about Paco. Both Teresa and Rosa Diaz had seemed impressed with the story, however, and Hector imagined they would spend much time pondering it in the days to come. In the meantime, Teresa had assured him that their entire family would be in attendance on Sunday.

Now Hector was home, and as he walked in the front door, his heart leaped at the sight of Marty sitting on the couch, surrounded by the three Rodriguez children. But one look into Marty's eyes told Hector that the news he was about to hear was not good.

Hector had always known that Chiapas State was a dangerous place for outsiders.

Chapter 23

HIS MOTHER WAS GONE. HE WANTED TO BELIEVE otherwise, to somehow convince himself that there had been a mistake and the woman who lay in the ground outside San Juan Chamula was not his mother... but he knew better. Hector had always known that Chiapas State—the San Juan Chamula area in particular—was a dangerous place for outsiders. This was particularly true if those outsiders were there with the goal of evangelizing the residents who already considered themselves followers of Christ, though their beliefs were nothing more than a mystical conglomeration of vague Catholic ideas and long-held Mayan practices. Occasional tourists visited the backward village, sure, but they did a bit of sightseeing, left a handful of dollars or pesos behind, and went on their way. No threat to the inhabitants—or the spirits they worshiped. But evangelical missionaries—*los evangelicos*—regardless of how they came packaged? That was another story altogether.

I thought You would protect her, Lord, Hector cried silently, as he knelt beside the desk in his office, his hands folded and resting in his chair. He had returned to the church soon after talking with Marty, needing to be alone in his grief, though he knew it was unfair to Mariana and the rest of the *familia*. He knew, too, that he must be the one to tell his brothers and sisters; he couldn't leave that to Marty. And yet...he needed time alone with God first.

Why, God? he prayed, echoing the universal question he had counseled so many others to let go of in their grief. But now it was his grief, his loss, and he wanted answers. His mother had been the godliest woman he had ever known. She had lost her husband to another woman but had still managed to raise nine children to love and serve God—no small feat! And Hector didn't doubt that Virginia Correo Rodriguez had settled near San Juan Chamula at the Lord's direction. Why, then, had He not protected her?

But the longer he cried out in his pain, demanding answers and questioning God's goodness, the less able he was to hear the still, small voice that called back to him.

Imix had never been more terrified in her life. She knew if any-one saw her or heard about what she was doing, she could be dead before the sun rose again over the treetops of San Juan Chamula. And yet she couldn't seem to stop herself. She had to find out, had to talk to the Campos family and ask if they still believed in the God mentioned in their version of the Scriptures, even now—now that the woman named Virginia was gone.

Imix had chosen to sneak out at night, while her mother and sisters slept. She could only hope they didn't awaken and find her gone. She also hoped—and even prayed, though she wasn't sure to whom—that the Campos family would be recep-tive to her visit.

Standing in front of the door to the house where she used to come each week to study the marks in the book, Imix found herself shivering, more from fear than the cold, though the dampness of the night fog made her wish she'd thrown a blanket over her shoulders before leaving. But then, she'd made the decision so quickly that there hadn't been time...

Raising her hand and willing it to stop shaking, she rapped lightly, realizing even as she did that no one would hear her, though she imagined that everyone within miles could hear the rapid pounding of her heart. When no one responded to her timid knock, she tried again, louder this time. A few moments later she heard a man's voice: "*Quien es?* Who is it? Who is there?"

Imix opened her mouth, but was stunned to realize that no sound came out. It was as if she had formed the words in her mind, but her tongue and throat would not cooperate. When the man called out again, she finally managed to gasp a one-word answer: "Imix."

She waited again, listening to the man speaking to someone, no doubt his wife, asking if she knew anyone named Imix. When the woman responded that she did and that she was one of the Mayan women who had attended Virginia's weekly classes, the door creaked open slightly. The man poked his head out. In the darkness, Imix could see little other than the whites of his eyes.

"What do you want?" the man asked.

"I..." She stopped. What did she want? She wanted to talk to them, to ask if... Her mind was blank. She was sure she had wanted to ask them something specific, but no matter how hard she tried, she couldn't remember what it was.

The man was growing impatient, and Imix was afraid he would send her away and close the door.

"Please," she said, her voice scarcely above a whisper, "I need to talk with you, with your wife, about...about the woman named Virginia."

A flicker of fear flashed in the man's eyes, but then slowly he stepped back and opened the door wide enough for Imix to enter. Relieved, the young Mayan woman hurried through the door.

It was nearly as dark inside as it had been outside the door, but as her eyes grew accustomed to the surroundings, Imix recognized the outline of a man and a woman, huddled together, watching her. Once again, she opened her mouth, determined to voice her question.

"I...came to ask about...about your God. The one in your Bible. The one the woman named Virginia spoke of."

This time she sensed rather than saw the flash of fear that followed the mentioning of Virginia's name, but it faded as quickly as it came. "Forgive us," the woman said at last. "We have not been good hosts. Please, sit down. I will heat some water for tea."

Imix held up her hand, even as *Señor* Campos lit a small candle and set it on the low-slung table by the stove, casting a small but welcome glow in its immediate vicinity. "No. Please," Imix protested, "don't bother. I know you would have to light the fire to heat the water, and I can't stay that long. I just..." She paused, allowing the Campos couple to escort her to the table where she sank down on the floor, grateful to rest her shaky legs. Now, what had she been about to say?

Before she could speak, *Señora* Campos reached across the table and placed her hand over Imix's. "Thank you for coming," she said, her smile soft in the candlelight. "You cared for Virginia, didn't you?"

Imix nodded, surprised at her response. She had been curious about the woman's beliefs, but she had never realized that she truly did care for her...until now. Imix just hoped they wouldn't ask if she had any knowledge of what had happened to Virginia. Truthfully, though Imix had her suspicions, she did not know for certain, and she was grateful for that.

"I...miss coming to the meetings," Imix confessed. "And...and I wonder about this God that Virginia spoke of when she read from the Bible. You, too, believe in Him, yes?"

The Campos couple exchanged glances, and then *Señor* Campos cleared his throat. "Yes, we do. We believe He is the one true God...the only God. The Scriptures tell us about

Him—how we are to worship, how we are to live." He paused. "And what happens to us when we die."

Imix's heart began to race. For as long as she could remember, she had been terrified at the thought of death. She had tried to stay busy, to keep her mind from dwelling on the inevitable, but always she returned to the frightening prospect of what would become of her after she took her last breath.

"Where do you believe...the woman called Virginia...is now?" Imix ventured.

Señora Campos smiled again. "We know where she is, Imix. She is with her Savior in heaven."

Imix felt her brows draw together. *Heaven.* She had heard the word but wasn't sure what it meant. Before she could ask, *Senora* Campos began to explain.

"Heaven is a beautiful place," she said, her hand still resting on Imix's. "It is a place where there is no sickness or tears or death, no fear or torment or pain. It is perfect, but only because God is there—the source of all light and life and joy. Would you like to know for certain that you, like Virginia, will go there when you die?"

Imix gasped. Was such a thing possible? How could it be? And where was this place? How would she get there? So many questions...and yet at that moment she knew only one thing for certain: Yes, she wanted to go there when she died.

She smiled and nodded, then felt her shoulders relax as *Señora* Campos explained to her about the One who had already secured her entrance into this perfect place.

He couldn't just stand there, staring at them.

Chapter 24

IT WAS SUNDAY MORNING, AND IT WAS THE FIRST time Hector had felt stymied about what to preach. He had spent the previous day in his office, praying, reading the Scriptures, and seeking God for direction, but by the end of the day, he had nothing. After tossing and turning most of the night, he had fallen asleep with the hope that he would awaken with at least the nugget of an idea in his mind, but it hadn't happened. And now he stood before the little congregation, wondering what had ever made him think he was called to be a pastor.

The eager eyes, the expectant faces, watching him and waiting to see where he would direct them in their Bibles, served only to make him feel more unworthy than ever. What would his flock think if they knew he stood before them, questioning everything he had ever proclaimed about a loving and sovereign God?

And yet he knew he had to do something. He couldn't just stand there, staring at them. What he really wanted was to hand his Bible to someone else and leave, to drive to the beach and walk on the sand and listen for God's voice. For truly the Lord had abandoned him—now, when He needed Him the most. How was that possible? How did a loving, caring, merciful God abandon His children in the midst of tragedy?

Hector despised himself for thinking that way, but he felt powerless to change it. His thoughts and emotions seemed to have taken on a life of their own since he heard the news about his mother. And yet, hadn't he expected as much? Hadn't he known from the very moment he realized he hadn't received his weekly letter? But until hearing the words from Marty upon his return from San Juan Chamula, Hector had been able to cling to hope, however thin and shaky. Now even that was gone, swallowed up in the words "disappeared…dead… buried."

His heart nearly imploded at the reminder, and to his horror, tears spilled from his eyes onto his cheeks, as his chest began to heave in uncontrollable sobs. His knees buckled, but before he hit the ground, he felt Mariana on one side and Marty on the other, holding him up and nearly carrying him to a chair. Within moments the entire congregation—including little Rosa and her mother, Teresa—had gathered around him. Those who were close enough reached out and laid their hands on him, while others who were farther back in the crowd raised their hands toward heaven. But all began to pray for the man who was their pastor, their shepherd, their brother…their friend. And in the midst of his pain, Hector rejoiced, knowing that God had not deserted him after all, for he could hear the Holy One's voice ringing out loud and clear through the prayers and petitions of His people.

Susana lay in her bed on Sunday night, pondering the events at church that morning. Her brother-in-law Hector had seemed to melt before their very eyes, as grief over the loss of his mother overwhelmed him. But then…a miracle, as the congregation prayed for him and healing flowed, not just to the heartbroken pastor but seemingly to all who were in attendance.

Susana herself had been stunned as she joined in the group prayer, only to find herself thinking thoughts that were too pure and powerful to be her own. In a split second of time, even as she prayed, she knew she was going to marry Marty Johnson—not wishful thinking, but a knowing that exceeded anything she had ever experienced before. She also knew that the two of them would one day go to San Juan Chamula to complete the work Virginia had started.

Now, in the semiprivacy of her bedroom, which she shared with her younger sister Lilliana, she wondered how God would accomplish such a thing. She had no doubt that it would be done—and that through no effort of her own—but it was difficult not to try to imagine what God might do to bring it about.

She had to admit, of course, that this was an easy revelation for her to accept—at least the part about marrying Marty. That possibility had already begun to tease its way into her consciousness, though she had never spoken of it to anyone. The part about going to Chamula in Chiapas State, however, was another matter entirely, and she was glad that the effecting of these events was up to God and not to her. Admittedly, if it were her idea and not something God had impressed on her heart, she would have left out the part about San Juan Chamula. But since she was confident that it was God's plan and not her own, she was at peace with all the details.

With that, she smiled and drifted off to sleep.

Rosa's birthday party had been the best ever. It was all she had thought of all week, even on Sunday morning when she and her mother visited the little church where the pastor smiled and made you feel welcome one day, and then cried and made you feel needed another. Rosa had already decided that she liked the little church very much and planned to go every chance she got.

As she lay in her bed, waiting for her mother to call her to breakfast, she marveled at how God had protected her, for surely that's what had happened. Though she had been disobedient and snuck outside at night, exposing herself to danger when she saw a man killed, God had heard her prayers and kept her from harm. The two men who had committed the crime right before her eyes were now dead, and Rosa could only hope and pray they hadn't told anyone else about her, for if they had, then she still wasn't safe.

Pushing that possibility from her mind, she thought about what the pastor had told her about the man named Roberto—how he had confessed his sins and turned to Jesus just before he died. Because of that, the pastor had assured her, Roberto was now in heaven. Rosa could only assume that the other man, Paco, was not in heaven, as he had died with a gun in his hand, ready to kill with his last breath.

The thought drove a spike of shivers down her spine, even under the warm covers of her bed. Never in her life had she considered killing anyone, but hadn't she sinned when she disobeyed her parents and went outside without permission? What about the times she had told lies to keep from getting in trouble? Or the time she took her sister's candy when she wasn't looking?

Rosa sighed. She might be ten years old now, but there were still so many things about life that confused her. Would she understand it all better when she was older? She hoped so, but from what she'd seen in some grown-ups, she wasn't so sure.

Imix was sure Kawak had figured out that she was still going to the Camposes' home on occasion, though not as regularly as when Virginia was there. The cold stare Imix received from her friend each time she passed her house made her skin prickle on the back of her neck. She regretted not being able to share her excitement and joy with Kawak, but she knew the stoic and devout Mayan would never accept Imix's conversion and acceptance of the *evangelicos'* form of Christianity. *Evangelicos* were the enemy, so far as Kawak and most other Mayans were concerned, nearly synonymous with *los conquistadores.* If they knew Imix had adopted their beliefs, they would consider her a traitor who deserved to suffer the same fate as the intruder named Virginia.

But though they couldn't possibly know for sure that Imix had become an *evangelico,* Kawak and others no doubt suspected as much. And that made every trip Imix made to the Camposes' home a dangerous excursion. Though she and the Campos family had agreed that Imix should come only when she could safely steal away at night and that their meetings would be brief—just long enough for a brief discussion of a verse or two of Scripture and a quick prayer—Imix knew she was risking her very life and the lives of the Campos family each time she took that first step toward their home. And yet her hunger to know more about this God who loved her and had forgiven her and made a way for her to be with Him forever drew her so strongly that she couldn't resist. Indeed, she had no desire to do so.

Tonight was no different. As she moved as stealthily and silently as possible, staying in the shadows and keeping an alert eye for anything unusual or suspicious, Imix's heart raced and her hands were damp with perspiration. But it was as much her desire to be with her new spiritual family as her fear of being caught that caused her to feel that way.

When at last she reached her friends' home, she scarcely had time to rap on the door before it opened and she was ushered inside and welcomed warmly, reaffirming her belief that the joy of fellowship with others who believed as she did was worth every risk.

Either God was sovereign, or He wasn't.

Chapter 25

MARIANA LAID HER HAND ON HECTOR'S ARM, invading the quiet bubble that surrounded him as he sat in the predawn hours at the kitchen table, staring at a cup of coffee that had long since grown cold. The children and Marty were all asleep, and he had thought Mariana was as well. He should have known she would wake up and notice the empty spot on his side of the bed.

He lifted his head and smiled at the woman who shared his heart, his home, his life. *Gracias a Dios* that she had recovered from the gunshot wound that could so easily have taken her life. How could his faith be so weak, so tentative, so conditional that he would praise and thank God one moment for sparing his beloved wife, and then doubt that same God when his mother's life ended in a faraway village full of pagan worshippers? Either God was sovereign, or He wasn't. Either their lives were in His hands—or they weren't. Which was it? And how could he, a pastor, still wrestle with such a fundamental question?

"I missed you," Mariana said, pulling a chair from the table and sitting down beside him.

"*Gracias, querida*," he said, laying his hand on hers. "For missing me, for loving me...for always being there."

She nodded. "There is nowhere else I want to be. Second only to being a child of God, I am your wife. My place is at your side."

Hector's heart squeezed. "And I am honored to have you there."

Mariana touched his cup. "Your coffee is cold. Shall I heat it for you?"

He shook his head. "I didn't really want it anyway. I just...I got up because..."

Her voice was soft as she clasped his hand in both of hers. "Because you were thinking of your mama—missing her, wishing you could see her again, hear her voice...hold her close."

Not trusting himself to speak, Hector nodded, even as the tears squeezed from his eyes and dripped down his face onto the table. Each time he thought he had cried until he had no more tears left to shed, a new flood poured forth from his heart. He had thought that surely after he broke down in front of his congregation, he would be able to get on with his life, move past this terrible pain and finally come to a place of rejoicing that his mother was at last in the presence of the Savior she loved so deeply; obviously not. If anything, the pain was greater than when he'd first heard Marty speak of Virginia's fate. How was that possible? How did a human being just disappear and die and end up in the ground? And how did such excruciating pain multiply daily?

How would he counsel one of his parishioners if they came to him with such a question? Surely he would listen and empathize, but wouldn't he also advise them to cling to Jesus and to allow God to heal the pain? Of course he would. So why was he unable to give himself the same advice?

"It would be easier if she were buried nearby, where we could go to visit the grave," he said suddenly, startling himself.

Until that moment he hadn't even realized the truth of that statement. But now he saw it clearly, and he began to cry again, harder now, as Mariana's arms wrapped around him and she leaned against his shoulder and wept softly, sharing his grief. It was the greatest gift she could have given him at the moment, as he pressed against her and stopped trying to fight the tears. Perhaps he had to let himself cry until the last of his doubts were washed away.

Marty lay in bed, listening to the soft sounds of weeping coming from the kitchen. How he ached to arise from his bedroll and go to his friend to comfort him, but the sound of voices intermingled among the sobs told him that Mariana had already filled that role.

As is right, he reminded himself. *Thank God Hector has such a devoted wife! Is there any greater gift God can give a man on this earth?*

As an image of Susana rolled through his mind, he thought of the verse in Genesis that declared, "It is not good for man to be alone."

How true, Lord. I can't imagine Hector going through losing his mother this way without having Mariana at his side. This is going to be so hard for them...for the entire Rodriguez family.

Again his mind focused on Susana, who was experiencing her own grief over losing Virginia, whom she had known since she was a little girl and had considered family even before Hector and Mariana were married. He could only imagine how many people would fill the little *Casa de Dios* church if they had a memorial service for the martyred woman.

He sat up so quickly he nearly knocked his head against an open drawer from the boys' shared dresser. Of course! Why hadn't he realized why Hector was struggling so desperately to deal with his mother's death? If she had died close to home, in

Tijuana where her family lived, they could have had a proper funeral service and burial, and though they would still miss her, the family could begin to heal. As it was, they could all be left hanging indefinitely in the abyss between grief and healing until they did something to finalize the situation.

Marty nodded, his mind made up. He would talk to Hector in the morning about arranging a memorial service for Virginia. If Hector didn't feel up to doing it himself, Marty would do it for him. He'd never officiated at any sort of formal service before, but he had just graduated from Bible college, so he should certainly be able to help his friend by conducting a proper farewell to a woman who had served God faithfully to her last breath.

Celeste was nearly certain she had lost her mind. What else could explain the fact that she had thrown a few things in a suitcase and climbed into her Mercedes to head south— across-the-border south, no less!—to find her son. She hadn't seen him in nearly a year, hadn't even bothered to go to his graduation from Bible college, which he had said was fine but she knew it wasn't, and now when she really wanted to speak with him, he had his cell phone shut off. And so she was driving down the California coast like a madwoman, determined to locate him.

But what in the world did she think she would say to him if and when she actually found him? She had no idea, and that was the craziest part of this entire escapade. And yet she kept driving, wondering if it was as much her need to escape her empty life as her need to see her son's face that pushed her forward.

Mile after mile, the tires rolled along, carrying Celeste past familiar landmarks, calling her to stop and eat or shop or browse, but she ignored the signs and kept going, stopping only for gas and restrooms. By the time she passed the San Diego County line marker, her head pounded and her eyes burned, but she pressed on. Oh, if only she'd listened to Marty and learned how to use email, maybe then they would be in touch more regularly! All she had now was an old letter in her purse that Marty had sent to her one summer while he was in Tijuana, and on it was the Rodriguez family's address. Surely someone would be able to help her find her way to their home once she had crossed the border, though for the first time in her life she wished she spoke at least a few fundamental words of Spanish.

He had risen early and left the house

while everyone else was asleep.

Chapter 26

HECTOR HAD ALWAYS AVOIDED THE TOURIST TRAP of downtown Tijuana, but today he felt the need to get lost in its hub. He had risen early and left the house while everyone else was asleep, and now he walked aimlessly up and down the relatively quiet Avenida Revolucion, not even seeing the closed shops and venders' booths that lined the way. In short order the sleepy scene would spring to life, with tourists looking for bargains and sellers looking for tourists, each hoping to get the best of the other.

None of that mattered to Hector. His mother was gone—dead. There, he'd said it, at least to himself. Virginia Correo Rodriguez, the woman who had given birth to and raised him and his eight siblings, was gone from this earth forever. Hector would not see her again until he crossed from this world into eternity.

And that wasn't the worst of it. In fact, if anything, knowing for certain that he would one day see her again was what kept him going, kept him putting one foot in front of the other, breathing out, breathing in. Their mutual assurance of eternity with God because of their faith in Christ was the good news! What tore at Hector's heart was the horror of what might have happened to his mother in her last hours or minutes of life. Had she suffered? Had she been tortured or humiliated? Had she even known what was happening to her, or did she at least die quickly and painlessly, passing into the Father's arms before she even realized what was going on?

Oh, how he hoped the latter was the case! Somehow he could better accept her fate if he could somehow know she hadn't suffered. But how could he? How could he ever be certain that his mother hadn't died alone except for her tormentors, and in agony?

Aye, Dios, he cried silently, *how can I stand the pain of not knowing? How can I trust You when I have no way to find out what happened to my mother, no body to bury, no grave to visit, at least not close by, where I can go to mourn and to grieve—and maybe someday to heal? How is this possible, Lord? How can You expect it of me?*

But no answer whispered to his heart or floated on the breeze, only the distant sound of a stray dog barking at an invisible danger. A lone shopkeeper stood on the corner, hanging his *"Abierto"* sign in front of his cart, as the smell of freshly baked *churros* teased Hector's nostrils. Though his stomach rebelled at the thought of eating one of the tasty pastries, his heart cried out at the memory of how his mother had sometimes surprised her children by having the sugar-sprinkled treats, warm from the oven, waiting for them when they returned home from school.

Never again, he thought. *Never again will I taste my mama's cooking or see her joyful smile or hear her gentle voice. Oh, Mama, why did you have to stay in San Juan Chamula? And why did I agree to take you there in the first place?*

Ignoring the *churro* vendor as he passed his stand, Hector walked straight ahead, his eyes blinded by the tears that stung his lids and dripped down onto his cheeks. He knew he should go home and check on Mariana and the children, on Marty, on his congregation, but first he needed to walk until he could walk no more. Then, perhaps, he would be able to go back and do what needed to be done, though for the first time in his life he questioned the meaning and importance of it all.

When Marty awoke and found Hector gone, he somehow sensed his friend had not gone to his office at the church. Though he wanted to go looking for him, he decided to stay and help Mariana with breakfast. She was doing much better, but he knew she still tired easily, and feeding three hungry and rambunctious children would tax what little strength she had.

"*Chorizo y juevos* are almost ready," he hollered from the kitchen, as he stirred the delicious concoction of eggs and spicy sausage in the pan, the aroma making his mouth water. "Who's going to help me warm the tortillas?"

All three children burst into the room at nearly the same time, all wanting to help fix their *desayuno*, though Marty knew they seldom showed up for breakfast with such enthusiasm. He assigned tortilla-warming and table-setting chores all the way around, and the food was on the table and ready to eat when Mariana joined them. She smiled as she wished them all a "*buenos dias*," but Marty saw the concern in her eyes.

That's when he decided. As soon as everyone had eaten and the dishes were done, he would excuse himself and go find Hector. Apparently God had brought him here for more than a time of reflection and direction seeking, Marty decided, and it was time he made himself useful.

Celeste had driven until she made it across the border and then, exhausted, had rented a room at the first decent hotel she could find. Locking herself inside, she had fallen across the bed and slept, unmoving, without even changing her clothes. When she finally awoke to the unwelcome glare of sunshine piercing the thin drapes that covered the window, she turned over on her back, groaning at her stiff joints that complained at her neglect.

Even my bones know I'm old, she thought. *So why can't I admit it?* She closed her eyes. No. Not yet. Surely she had a few more years before being relegated to the stockpile of AARP members whose greatest joy was getting a 10 percent discount at a local department store on Tuesdays.

Pulling herself to a sitting position, she yawned. Coffee would help. She had made a point to confirm that the hotel had a restaurant on the premises and that it was open twenty-four hours. A shower and then some food would clear her head. Now if only Marty would turn on his cell phone and make her task so much easier...

Somehow Marty had known that sooner or later Hector would show up at the familiar strip of beach at Puerto Nuevo, so he wasn't surprised when he finally saw his friend pull his once-blue beater into the parking lot and kill the engine, though it continued to spit and sputter for a few seconds afterward.

Marty watched Hector sit for a moment behind the wheel, his face drawn and dotted with dark stubble. The young Americano wondered — marveled, even — at the attachment his friend had for his mother, since Marty had never experienced such a relationship. True, he would feel bad if something happened to his mother, but he doubted it would change his life much, since she'd never really been a part of it.

Stepping out of his El Camino, Marty stood beside the open door and waited. He wanted Hector to see him, but he didn't want to rush their meeting. As it was, Marty had been sitting in his car for nearly an hour, waiting. Now his waiting had paid off. Hector was here. All Marty had to do now was figure out what he would say to his brokenhearted *amigo*.

At last Hector opened his car door, the squeak of rusted metal grinding Marty's teeth. His El Camino was old, but he'd never let it fall into disrepair. Though he often referred to it as "the beast," it was more accurately his "baby," and he cared for it accordingly. The thought brought a swift point of correction to his heart, which he acknowledged and then scolded himself for misplaced priorities.

Hector appeared to be scanning the horizon when his eyes landed on Marty. The smile that lit Hector's face reassured Marty that he had been right to come here. His friend needed him. What he said or did wasn't nearly as important as the fact that he was here. Marty's presence told Hector he cared, and Hector's response assured Marty that his presence was appreciated.

The two men greeted one another wordlessly, a hearty hug and back-slapping conveying all that needed to be said. They would walk the beach together, speaking if necessary, sharing silence if preferred. The rest was up to God.

Marty couldn't help but marvel at the depth of attachment between Hector and his mother.

Chapter 27

ELESTE NURSED HER THIRD CUP OF COFFEE, AS she used her fork to push the now-cold *juevos rancheros* around her plate. What had made her think she wanted a Mexican-style breakfast just because she was in Mexico? Two or three bites into the admittedly tasty offering, she had lost her appetite, choosing instead to stare out the window at the growing foot traffic that passed by the hotel restaurant. She imagined that nearly everyone she saw was either a tourist or someone working in the tourist industry, as she couldn't think of much else that went on in this teeming border town. Of course, she'd never really spent time exploring the city or studying about it; she had, in fact, shown little or no interest in the town that had become a second home to her only child. She'd heard there were nice places in and around Tijuana, but she found that tidbit of information doubtful at best.

Her hotel certainly hadn't improved her opinion of the place. Though it had been neat and clean, there were no added amenities beyond the perfunctory bar of bath soap and a couple of towels. But it had served its purpose. Now, though, she was determined to remain in Tijuana for however long it took to find her son and spend some time with him, she also planned to immediately locate somewhere nicer to stay.

She sighed. Where to begin? The entire process would be simplified if Marty would turn on his cell phone, or at least check his messages. She had left several, but no response. Her only other option seemed to be to find someone who knew the city well enough to direct her to the address on Marty's letter, though she didn't relish the idea of driving through unknown territory, particularly since she had no idea what sort of neighborhood these Rodriguez people lived in.

What was wrong with Marty anyway? Why would he give up so much to gain so little? Hadn't he been raised with the finest of everything? Why, then, would he apparently feel the need to go searching for something more?

First, he had gotten involved in that religious thing when he was only ten. Celeste didn't mind if he wanted to go to church on occasion; she had even done that once or twice herself. And she had been certain it was a phase Marty would outgrow. But he hadn't—at least not yet.

Still, she could have accepted her son's obsession with attending church and identifying himself as a Christian. It was a free country, after all. But then he started talking about "mission fields" and Bible college, and the next thing Celeste knew, her son was spending time living in the slums of a nearly third-world country. Who knew what he might do next?

Why couldn't he just be satisfied with what he had? she wondered. And then she remembered: she wasn't satisfied with her own life or she wouldn't be sitting in this dump of a place all alone, wondering how to find her son. But she was, and there had to be a reason for it. She only hoped she would discover what it was without wasting too much time in a town where she knew no one and where she didn't even speak the language.

Marty and Hector hadn't walked far before they parked themselves on an isolated sand dune to watch the tide roll in and out, as the midmorning sun sparkled off the gray water and the whitecaps settled down to race like frothy bubbles across the packed, wet sand. Marty couldn't help but compare the cold Pacific Ocean to the warm, turquoise seas of the Caribbean, where his mother had taken him on vacations as a child. He had to admit, it was much easier to dive into those sun-warmed waves off the beaches of San Juan or St. Thomas than the sometimes harsh and even frigid waters of Southern California or Baja. And yet he loved it here, where the beauty was more rugged than relaxed, challenging him to think beyond himself.

That's what he was doing as he sat next to his friend and shared his grief in unspoken camaraderie. Marty knew that Hector communed with God, letting his aching heart utter the words that he was unable to formulate in his mind or speak with his lips—and then listening for the answer on the *whoosh* of an incoming wave. God was always right and always on time, but oh, how difficult it was to transfer that thought from the mind to the heart! It was a process, Marty knew, and a lifetime one at that. He also knew that Hector was much further along in that process than he, and yet there were times when even the younger and more immature believers had to come alongside the older ones to help carry the burdens that life in a broken world imposed.

It was obvious that Hector's thoughts were on his mother, the woman who had raised and loved him, as well as her other eight children, despite the fact that she had been abandoned by those children's father. Marty couldn't help but marvel at the depth of attachment between Hector and his mother. He even felt a stab of jealousy as he wondered how different his own life might have been—might still be, for that matter—

if he and his own mother had that sort of close bond. Marty supposed that he loved his mother, and he imagined that in her own way she loved him as well. But a bond, a connection that went beyond the physical aspect of her having given birth to him twenty-two years earlier? No. It simply did not exist.

Marty's heart squeezed at the thought. What was that old saying—that it was better to have loved and lost than not to have loved at all? He knew that was meant to apply to romantic love, but couldn't it apply to other types of relationships as well? True, Hector was hurting deeply because he had lost his mother, but at least they had shared a close mother-son relationship for many years before the loss. In Marty's case, he wondered what, if anything, he would feel if he lost his mother. And then he wondered if it was possible to lose something you'd never had in the first place.

He reached up and laid his hand on Hector's shoulder, giving him a pat of reassurance before removing it once again. Hector nodded in affirmation, and Marty tilted his head to the sky and smiled in gratitude.

La abuela was alone in the house once again, thinking, praying…remembering. Just the previous day she had seen the pastor's wife at *la tienda*, where they were each purchasing fruits and vegetables for the day. The elderly woman had always thought Mariana Rodriguez was a kind and beautiful woman, with a heart for her husband, her children, and most of all, for God. That opinion was strengthened when Mariana told *la abuela* about Hector's mother, Virginia, a woman *Señora* Mesa knew well and had long admired, and whom Mariana had honored throughout the years Virginia had been her mother-in-law.

Now, it seemed, Virginia Correo Rodriguez was gone, her life sacrificed as so many others through the centuries to preach the gospel to those who so desperately needed to hear it. *Señora* Mesa knew Virginia had not died in vain or apart from God's knowledge and mercy; she also knew it was a terrible loss for her entire family. And so she would pray for them, even as she did for her own family, now that her beloved Roberto had gone home to be with the Savior. How *la abuela* longed to join her *nieto* in that wonderful place! *I am an old woman*, she prayed, *a* vieja. *Is it not time for me to come home?*

But there was no answer, and so she continued to pray for the others, her greatest pain not so much for those who had gone ahead of them to eternity, but for those who remained behind and were not yet ready to do so.

If ever Hector Correo Rodriguez needed God's

strength poured out to him . . . . it was now.

Chapter 28

LEAVING THE RESTAURANT FEELING AS EMPTY AS when she'd first arrived, Celeste pondered her next move. She'd tried Marty's phone twice already that morning, and the only information she'd gleaned was that his voice mailbox was full. Now what?

She climbed into her car and rummaged in her purse for the envelope with the Rodriguez family's return address. Why hadn't she thought to try to get someone to help her obtain directions before leaving home? Because she hadn't been thinking at all, she reminded herself—only reacting. Now she was in Tijuana, with no idea how to find her son in this quickly-coming-to-life tourist trap of a town. Surely someone knew how to get to the address where Marty was staying.

Celeste sighed. She'd tried the obvious—asking the clerk at the hotel where she had spent the night. But he'd been no help at all, except to answer her question about how to get to the nearest police station. She decided that was her best option after all and started the engine.

Her mind filled with thoughts of the previous day's drive and the uncertainty of what lay ahead, she was rocked back into reality when a jolting crash threw her forward into the steering wheel, triggering an air bag explosion that slammed her back against the headrest. Blinding, white-hot pain ricocheted from her nose to her neck, triggering a warm gush of blood from her nostrils. Her last thought before slipping into unconsciousness was that she should have thought to stop north of the border to buy Mexican car insurance.

By the time Hector pulled up in front of his house, with Marty following directly behind in his rumbling El Camino, he had decided to accept his young friend's suggestion of having a memorial service for his mother. A funeral was out of the question, as the body had already been buried many miles away, but at least a gathering of friends and family who had known and loved Virginia would give them something tangible where they could put her to rest in this life and rejoice that she had gone on to be with the Lord she had faithfully loved and served for so many years.

He was still resisting the idea of having Marty officiate at the service, however. After all, Hector was the pastor of the church that would host the event, and Virginia was his mother. Shouldn't he be the one to lead the ceremony? Wouldn't his parishioners expect it?

No. He shut off the engine, waiting a moment until the vehicle stopped its coughing and sputtering before opening the door. Of course it should be someone other than himself; the only reason he was hanging on to the idea of doing it himself was pride—pride that he was the pastor, the loving yet bereaved son, the one in control, when in fact he could scarcely put one foot in front of the other. If ever Hector Correo Rodriguez needed God's strength poured out to him in the form of love and help from other people, it was now. This was no time to pretend with anyone. He was crushed over the loss of his mother, particularly the way it had happened, and there was no reason to continue to try to convince others that he was handling that loss with any sort of grace or dignity. Hadn't everyone in his congregation already seen him break down on Sunday? Whom did he think he was kidding? Certainly not Mariana, who most likely knew him better than he knew himself. And after his talk with Marty today, it was obvious the young *gringo* also knew what was really going on in Hector's heart. If they knew, others surely knew as well. And wasn't it more important to allow those others—particularly his children and congregation—to see that in his weakness he leaned on Jesus, rather than himself?

Yes. It was time to lay down his pastor's hat and allow someone else to carry the burden of officiating at the memorial service. Since Marty had offered, he was the logical choice, and Hector felt a sense of heaviness lift from his chest at the temporary transfer of responsibility.

Gracias a Dios, he thought, as he stepped from the car to head into the house and tell Mariana of his decision. *You have sent Marty to us at just the right time, Lord. Thank You.*

Kawak was angry. She had gone to great lengths to assure that Imix would not be drawn into the web of lies spun by the woman named Virginia, using the book and the stories of *los conquistadores* that had nearly destroyed their ancestors' culture. If it weren't for the faithful *curanderos*, particularly Evita, who oversaw the spiritual welfare of the people of San Juan Chamula, their enemies would have been successful and there would be no Mayan culture today. Thankfully there were still those in their little village who clung to and preserved the ancient ways, but it appeared that Imix was not going to remain one of them.

Two nights earlier Kawak had been unable to sleep. She had finally pulled herself up from her sleeping mat on the floor and gone to stand in the doorway of the tiny home she shared with her family. As the cool night air washed over her, she spotted a figure moving quickly but silently through the darkness. Though she could not make out the person's features, it was obvious from the shape and way of walking that it was a woman, cloaked in a blanket that covered her head and shoulders. Something familiar about the figure nagged at Kawak, but it wasn't until she was out of sight that Kawak realized it was probably Imix. But where would she be going in the middle of the night—and why?

The answer began to take shape as Kawak stared into the darkness, watching a dog skulk along the deserted dirt road, searching for food scraps. Surely the figure Kawak had seen was, indeed, Imix, and no doubt her friend was stealing away to meet with the Campos family to study the treacherous book and to plot how they might at last complete the mission of wiping out the Mayan culture once and for all.

Kawak made a decision at that moment. She would continue to watch during the night until she spotted the figure once again. Then she would venture out into the darkness and follow the lone figure to confirm her suspicions. If the situation was truly what she thought it was, then she would be forced to pay another visit to the shaman.

Alberto still struggled with the passing of day and night and the understanding of how many twenty-four-hour periods had elapsed, but one thing he knew for certain: neither Hector nor his young *gringo* friend had come to see him in quite some time. Why? Had something happened? Hadn't the *Americano* said he was going to Tijuana to visit Hector and his family? Was it because of that visit that neither had been to see him? Or was there some sort of problem? Surely Virginia was all right, as Alberto still had her letter tucked safely inside the drawer beside his bed. Though his eyes were too far gone to focus on her words and read them himself, he often took the letter from its place of safekeeping and clutched it to his chest, remembering the words the nurse had read to him from the two handwritten pages.

Virginia, his true *amor*, his *esposa* and the *madre* of his *hijos*, had forgiven him. Though she had said so much more, that was the statement that had stood out to him above all else — that and the fact that she had never remarried because she still considered him, Alberto Javier Rodriguez, her *esposo*. It was a miracle so amazing that Alberto found it difficult to believe. When he had doubts, he clutched the letter, overjoyed to have something in his hand that had recently been held by the woman he had so wronged.

Retrieving the precious note, which had now become his most prized possession, Alberto felt the tears burning his eyes, as the miracle of Virginia's forgiveness led him, as it always did, to the next logical question: If his wife could forgive him such a grievous sin, was it possible that God could as well?

Oh, if only Hector would come to see him again — to speak to him of God's love, to offer to pray with him just once more! For this time Hector would surely accept.

"The police?" Celeste felt her heart leap.

Chapter 29

CELESTE, WAKE UP. TALK TO ME. CELESTE, IT'S ME, Byron. Open your eyes and tell me you're all right. Celeste!"

Byron. She knew the name...even knew the voice. But who was he? And why was he calling her? Where was she, and why did she feel as if she'd been kicked in the head by a very large mule?

She tried to will her eyelids open, but the effort was exhausting, and she somehow sensed that the light was going to hurt.

"Celeste?"

Obviously this Byron person wasn't going to go away. Resisting the urge to reach up and use her fingers to pry open her lids, she managed to open them enough to peer through miniscule slits at the face that belonged to the voice. Aha. Byron, of course! Her attorney, the man who had been at her side longer than her husband, who had hung around only long enough to give her a child and then beat a hasty exit, stage left.

Sure, she knew it was illogical to blame someone for dying, but she just couldn't seem to stop being angry at Martin for deserting her when she'd needed him most.

Back to the problem at hand, she managed what she imagined to be a tepid, tight-lipped smile. "Byron," she croaked. "Thank you so much for coming. However did you find me...and where am I, anyway?"

Byron's smile was wider and warmer than her own had been, as what was no doubt a wave of relief washed over his plain but concerned face. Though Celeste had never considered him an attractive man, his familiarity made him appear quite handsome at the moment.

"You don't remember?" He was still smiling, but his brows were drawn together over his dark brown eyes. The ridiculous thought darted through Celeste's mind that a man who had no hair on top of his head shouldn't have such heavy eyebrows, but she scolded herself for being critical and dismissed the notion as quickly as it had appeared. After all, Byron Moore had been Martin's best friend, and had helped her with her legal affairs and finances since she'd become a widow. No one had been more reliable or loyal than Byron, and her relief at seeing him perched on the edge of her hospital bed was almost palpable.

Hospital bed? Ah, it was coming back to her now—her spur-of-the-moment drive to Tijuana, the night in the hotel, breakfast in the restaurant, and then...then she'd been about to back her car out of the parking space and look for a police station. Instead she'd been catapulted into a world of pain, which now seemed only somewhat lessened by medication, which would account for the heaviness of her eyelids and the almost irresistible call to sleep.

"I wanted to find Marty," she mumbled, her words sounding slurred and foreign to her ears, as if they had been spoken into a tin can.

Byron nodded. "I figured as much, especially when they gave me the letter from your purse. They said they were going to try to contact the Rodriguez family first, but then they found the notation in your wallet to call me in case of an emergency. I came as quickly as I could."

They. Obviously Byron was talking about the hospital personnel. So they had followed her in-case-of-emergency instructions and called her lawyer, who apparently had immediately hopped into his car and sped to her rescue. Dear Byron. Whatever would she do without him?

The memory of the moment of impact in the parking lot was growing clearer, and Celeste felt her eyes widen at the possibilities. "What did I hit?" she asked, nearly holding her breath as she awaited the answer.

"A pole," Byron answered, smiling again. "Don't worry. No other cars were involved, and no one else was injured."

Celeste felt her shoulders relax, as she exhaled and nodded at the good news. And yet...

"My car? How bad is it?"

Byron's smile faded. "Bad. Bad enough that it's not drivable. The police said—"

"The police?" Celeste felt her heart leap, as she remembered wishing she'd purchased Mexican car insurance before crossing the border. She'd heard horror stories of what could happen to tourists who got into car accidents in Mexico without the proper insurance.

Byron laid his hand on her arm. "It's all right," he soothed. "Don't worry about it. I've already taken care of it. I've had the car towed to a garage in San Diego. It'll be ready to pick up in a week or so."

"But—" She stopped, confused. "You said the police were called, and—"

"Of course. They had to be, along with an ambulance. But since no one else was involved, they simply impounded the car, though there are no charges against you." He shrugged. "I couldn't get them to dismiss the fine, though. It was pretty hefty."

Celeste could only imagine. And then, for no apparent reason, the ironic thought occurred to her that she had been about to go looking for the police, but instead they had come to her. A bubble of laughter rolled up from her chest to her lips, but when she cracked a smile to let it escape, the pain in her neck and nose intensified.

"Ow," she complained, gingerly touching her nose, which surprisingly wasn't covered in bandages. "How bad am I?"

"Your nose isn't broken, if that's what you mean," Byron said. "Just very sore and tender. The air bag hit you in the face, so it could have been a lot worse."

Well, at least she could be thankful for that. It was one thing to look old, quite another to look like an old, broken-down boxer. That would have been more than she could bear! And all because she'd decided to come looking for Marty. When would she learn to leave well enough alone?

Rosa sat under the tree, leaning against its trunk and remembering how scared she had been when she sat in this very spot and watched a man beg for his life. The two men with the guns hadn't paid any attention to him, and the next thing Rosa knew, she had seen someone shot. Even now, in the afternoon sun, she shivered. Though she knew one of those two men with the guns had died in a car wreck in front of her house and the other one had died protecting her, she had come to believe the world really wasn't a safe place to live. She couldn't always count on someone like the man named Roberto being around to take a bullet for her. What if she begged for her life like the man had that night, but no one paid attention?

She sighed. Death was something she'd never thought much about until that night, but now it seemed to be all around her. Even the nice pastor of the little church that she liked to go to so much had cried in front of everyone because his mama had died.

Rosa frowned. After church on Sunday, when they'd all gathered around the pastor to pray for him and his family, Rosa had asked how the lady died, but her mama had quickly changed the subject. Later that afternoon, however, Rosa had overheard her mama talking with the neighbor, telling her what had happened at church that morning. Rosa wasn't close enough to hear everything that was said, but she did catch a few words, like "disappeared" and "murdered" and "Mayan *curanderos*." None of it made much sense to Rosa, but she knew enough to realize that something bad had happened to the pastor's mama.

Now it was Friday, nearly a week since they had gone to the little *Casa de Dios* church, and Rosa pondered the words she had heard her mama speak to her papa just the night before. Rosa had been in bed, but her door was open and she could overhear her parents talking.

"There's going to be a service," her mama had said. "This Saturday. I think we should go."

Rosa could almost see her papa's shoulders shrug. "*Porque?* Why? You just started going to that church, and we hardly knew the woman. Sure, we know who she was—her name and what she looked like and where she lived—but we weren't close to her. So why go?"

"*Porque* I like the pastor—and his family too. Virginia Rodriguez was a good Christian woman, and she died for her faith. We should honor that."

"*Humph.*" Rosa's papa dismissed the thought with a sound, which didn't surprise the little girl. She knew her mama considered herself a Christian and had tried to teach Rosa about Jesus, taking her to church now and then and even reading to her from the Bible once in a while. But Rosa's papa had never even pretended to believe in God, let alone attend church, so it was no surprise that he wouldn't feel obligated to attend the service for the pastor's mama.

"If you and Rosa want to go, that's fine," he grumbled, "but don't think you're going to drag me along."

Rosa imagined her mama's beautiful face breaking into a smile. "*Gracias, esposo,*" she said, her voice so low Rosa almost couldn't discern the words. "*Gracias.* Rosa and I will go, then."

The issue had been settled, as all issues in Rosa's home were settled—by her mama talking with her papa and gaining permission to do what she requested. Rosa didn't remember many times when her papa had denied even one of her mama's requests, but always Mama obtained his approval before doing what she wanted. It seemed to work well for them, though it also seemed they had more differences than common interests.

Now, sitting under the tree and remembering the exchange between her parents, Rosa wondered what it would be like to go back to the little church for what her mama had called a memorial service. Rosa couldn't remember ever attending such a thing, though a couple of years earlier she had gone with both her parents to a funeral at a Catholic church that was huge in comparison to the *Casa de Dios*. The funeral had been for Rosa's *abuelo*, the *padre* of her papa, who cried all the time the priest was speaking, making Rosa very uncomfortable. Besides that time, she couldn't remember ever seeing her papa in church.

She sighed. Though she had no idea why, she somehow imagined this service on *el Sabado*, Saturday, would be quite different than the one for her *abuelo*. She wondered if many people would attend, and if so, where they would sit in such a tiny building.

He choked back a sob, and
Mariana squeezed his hand.

Chapter 30

THE BACKGROUND MUSIC WAS SOFT BUT NOT SAD OR depressing. *As Mama would have wanted it*, Hector thought. *Music of rejoicing and celebration, of victory and triumph. She always said she wanted to give her life for God's service, and when He was done with her, she wanted to go home...*

He choked back a sob, and Mariana squeezed his hand. How would he ever get through this day without his beloved *esposa* at his side? *Gracias a Dios* that she was always there for him! It was as if her strength flowed from her hand to his, as they sat in the front row of the little church where he had preached his weekly sermons, joined couples in holy matrimony, and helped the members of the congregation say good-bye to loved ones who had gone on ahead of them. But it was also the house where he had grown up, and the bittersweet memories were nearly more than he could bear.

He supposed it was appropriate that he and his siblings would be gathered together here with other family members and friends to say good-bye to the woman who had lived in this very house and had given so much love to so many over the years. Now she had gone to be with her Savior, and Hector would not see her face or hear her voice again until he, too, had left the temporal behind to live in the eternal.

There was no doubt in Hector's mind that his mother was happier at this moment than she had ever been during her lifetime here on earth, and he truly did rejoice for her in that. But oh, how difficult it was for those who remained!

He glanced behind him and was stunned at the sea of humanity that continued to flow through the front door as he prayed and waited. Where had they all come from? And how would they possibly seat them all?

As pastor, he found himself starting to rise from his seat, to go to the back of the room where already people were standing shoulder to shoulder against the walls, even as others continued to stream in the open door. He felt it was his responsibility to help find places for all who had come, but Mariana stopped him with a touch on his arm. When he turned to her, she gently shook her head.

"They are fine, *querido*," she whispered. "God will take care of them. You just sit here beside me and say good-bye to your precious mama."

Hector felt the all too familiar tears pooling in his eyes once again, and he nodded. As usual, Mariana was right. God cared more for the people who had gathered at *Casa de Dios* than he as a pastor ever could. Hector needed to learn to let go and leave the others to rest in the Savior's nail-pierced hands. In fact, he needed to remember to practice that himself...

Señora Mesa's heart was weary with the good-byes. It seemed the older she got, the more often she found herself saying *adios* to yet another friend or relative. She knew, of course, that for those who had received Jesus before dying, this wasn't the end and she would certainly see them again.

Soon, Lord? As it did so often these days, the longing and homesickness swept over her. *So many have gone on ahead of me, and yet still I remain.* Porque, *Lord? Why? What is my purpose? I know there must be one or I wouldn't still be here, so I submit myself to fulfill that purpose, whatever it is. Just make it clear to me,* por favor, *please, and I will do it.*

An image of Roberto floated in her mind, and though the pain of missing him and the memory of the quiet memorial service that had been held for him in this very room so recently brought fresh tears to her eyes, she knew God was reminding her that even as she had prayed for her *nieto*, she was to pray for others.

She nodded, committed to spend her remaining time on earth in intercession for those who did not yet know the Savior. Unable to travel to distant lands, it was obvious that the little neighborhood where she and her family lived was her mission field. So many souls who needed to know Jesus as she did—as Roberto did in his last hours of life. As Virginia Correo Rodriguez had known Him for so many years and had devoted those years to leading others to that same knowledge.

La abuela smiled, as she realized yet again God's goodness in allowing Virginia to live and die in service to her Lord. What a joyous moment it must have been when she heard the precious words, "Well done, good and faithful servant. Enter into the joy of your Lord."

One day soon, she thought, *I, too, will hear those words. Until then, I will continue to pray.*

Rosa squirmed in her seat, wondering how adults could sit still so long. The service hadn't even started yet, and already she wished she could get up to offer her chair to one of the many people now standing around the back and sides of the room, leaning against the walls. But when she had tried to suggest it, her mother had told her to hush and be still. And so she sat, waiting.

From her vantage point she could see the backs of the pastor and his family, and she recognized the two boys from school, though she'd never really spoken to them. Rosa and her *amigas* tended to avoid boys at all costs, whether on the school playground or if they ran into them somewhere else. Boys were loud and sometimes didn't smell too good, but she felt sorry for Hector Jr. and Manolo at the moment. She knew how they must be feeling because she still remembered how her heart ached when her own *abuelo* died. She had never known her other grandparents, who all died before she was born, and she wondered if that was sadder than having them die after you'd spent several years with them.

When the man with the light-colored hair stood up and walked to the front, carrying his Bible, Rosa abandoned her daydreaming and sat up a bit straighter. Why was this *gringo* standing in the pastor's place? What could he possibly have to say to any of them?

Curious, she perked up her ears and listened. Even her mother seemed to lean forward in anticipation, as the background music stopped and the man with the Bible bowed his head in silent prayer.

What was I thinking when I offered to do this service? Marty wondered. *Help me, Lord! You know my Spanish is only passable. Please guide me in what You want me to say. Help me remember the words, and help these people to understand me, Father.*

With that, Marty opened his Bible to 1 Thessalonians 4 and read verses 13–18, praying his Spanish would be recognizable to his listeners:

But I do not want you to be ignorant, brethren, concerning those who have fallen asleep, lest you sorrow as others who have no hope. For if we believe that Jesus died and rose again, even so God will bring with Him those who sleep in Jesus. For this we say to you by the word of the Lord, that we who are alive and remain until the coming of the Lord will by no means precede those who are asleep. For the Lord Himself will descend from heaven with a shout, with the voice of an archangel, and with the trumpet of God. And the dead in Christ will rise first. Then we who are alive and remain shall be caught up together with them in the clouds to meet the Lord in the air. And thus we shall always be with the Lord. Therefore comfort one another with these words.

He closed the book and looked out at the crowd, which now filled every available inch of space and spilled out onto the front porch through the open door. The overhead fan wobbled as it spun at full speed, trying in vain to cool the stuffy room. Marty could already feel the sweat trickling down his face and plastering his shirt to his back, whether from the heat or from nerves he wasn't sure.

"Lest you sorrow as those who have no hope," he said, relieved that the foreign words had come easily to him. "There is nothing sadder than losing a loved one who is not a believer in Jesus Christ, for there truly is no hope in such a tragic situation. But we know that wasn't the case with Virginia Correo Rodriguez, who received Jesus as her Savior when she was a young woman, just beginning her family. And she raised that family faithfully in the Word of God, leading each one of her nine children to a vibrant, lasting relationship with Jesus. For that reason, though we will all miss Virginia, we can also rejoice to know with certainty that we will see her again."

A little girl with dark eyes that looked too big for her face caught Marty's attention. Recognizing her from the previous Sunday's service, he realized she was hanging on his every word. *Draw her, Father*, he prayed. *Call her to Your heart…*

"And so," Marty continued, "though we have sorrow because we can no longer see or talk with Virginia, we also have hope—a real, sure hope without any doubt—that we will see her again, so long as we, too, know the Savior as she did."

Marty was amazed. His Spanish seemed to be flowing as if it were his first language. He wasn't stumbling or faltering, as he'd been concerned he might do. And as he continued the short message he had prepared, he knew God was working to bring forth His desired results—whatever they might be.

La abuela smiled as she hobbled home.

Chapter 31

CELESTE KNEW SHE SHOULD TAKE BYRON'S ADVICE and get out of the country as quickly as possible, but she simply couldn't leave without at least trying to find Marty. Reluctantly, Byron had agreed, helping her get set up at a good hotel and promising to be no more than a phone call away if she needed him. Now she wondered if she'd made a serious mistake in not taking his advice and leaving with him.

Byron. What would she do without him? Even now he had taken charge, having had her car taken north of the border for repair, plus arranging for a rental in the meantime. Thank goodness no one had been hurt in the accident, or there could have been serious repercussions, since she hadn't thought to get the required Mexican car insurance. She would have to be more responsible in the future.

For now, however, she felt driven to see her son. Byron had gotten the directions to the Rodriguez home for her; now all she needed to do was get up the nerve to actually go there. Byron had even offered to stay longer and go with her, but she had declined, sensing she needed to make the initial contact alone.

It was Saturday afternoon, and she hoped she would find someone at home, though it would certainly be easier if Marty had his phone on and she could call first. Of course, then she wouldn't have to go at all; she could simply have Marty meet her at her hotel. But because that wasn't an option, she decided there was no sense putting it off any longer. She'd been out of the hospital for a full day now and was feeling much better, though her neck was still a bit stiff and her nose was tender.

Gathering together her purse and cell phone, she took one last look in the full-length mirror and realized she'd better keep her sunglasses on at all times, as her makeup wasn't doing what she'd hoped in hiding the puffiness and color around her eyes.

Great, she thought. *If I do manage to find Marty, he's going to think I've been in a fight. Maybe I should wait until—* She shook her head and sighed. *No. I've come this far; I may as well finish what I've started.*

Stepping out into the hallway, she held herself as erect as her painful neck and shoulders would allow, and headed for the elevator.

Marty watched the little girl named Rosa walk down the street with her mother, away from the church and toward their home. His heart still soared at the implications of what had transpired at the end of the memorial service for Virginia. By the time he had finished giving his brief message, he knew without a doubt that the little girl had soaked in every word. After several in the gathering got up to share their memories of the woman they had gathered to honor, Marty resumed his position in front of the room and asked if there was anyone present who did not have the assurance that when they died, they would see Virginia again. The little girl hesitantly raised her thin arm, her already large eyes widening as they filled with tears.

Marty had smiled and nodded at her. "Would you like to have that assurance?" he asked. "Would you like to know that when your life is through here on this earth, you will go immediately to be with Jesus?"

The little girl nodded, and Marty had called her to the front, where he asked her name and then put his hand on her shoulder and drew her close while he explained the simple plan of salvation to her and to the entire room. "If there is anyone else who would like to join Rosa in making the most important decision of your life..."

No one had come forward, and so he had led Rosa in a prayer of repentance and commitment to Jesus Christ, forgetting for a time that he usually struggled when he spoke Spanish for such long intervals. By the time they were through, it seemed the entire congregation was rejoicing that a young girl had been born into the kingdom, even as they gathered to say a temporary good-bye to a woman who had served so faithfully in that same kingdom, setting a godly example for others to follow. Marty knew it was the greatest gift of comfort that Hector and his siblings could ever receive in the midst of Virginia's memorial service.

When the service ended, many had milled around to chat with the family and to snack on the food prepared by some of the women in the congregation. But Rosa and her mother had excused themselves, saying they needed to get back home. Now, as Marty stood in front of the church, watching them leave, he couldn't help but notice the close bond they obviously shared, and it reminded him of the close relationship Virginia had cultivated with her own children.

A stab of regret pierced his heart as he thought of his own mother, who was no doubt off on some cruise or in the midst of planning another society event. If only the two of them could have had such a relationship!

He sighed. The fact that they hadn't was just one of those things he would have to accept—and for the most part, he had. But it was at times like this...

"That was beautiful," a soft voice said, interrupting his thoughts. He turned to see Susana standing beside him. "What happened in there with Rosa."

Marty nodded. "Yes, it was," he answered. *And so are you*, he thought, though he dared not say it. One day soon, though, he hoped to work up the courage to do so.

La abuela smiled as she hobbled home. Just about the time it seemed she had outlived her purpose, God called her to something special. There she had sat in that memorial service, asking God to show her what to do, and a light had begun to shine around the little girl in such a way that *Señora* Mesa knew she was to pray for her. And so she had—throughout the service, continually, until Rosa had gone forward to receive Jesus as her Lord and Savior. How the old lady's heart had soared as she realized God had allowed her to be a part of such a great miracle—and in the life of the little girl who had once been so terrified of her *nieto* Roberto! God was truly amazing, His ways so far above her own, so past her understanding...

"*Gracias*," she whispered as she walked. "Thank You for allowing me to pray for that little girl, and to see the results. May I not forget to pray for her each day until my time on earth is finished. It is a glorious thing, Lord, to be used by You. A glorious thing."

Still smiling, she continued on, praying also for the young man named Marty who had so graciously led the service. It was obvious that God had His hand on him, and it was also obvious that the pastor's sister-in-law had noticed him as well. Might there be something special in their future—together? *La abuela* would not be surprised at all if that proved to be the case. Another point for prayer.

Hector was feeling overwhelmed—by the simple beauty of the memorial service, by little Rosa's response, by the kind and encouraging words of those who had attended, and by the love and care he felt from his family and from the Lord. Though his heart still ached at the knowledge that he would not see his mother again this side of heaven, he rested in the words Marty had shared about not sorrowing or grieving as those who have no hope. He had, indeed, been comforted with that great truth of Scripture.

Stepping outside to get a breath of air, he noticed Marty and Susana standing together in the yard. Hector smiled. They seemed so natural together, so...right. And Hector couldn't think of anything that would make him happier than if the two of them decided to get married. He knew Mariana would agree, though she had her reservations about where such a life might take her younger sister. Marty had never made any secret of his desire to serve on the mission field, and he would never even consider getting married unless his wife shared the same passion. Would Mariana be able to let go of Susana if she and Marty made such a decision? Would Hector himself be able to do so, particularly now that he had lost his mother in a similar situation?

It was a question worth considering—and yet one that really had no place in his life. After all, didn't the Scriptures declare that the lives of believers belonged to God and not to themselves, that they had been purchased with a costly price? Yes, they did. And even as the thought caused Hector's heart to race, he sensed he would somehow be put to the test of his belief in those words very soon.

*And then she turned the corner
and slammed on the brakes.*

Chapter 32

WHEN THE STREETS CHANGED FROM BLACKTOP TO dirt, Celeste knew she was in trouble. But the directions she had gotten from Byron were explicit, so she also knew she was on the right track.

The rental car, which Celeste imagined was several years old and had already weathered far too many of these rough, bouncy roads, jounced along gingerly as she kept a light foot on the gas and strained her eyes for an occasional street sign. Didn't these people believe in posting their addresses? How was anyone supposed to find their way around?

And then she turned the corner and slammed on the brakes, nearly repeating the incident in the parking lot by smashing herself into the steering wheel. Thankfully no air bags burst out to greet her. The old car probably didn't even have any, she thought, as she caught her breath and pushed herself upright to stare at the gathering of people in front of the building just a few houses beyond her. *"Casa de Dios"* the hand-painted sign read, but it was not the sign that had snagged her attention.

Though still several blocks from her destination, Celeste knew she was in the right place. For there in front of her very eyes was Marty, tall and handsome, standing with a Bible in one hand and the other hand in his pocket, his blond hair ruffling in the breeze. A strikingly beautiful young woman stood facing him, as they spoke to one another with obvious familiarity. Their mutual attention was so complete that they appeared to be oblivious to everyone else around them.

Celeste took her foot off the brake and slowly continued her approach, stopping just yards from her son and the woman who gazed up at him with a look Celeste knew only too well. She now realized she had arrived just in time to rescue her son from making a tragic mistake, and even before she shut off the engine and opened the door, she resolved to do whatever was necessary to make sure she got him out of there unscathed.

"Marty?"

The word caught his attention in the same way as if he'd heard a grizzly bear growling nearby or a wave breaking where there was no shore. It was out of place, foreign, and yet he recognized it the moment the sound invaded his consciousness.

"Mother?"

He turned, feeling his eyes go wide and flat at the sight of the woman who considered eating at a fast-food restaurant on a par with visiting a third-world country, standing beside an unwashed car with Mexican plates, glaring at him as if she'd just caught him with his hand in the proverbial cookie jar.

Second only to his shock at seeing his mother under such bizarre circumstances was his concern at how her sudden appearance would ultimately affect his relationship with Susana.

"Mother?" he repeated, taking a step in her direction, wondering if even now she might disappear and he would realize he had been hallucinating.

But she didn't disappear. Instead, being careful not to scuff her white heels, Celeste Johnson smoothed her perfectly tailored lavender-colored pantsuit and carefully picked her way through the dirt until she stood directly in front of Marty. When she lifted her face to his and removed her sunglasses, Marty was shocked to see the swelling and discoloration around her eyes. Even her nose looked puffy. Had she been in some sort of altercation, an accident perhaps?

"I backed into a pole," she said, answering his unasked question. "In a parking lot at the hotel where I stayed the first night I arrived in this dreadful town. What you find here that continually pulls you back is beyond me."

She stopped and cut her eyes to Susana, giving her a quick once-over before returning her attention to her son. "Then again, maybe it's not such a mystery after all."

Marty felt the old resentment rising up to grip his throat, and he took a deep breath before saying something he would regret. "This is Susana Lopez, Mother, and you will treat her with respect if you expect me to continue this conversation with you."

Celeste raised her perfectly arched brows but winced and quickly lowered them again. "Of course," she said, her voice cool. "Why would I do anything else?"

She smiled then. "As I was saying, I backed into a pole and spent the next couple of days at the hospital. Byron came and took care of the car issue for me, and also checked me into a better hotel. Then he got directions to the Rodriguez home so I could try to find you—which I wouldn't have had to do if you'd had your cell phone on, by the way—but imagine my surprise when along the way I spotted you and"—she paused and tossed a condescending smile at Susana— "and your friend here."

Marty opened his mouth, but before he could say a word, Susana cleared her throat. He turned to her and realized she wanted to be introduced. Marty sighed. Poor Susana. She didn't know what she was getting herself into.

He forced a smile. "Forgive me, Susana," he said. "I told Mother your name but didn't tell you hers. This, if you haven't already guessed, is my mother, Celeste Johnson, who apparently has decided to come for an unannounced visit."

With a much more genuine smile than his own, Susana reached out her hand. "Hello, Mrs. Johnson," she said, her English far from impeccable but certainly clear. "It is so nice to meet you."

After a brief hesitation, Celeste took Susana's hand. "Likewise, I'm sure," she said. Then, dropping Susana's hand, Celeste turned her full attention back to Marty.

"You're right, of course, that my visit was unannounced, but why do you suppose that is? As I said, you would have simplified this entire situation if you'd simply had your cell phone turned on. Isn't that what cell phones are for, so we can be in touch with people even when they're not at home?"

Marty sighed. She had a point. Then again, how often did she actually call him? Three or four times a year—at most? And then for a perfunctory "Merry Christmas" or "Happy Birthday" greeting. So what was so important that she would drive all the way to Tijuana to see him?

That was the sixty-four-thousand-dollar question, and Marty intended to find out the answer as quickly as possible.

It had taken nearly a week of stealthy watching and patient waiting, but at last Kawak had spotted the same lone figure stealing down the street at night, heading in the direction of the Camposes' home. Quickly the young woman had grabbed a *serape* to cover her head and shoulders and slipped out into the night, keeping just enough distance between herself and the one she followed to prevent detection.

As she had suspected, the excursion took them straight to the Camposes' neighborhood and then to their home, where the figure rapped softly on the door and then slipped inside quickly only seconds later. All Kawak had to do now was to wait until the figure re-emerged and then confront the one who was almost certainly Imix.

The thought made the waiting bearable, for Kawak's anger simmered and grew with each passing moment. Hadn't she swallowed her own fears and gone to *la curandera* on Imix's behalf, daring to tell the shaman what was taking place at the Camposes' home, with the intruder named Virginia leading the treachery? And hadn't Evita taken care of the problem, just as she'd said she would, eliminating the threat and enabling Imix to be set free from the spell that had so obviously been cast upon her? And what thanks did Kawak get? Imix continued to go to the home of the traitors, those who had invited the outsider into their lives and into the Mayan community, tainting what little remained of their culture and religion. Something told Kawak that *la curandera* would not take kindly to this revelation, and that she would deal even more harshly with the situation this time around.

And yet Kawak still cared for her friend and wanted to give her every chance to reject the lies of those who carried the name and the beliefs of the *evangelicos*. When Imix emerged from the Camposes' home — and Kawak was nearly certain that her friend and the figure she had seen enter the house were one and the same — Kawak would give her one last chance to turn her back on the traitors and affirm her loyalty to her own people. If she refused, then Kawak knew what she had to do.

But there was no sense or reason to postpone

what should be done immediately.

Chapter 33

LUPITA STOOD IN FRONT OF HECTOR, HER WIDE, DARK eyes gazing up at him. It had been a long day, and it was time for the little girl to go to bed, but Hector recognized that there was something on her young heart that needed to be settled before sleep would come. He only hoped he was able to help her.

"What is it, *mijita*?" he asked, leaning forward in his chair beside the kitchen table where his as yet untouched cup of coffee sat cooling. "Do you wish to ask me something?"

Lupita nodded. "Is *Abuela* Virginia in heaven with Jesus?"

Hector smiled. This one he could answer with certainty. "*Sí, Lupita. Su abuela* is truly in heaven with Jesus."

A smile passed over the little girl's face, but it was obvious she wasn't through yet. "Is she happy there?"

"Oh, *sí*, she is very happy!"

The smile returned but faded again. "Will I be able to see her when I go to heaven?"

Hector reached out and lifted his daughter onto his lap, situating her on one knee so she could look up at him while he spoke. "Lupita, when you get to heaven, the first One you will want to see is Jesus—and you will! Then you will be able to see all your friends and family who are already there."

"*Abuela* Virginia *tambien*?"

Hector laughed, surprised at the sound and at the realization that it was the first time he had done so since learning of his mother's fate. "*Sí, mija. Abuela* Virginia also."

Lupita's smile was full this time, satisfied and perhaps a bit relieved. Hector marveled at the thoughts that passed through the mind of this child who had not yet lived even five years on this earth.

"*Abuela* Virginia was your mama, *sí*, Papa?"

Hector nodded. "*Sí.*"

Lupita's smile faded and her lower lip trembled. "Are you *triste*, Papa?"

Hector's heart squeezed at his daughter's tenderness and concern. "*Sí*," he said, his voice low. "I am sad, *mijita*, because I miss her very much."

The little girl reached her tiny hand to his face and patted his cheek. "I will help you, Papa, so you won't be *triste*."

Tears stung his eyes as he pulled her against his chest. What a blessing to have such a close and loving family! "Thank You, Lord," he whispered, kissing the top of Lupita's head.

When she pulled back and looked up at him, Hector smiled. "You are a great gift to me, *mija*. And I am so grateful."

Lupita nodded, and Hector sensed that she understood more than he would have imagined her capable of. And then she asked, "What about *Tío* Marty's mama?"

Hector raised his eyebrows. Though they had all met the woman briefly after the service and before Marty had excused himself to spend some time with her, they really hadn't had any time to get to know her. Hector had wondered about Marty's mother many times, particularly since the young *Americano* seldom spoke about her. The cool reunion between mother and son had reinforced Hector's suspicions that the relationship was not a close one, and now he wondered how difficult it must have been for Marty to grow up with such a void in his life. How did family members remain aloof from their own flesh and blood?

And then, as if a light had suddenly come on in his mind, his father's face flashed before his eyes, and a horrible realization dawned in his heart. Not only had he neglected to visit his father in quite some time, he had failed to tell him of his wife's fate! Though the two had been apart these many years, they were still legally man and wife, and they shared nine children together. Alberto Javier Rodriguez had a right to know what had happened to his *esposa*.

With a heavy heart, Hector once again pulled Lupita against his chest, as if to draw strength and comfort from the love they shared together. The thought of driving across the border the next day to tell his father the news seemed somehow more daunting than anything he had endured since first suspecting that something had happened to his mother. At least he knew that she was safe in the arms of Jesus, but his father? That was another story entirely. But there was no sense or reason to postpone what should be done immediately.

"Papa?"

Hector realized then that Lupita was still waiting for an answer to her most recent question. What had she asked? Oh, yes. About Marty's mother.

"You want to know something about *Tio* Marty's mother?" he asked, hoping to clarify the little girl's question before responding.

She nodded. "Does she think Marty is a great gift to her?"

Hector paused. That was indeed a good question. He would like to be able to say that of course, all parents considered their children gifts and were appreciative to have them! But sadly, he had seen too many instances over the years where that was not the case. He only hoped that wasn't so with Marty and his mother.

"I'm sure she does," he answered, wording his statement carefully. "After all, your *Tio* Marty is a great gift to all of us, *sí*?"

Lupita's nod was more vigorous this time. "*Sí*, Papa! *Tío* Marty is my very favorite *tío* of all!"

Hector laughed, wondering what his *hermanos* would think if they found out they had lost their most honored *tío* position to a *gringo* from north of the border—a blond-haired, blue-eyed *gringo* at that! Then again, not only his *hermanos* but Mariana's as well already considered Marty part of *la familia*, so Hector was sure they wouldn't mind.

Remembering how Marty and Susana had looked as they stood together outside the church earlier that day, gazing into one another's *ojos* as they talked, Hector couldn't help but wonder if Marty would make that family membership official in the very near future.

Marty had driven his mother's rental car south from Tijuana to the spot where he went so often with Hector in Puerto Nuevo. The day couldn't have been more perfect, with the afternoon sun glinting off the water as they followed the coastline southward. Marty wondered how his mother could miss such beauty, but it seemed she did, as each time he commented on the nice weather or the amazing scenery, she simply grunted and stayed hidden behind her sunglasses.

He was glad, of course, that she hadn't been seriously injured in her accident, but he still couldn't imagine why she had come at all. This was so out of character for her! Since graduating from high school and leaving home, it had been he who usually initiated contact—and he who usually regretted having done so. He supposed he loved his mother, and he hoped she loved him, but spending time together was quite obviously something that neither of them truly enjoyed.

That truth made Marty sad, particularly when he considered the close relationship Hector had enjoyed with his mother.

But it was simply the way things were, and Marty imagined that it was far too late to change anything now.

And so they had driven in relative silence until reaching the familiar parking lot in Puerto Nuevo, where Marty planned to deposit his mother's rental car before taking her for a walk on the beach. He'd forgotten about the crowds that gathered on Saturday, however, and so he'd had to scavenge a bit before finding a spot where he could squeeze the car in between two other vehicles parked at the curb and still leave room for them to open the doors and pile out.

The stroll on the damp, hard-packed sand hadn't been any more fulfilling or productive than their ride in the car. It was obvious Celeste hadn't expected such an excursion, and she made her displeasure evident by the way she picked her way across the sand, careful to avoid pebbles and shells, and particularly the piles of seaweed and brown kelp that seemed to offer an open invitation to every fly within a twenty-mile radius.

At last Marty had conceded defeat and proposed they return to the shops and restaurants where he offered to buy her a lobster. Even that had caused her to turn up her nose. "You know I like lobster," she'd said at his suggestion, "but I'm not so sure I trust their methods of catching and cooking them here. Have you eaten at these restaurants before?"

"Many times," he assured her. "And they're all delicious."

She raised her eyebrows, and then finally nodded her assent. "All right. I suppose we can give it a try. But please, let's find the cleanest place available, shall we?"

And so they now sat at a table by the window in an immaculate restaurant, playing with their food and alternately gazing out at the rolling breakers and frolicking tourists, and making pathetic attempts at conversation.

Finally he could stand it no longer. "Mom," he said, focusing his eyes on the top of her head, which was currently bent down toward her plate, "why did you come? I mean, it's not like you make a habit of doing things like this. So why are you here? I'm not trying to be rude, and I'm glad to see you, of course, but"—he shook his head—"I have to admit, I just don't get it."

Slowly she raised her head, and Marty was surprised to see a hint of tears in her blue eyes. Chastened without words, he dropped his defenses and waited. Perhaps there was bad news. Was she seriously ill? Is that what she'd come to tell him?

"I..." She cleared her throat. Still holding her fork, she tried again. "I missed you. I...needed to see you. I can't explain it, but..." She took a deep breath and laid the fork on her plate, then folded her hands in front of her as if she were about to pray. "I don't understand it any better than you do—truly I don't. I only know that I've been thinking a lot lately about growing old." She dropped her eyes before raising them again to continue. "I am getting old, you know. And I won't deny that I'm not too happy about that fact. But I'm also enough of a realist to know that there's nothing I can do to outrun it. I've done the facelifts and neck tucks, have my hair dyed regularly to cover the gray, and I do everything I can to try to maintain my weight, though it seems that's becoming a losing battle. All of it is, for that matter. My looks are fading, Marty, and I just don't know what to do about it. It's as if...as if I'm losing me. As if there won't be any of me left once I'm old and wrinkled and no one finds me attractive anymore. Does that make any sense?"

Only if you're a narcissistic egomaniac, Marty wanted to say, but of course he didn't. And then he felt ashamed for even thinking it. Still, what else could he say? What words could he offer her to counter the inevitable, universal truth that every human being had to face at one time or another—their own mortality? The one answer—the only answer—that could give her the hope she was looking for was something she had never wanted to hear. Was it possible her heart had changed and she was now open to that truth? Did he dare broach the topic of her eternal destiny and her need for a Savior? He had tried before, countless times, and had never gotten past square one. Was there any reason to think today might be different?

And then he thought of the words he had spoken just a couple of hours earlier, as the little *Casa de Dios* congregation had said *adios* to Virginia, that faithful servant of God who had devoted her life to leading others to Jesus. Marty knew at that moment that the question was not whether he dared to speak to his mother of her need for a Savior, but whether he dared not to. There was no doubt which option God had called him to obey, regardless of his mother's response.

He smiled, his heart at peace then as he reached across the table and took his mother's hand, ready to share yet again the message of hope in the midst of sorrow that he had just preached as a farewell to Virginia Correo Rodriguez.

Kawak had spoken only one word,
but the figure had stopped immediately.

Chapter 34

KAWAK WAS UPSET. JUST AS SHE HAD SUSPECTED, the figure stealing through town during the night to slip in and out of the Camposes' home was, indeed, her friend Imix. After nearly an hour, Kawak's wait in the shadows had been rewarded when the Camposes' front door had opened and the lone figure had snuck back onto the street, passing by Kawak's hiding place within seconds.

"Imix."

Kawak had spoken only one word, but the figure had stopped immediately, turning toward the sound of Kawak's voice. Any doubt Kawak had retained as to the mysterious person's identity vanished in that moment, as she stepped out from her hiding place and moved to within inches of her friend who stood, unmoving, in the moonlight. As Imix looked out from beneath the *serape* that covered her head and shoulders, Kawak could see the fear in her eyes, and for a moment she regretted that she had followed her and discovered her secret. But she was doing it for Imix's own good, trying to help her break away from the spell cast over her by the traitors who had housed the outsider in their home. Kawak wanted Imix to return to the Mayan form of Catholicism practiced by her people—their people—and stay away from the Camposes and others like them who stirred up trouble and tried to pull the few true Mayans who were left from the culture and traditions of the ancient ones.

"What are you doing here?" Imix asked. "What do you want from me?"

Kawak shook her head. She wasn't going to be turned from her mission. "It is not I who should explain my actions or my motives; it is you, who betrays your people by sneaking out at night to learn of the blasphemous ways of the *evangelicos*."

Imix paused, offering no response, and then turned as if to leave. Kawak caught her shoulder and spun her back. "I won't allow you to leave without answering me. You have no right to be meeting with those people. What do you think the shaman would say if she knew?"

A flash of fear returned to Imix's eyes, and Kawak knew she had struck her friend in the heart. Good. That is what she wanted to do, what she must do if she was to turn Imix away from the enemy of their people.

Then, as suddenly as the flash of fear had appeared, it vanished, and Imix's shoulders slumped in what appeared to be resignation. She nodded and opened her mouth to speak.

"You are right, my friend," she said. "It is I who need to explain myself to you, not the other way around. It is I who have turned my back on the beliefs of our people, and I suppose I knew that sooner or later someone would find out. I suppose I'm glad it is you, my closest friend. I only hope you can try to understand."

Kawak hardened her heart against Imix's call to friendship. Kawak had no intention of trying to understand why Imix had done such a thing—unless she was willing to admit her wrong and cut off all contact with those who challenged the beliefs and ways of their ancestors. But if not, Kawak would listen to Imix anyway so she could better understand what to tell the shaman when she reported to her the next day. Meanwhile, they would walk together in the moonlight while Imix attempted to explain herself.

Marty lay on his bedroll, staring into the darkness and wondering what it would take to get through to his mother. He had laid out the gospel as clearly and simply as he could, and it seemed she had listened. But when he finished and asked how she felt about what she had heard, she simply shrugged and said it was fine for him, but not for her. She preferred to depend on her own strength and not rely on a "crutch," as she more than once had labeled Christianity. Coming from a woman who had admitted to being nearly obsessed with worry over the fact that she was getting old and losing her looks, her reasoning could only be described as ridiculous. Quite obviously she preferred to continue worshiping at the altar of narcissism and self-adulation, so Marty had resolved to back off—at least for now.

Why, then, had she come? If she wasn't going to listen to what he had to say, why go to such lengths to seek him out? Why not just remain in her cold, empty, immaculate mansion where others spent their time cooking for her, cleaning up after her, and driving her where she wanted to go? Why, of all places, come to Tijuana?

And yet, despite Celeste's insistence that she wasn't interested in anything Marty had to say about God, he concluded that she had at least a nugget of curiosity about it, and so he would not give up hope. Whether or not he ever had a close relationship with his mother, he would always pray for her salvation, for ultimately that was the only thing that truly mattered.

His mind wandered then to the second portion of their conversation over their mostly uneaten lobster meals. Once she had closed the door to any further discussion of faith or God or anything even remotely religious, Celeste had moved on like a steamroller to bring up the question of the young woman named Susana and why she and Marty had appeared to be so enrapt with one another.

Marty had to admit that the word *enrapt* caught his attention. It most certainly described his feelings for Susana, but had it been that evident to others that Susana felt the same about him? Did he dare hope that she shared the attraction that seemed to grow in his heart daily?

Of course, if she did, his mother had made it quite clear that it would not be a welcome relationship in her corner of the world. Celeste Johnson, though scarcely involved in her only child's life, would want a huge society wedding, centered around an "acceptable" bride, which clearly eliminated an attractive young lady from a poor neighborhood and a humble family in Mexico. But that didn't discourage Marty one bit. All he could focus on was the fact that his mother had seen something mutual and intimate between Marty and Susana, and for the first time he was ready to start praying seriously about where his relationship with Susana might be headed.

Marty smiled. What would his mother say if she knew it was her very words that had opened this possibility in his mind? He doubted she'd be pleased, but then he never had done much in his lifetime that pleased her anyway. The only approval he was truly concerned with at that point was his heavenly Father's.

Closing his eyes, he began to pray...

Imix still shivered, long after she'd returned to her home and crawled back into her bed with the covers pulled up around her neck. Though she knew she'd taken a huge risk each time she snuck out of her home to visit the Camposes and to learn from them about the God of the Bible, she had never imagined that it would be Kawak who would discover her.

Would her longtime friend betray her? Imix suspected she would. After all, Kawak felt that Imix had already betrayed her own people, so she would no doubt feel she was doing the right thing by telling *la curandera* about Imix's defection.

What would happen to her? Would she experience the same fate as the woman named Virginia? Would her death be quick and painless, or would she linger, paying slowly and miserably for abandoning the faith of her people? Imix no longer feared death as she once had, but she had to admit that she didn't like the idea of suffering.

I am a coward, God, she prayed silently. *Help me to be brave and courageous! I do not wish to shame You, Lord.*

The voice came softly, like a gentle caress against her skin: *You are My daughter. I will hold you in My hand.*

Tears sprang to her eyes, as waves of joy washed over her, warming her and stilling her shivering as no blanket could ever do. She had come to believe in the God of the *evangelicos* and to trust His Son as her Savior, but this was the first time she had ever heard him call her "daughter." At that moment, all fear melted away, as her longing to be with the Father overshadowed all else.

"Thank You, my Father," she dared to whisper. "To be Your daughter is enough. I no longer need anything else."

And in her heart of hearts, she knew she had spoken the truth.

"But I must go tell him, querida," Hector argued.

Chapter 35

AS CELESTE LAY IN THE DARKNESS OF HER HOTEL room, she knew she had blown it, but it seemed she just couldn't stop herself. She had fought the rising emotion in her chest as Marty spoke to her about a loving and forgiving God, refusing to give in to the emotionalism of religious faith that countless others seemed to fall on in their latter years. It would have been easy to do, and she could certainly understand why so many bought into that so-called pie-in-the-sky talk that promised a happily-ever-after existence to anyone who would jump through certain religious hoops. And though Marty presented a good case, Celeste realized as he spoke that she just wasn't ready to give up the fight—at least not yet. Surely she still had a few good years left in her, and she wasn't about to spend them on the back pew of some stuffy old church with a bunch of other wrinkled hags who had long since forgotten how to have fun and enjoy life.

Besides, Celeste had an advantage over most everyone else who came to the end of their life with little money and few possessions. She had both, everything she could possibly need to spend her last years in relative comfort and ease. No two-bit nursing home in her future, that was for certain.

So why had she driven to Mexico to find Marty? If it wasn't to talk with him about his faith and find some comfort for her own aging life, perhaps she had just sensed the need to strengthen their relationship while there was still time. But was it already too late? She certainly hadn't done a very good job of getting closer to her son during their visit that day. First she had resisted his attempts to convince her that she needed to repent and "accept Jesus as Savior." It was obvious she had disappointed him by her lack of response.

Then she had ventured into personal waters, and she had known almost immediately that she had made a big mistake. The moment she asked about "this Susana person," Marty's face had changed. No longer was he a son concerned with his mother's eternal standing; rather he was young man defending the woman he loved from an intruder. And yes, *love* was the appropriate word for Marty's feelings for Susana; Celeste had seen it written all over his face. Her concern over her son's involvement with someone who was obviously beneath him had been interpreted as an attack, and he had quickly risen to the occasion.

Celeste sighed. She'd never really been able to talk to Marty. It seemed no matter how she tried, she always handled things badly. Though she had told herself it would be different this time, it wasn't. And now the wall between them had become higher and more impenetrable than ever.

She glanced at the clock: 2:00 A.M. She'd been lying there for several hours now and was no closer to drifting off to sleep than when she'd first climbed into bed. Perhaps a couple of drinks from the room's minibar would help. After all, she had no plans for the early morning hours, so she could sleep in as late as she wanted. And then she would relax around the pool for a while until Marty picked her up for their preplanned dinner date. He had asked if he could bring Susana along, and Celeste had grudgingly agreed, but she hoped he would think better of it and come alone. Then again, if the girl accompanied him, perhaps Marty would see the contrast between someone so uncultured and the mother who represented all the good things in life that he had appreciated while growing up. Surely that would open his eyes to what a terrible mistake it would be to pursue this ill-suited relationship.

"But I must go tell him, *querida*," Hector argued. "He has a right to know. I don't know why I didn't do it sooner."

Mariana sat beside him at the table, as the two of them shared their morning coffee before the rest of the household joined them. She laid her hand on his. "Of course you do," she said. "I'm not arguing that point. And don't blame yourself for not thinking of it before this. After all, it isn't as if he's been involved in your lives all these years. And you were dealing with all the emotional stress of suspecting something had happened to your mother...and then finding out you were right. Who would expect you to remember every detail in the middle of all that?"

She leaned in to kiss his cheek, her softness warming his heart. "I'm only suggesting that you give the rest of your family a chance to go with you to break the news."

Hector sighed. As usual, his *esposa* was right. Many times he had thought he should invite some of his brothers and sisters to accompany him when he crossed the border to visit his father, but he rationalized that they should have asked to come along. Since they didn't, he assumed they didn't want to.

This was different, though. Their mother was dead, and their father had a right to know—and to hear the news from the children he and Virginia had produced together. Now all he had to do was contact all eight siblings and find out which, if any, wanted to come along on this trip. And if some or all of them did, how would they ever find a time that would be convenient for everyone concerned?

He started to open his mouth and voice his doubts about the practicality of inviting others to accompany him, but he knew Mariana would tell him to let God work out the details.

Susana was nervous. Marty had invited her to dinner with him and his mother that evening, even though he'd admitted his visit with her the previous day had been anything but successful.

How was it possible for a mother and son to be so unattached? she wondered as she stood in front of the bathroom mirror brushing her long, thick hair and considering the possible implications of this three-way meal. Perhaps she should suggest they bring Lupita or someone else along as a buffer or a chaperone, or...

No. Definitely not Lupita. Marty had made it clear that his mother was uncomfortable around children. Besides, the meal would be at a nice restaurant, and Lupita would never be able to be still and quiet long enough to get through the ordeal.

Maybe she herself should not go. She could tell Marty that it would be better for him to go without her—which was no doubt true. Yet she knew Marty wouldn't have invited her if he didn't want her there. But why? What purpose did he have in wanting his mother to get to know her? Did she dare hope that Marty's feelings for her were getting serious enough that he was considering asking her to marry him?

She plunked the brush down on the bathroom counter and shook her head. *Stop thinking that way*, she ordered herself. *You're only nineteen years old—though Mama married Papa before she was that age. Still, Marty just finished Bible college and wants to go to the mission field. He's not thinking about marriage...*

And then she remembered the Sunday service when she had suddenly known without explanation that she would one day marry Marty Johnson and go to San Juan Chamula to carry on the work Virginia had started.

When? Her thought was more of a silent prayer, but a bubble of excitement rolled around in her stomach even as the question formed in her mind. How soon would she become Marty's wife and go off to begin a new and exciting — if somewhat dangerous — life with him?

She smiled. *The sooner the better*, she thought, and yanked the string to turn off the bathroom light.

She had fought for sleep but to no avail.

Chapter 36

KAWAK WAS EXHAUSTED. AFTER RETURNING FROM her confrontation with Imix, she had fought for sleep but to no avail. When the sun finally broke over the treetops and invaded the tiny window above her bed, she had given up, rising quickly and grabbing a meager breakfast of vegetables so she could escape outside before anyone else was awake.

Now, weary and confused, she sat on a rock beneath the trees, on a slight rise overlooking the village below. All appeared peaceful, with most of the residents of San Juan Chamula just now awakening to begin the new day. From her vantage point Kawak could see the spot where she had stood in the street and spoken with Imix only hours earlier, and her heart ached at the thought of what she knew she must do. Hadn't she tried to warn her friend, to dissuade her from following after these foreign ways and beliefs, even to the point of reporting the goings-on at the Camposes' home to the shaman? The outsider was gone now. Why couldn't that be enough? Why did Imix have to continue pursuing the blasphemous teachings of the *evangelicos*? Everyone knew foreign teachings like that had nearly destroyed their ancient culture. What was wrong with Imix that she couldn't see that? Had the outsider and her adopted Campos family truly put a hex on Kawak's friend?

She sighed. There was no other explanation. And now there was no other recourse. She would have to return to the shaman and report to her about Imix's continued treachery. Kawak could only hope that the fallout would be limited to the family who had beguiled Imix, and not extend to Imix herself.

Marty's nerves jangled like wind chimes in a storm. Why did he let his mother get to him like this? After all these years, why hadn't he learned to ignore her haughty attitude and snide remarks?

He shook his head, buttoning his shirt as he prepared to pick up Susana and take her to his mother's hotel. That was what bothered him most, he decided. It wasn't so much that he couldn't get through the evening himself; it was that he didn't want Susana to be hurt by his mother's condescending barbs.

If only he hadn't mentioned the invitation to Susana. How much easier it would be to simply meet his mother for dinner and tell her Susana couldn't come. But it was too late now. Susana had been invited, and she had accepted. His only hope was that she would have second thoughts and opt to stay home. Though he would miss her company, it would be better to go without her than to subject her to what would no doubt be a long and uncomfortable evening.

As usual, when he considered how unlike he was from his mother, Marty thought of his father, whom he'd never really known. How different might his life have been if his father had lived? His mother often said that Marty was like Martin

Sr. both in looks and personality, and Marty imagined it must be true, as he had so little in common with his socialite, materialistic mother.

He sighed. But she was, in fact, his mother, and he needed to honor that fact. And he would, so long as she didn't cross the line with Susana. He knew his protective instincts would never allow that, even if his defense of the woman he loved caused permanent damage to his relationship with his mother.

His fingers stopped buttoning at the thought. *The woman he loved?* The words had passed through his mind as clearly and simply as if they belonged there. He smiled. Apparently they did. Why not just admit it? He loved Susana, and if his suspicions were correct, she felt the same about him. Therefore, what did it matter what his mother thought? Though he would like for his mother to accept Susana and even to welcome her into the family—and now he was taking this to the next step!—he knew at that moment that he was going to broach this subject with Susana very soon, whether his mother approved or not.

With that settled, he grabbed the keys to his El Camino and whistled his way to the front door.

Susana felt her eyes widen at the sight of Celeste Johnson, positioned like a queen holding court on the high-backed chair in the best spot in the restaurant. It was as if she had staged the entire scene, and from Marty's warning, Susana knew she might very well have done so.

Susana forced a smile, feeling small and completely underdressed for the occasion, though she had donned her best church clothes and done her hair up with a matching red ribbon. Marty's eyes had widened when he saw her, and her heart had soared at his enthusiastic compliment, but now it plummeted back to earth as she read the disapproval in his mother's eyes.

At least she has her sunglasses off tonight, Susana thought, pleased to see that the puffiness and discoloration had lessened. Should she mention it? No. Somehow she knew *Señora* Johnson would not appreciate the reminder that she looked anything less than perfect.

"Hello, Mom," Marty said, bending down to kiss the cheek she had so properly offered to him.

"Marty," she said in reply, kissing the air. "You look nice this evening. Is that a new shirt?"

Marty's eyebrows arched as he glanced down at his clothing. "This? I've had it for months."

Celeste's smile was cool. "Of course." She turned her gaze toward Susana, who suddenly found herself wishing she'd worn something more subdued. She imagined her red dress must be flashing like Christmas lights.

"Hello again, my dear," she said, her smile unmoving as she spoke. "You look . . . lovely. What a quaint dress!"

Before Susana could reply, Marty pulled out a chair for her and indicated with a nod that she should be seated. "She is lovely, isn't she?" he said, his eyes on Susana even as he directed the words at his mother. "I never realized until tonight that red is my favorite color."

Susana felt her cheeks warm, not only at the compliment but because she knew Marty was already rising to her defense. She smiled at him as he took a seat beside her.

"So," he said, "how are you feeling, Mom? You look a bit better today."

Celeste raised her perfectly arched eyebrows. "Yes, thank you, I am better. So much so that I'm thinking of returning home tomorrow, in fact. I believe I'll just call Byron to come and pick me up."

Marty had filled Susana in on the man named Byron, and she couldn't help but agree that the man must have more than professional feelings for Celeste to be so ready and willing to come to her side at a moment's notice. Yet Marty said his mother had never shown any interest in the man beyond his legal advice and assistance.

How is it possible to be so cool and detached? Susana wondered. *And even if it's possible, why would anyone want to be? What good is life without relationships? Is she afraid of caring? Is that why she holds herself back, even from her own son? Is it fear that holds her back, even from God?*

Susana's heart went out then to the attractive but aging woman who seemed fearful to love or be loved. What an awful way to live! Susana determined at that moment to do everything possible to befriend Marty's mother, whether she responded or not, and to pray for her daily. Regardless of whether or not she was able to break through the wall Celeste Johnson had so obviously constructed around herself, there was no doubt in Susana's mind that the woman needed all the love she could get.

What a disaster! The entire evening—this entire trip, for that matter—was a complete waste of time, Celeste thought. *Why did I even bother to come?*

She used her room key to open the minibar and then extracted two small bottles of wine. No doubt she would need them to fall asleep after such a dismal dinner with her son and that girl with whom he was so obviously smitten. Celeste could understand that he might be drawn to her beauty, such as it was, but why not just enjoy her for a time and then move on, as most men did? She had seen it in Marty's eyes, though, and he had much more than a temporary fling in mind.

Great, she thought, opening the first bottle and filling her glass before plunking down on the small sofa in front of the television, which she hadn't bothered to turn on. *That's all I need—a daughter-in-law who can scarcely speak English and who lives in a hovel with a dozen other people. What is wrong with Marty that he can't see what a dead-end life that would be? And what am I to do if they show up on my doorstep one day with a tribe of their own—my grandchildren?*

She shuddered, downing the contents of the glass without even tasting it and then pouring more. Perhaps Byron would have an idea or two on how to avert this catastrophe. Spying the phone on the end table beside the couch, she snatched it up and punched in his number. Not only would she tell him she was ready for him to come and pick her up and take her home, but she would use their driving time to explore his legal brain for some answers.

This was too important to run ahead of God,

even with one step.

Chapter 37

ROSA HAD NEVER BEEN HAPPIER. THOUGH NOTHING had changed at home, it seemed as if everything was different—better—since she'd prayed with the *gringo* pastor about accepting Jesus as her Savior. Even now, as Rosa lay in bed, waiting for her mother to call her to breakfast, her heart felt light, as if it were being held up by balloons. And though the thought wasn't really funny, it made her want to laugh out loud. Of course, she didn't because her *hermanas* were still sleeping.

I like being Your child, she prayed silently, remembering how the pastor had explained to her that God was now her Father. *For the first time, I feel safe. No matter what happens, even if more of* los malos *come looking for me someday, I know You will take care of me.*

She smiled. Being ten years old wasn't so scary when you knew that God Himself was looking out for you. Now if she could only convince her papa that he, too, could feel as if his heart were being held up by balloons...

Celeste's head felt as if it were going to explode. She should have known better than to drink all that wine on top of the pain pills the doctor had given her. But at least she'd slept soundly, which was rare these days. By the time she had drug herself out of bed, it was nearly noon, and she'd scarcely had time to shower and dress before Byron arrived to drive her home.

Dear Byron, she thought, keeping her eyes closed behind her sunglasses and leaning her head back against the headrest as he maneuvered his car through town toward the border crossing that would take them back into the States. *He's always there for me. He must have started driving south the moment I called him last night, and now here he is driving me all the way home — obviously with no sleep at all. But he never complains. Of course, I pay him handsomely for his services, but he's always made it perfectly clear that he would like our relationship to be more than professional. Why in the world haven't I taken him up on it by now? He's certainly worth a dozen of those losers I've dated over the years.*

She suppressed a sigh, preferring to let Byron believe she was sleeping. She wasn't ready to talk yet. There would be time for that after the aspirin she'd taken just before leaving the hotel had time to kick in and clear her head. Of course, she knew that initially Byron would try to convince her to leave Marty and Susana alone. Hadn't he always told her she was too controlling and that she needed to let Marty lead his own life?

"He's a good boy, Celeste," Byron had repeated countless times. "Trust him to make the right decisions."

The right decisions? Throwing his life away by going to some two-bit Bible college instead of one of the finest universities in the country? And now getting involved with some peon who wasn't even an American citizen? Did Byron or anyone else actually believe she could stand by and let her only child throw his life away without at least trying to stop him?

The car rolled to a near halt, and Celeste peeked out from behind her sunglasses through the windshield at the line of cars ahead of them, as well as on each side. They had reached the border. Perhaps by the time they managed to crawl to the other side, her headache would be gone and she could convince Byron to help her prevent Marty from making the biggest mistake of his life.

It had taken longer than expected to make it across the border that day, but at last Hector and Jorge, along with their other seven siblings, had all streamed across in their caravan of three old cars. Now they were headed for the hospice facility and what they had all prayed would be a meeting with their AWOL father that would prepare his heart to meet God before it was too late.

Hector was still stunned that all eight of his *hermanos y hermanas* had agreed to give up their plans for the afternoon and accompany Hector on this mission of mercy. In the past he had halfheartedly invited one or more of them on several occasions, but always they had declined for one reason or another. This time it was as if God had gone ahead of Hector to prepare their hearts, as each one readily accepted when he explained to them how he felt they should all go together to tell Alberto Javier Rodriguez about his wife—and to try once more to convince him to give his heart to the Savior who waited with outstretched arms.

Oh, Father, he prayed silently, *por favor, please, go ahead of us yet again and open* mi padre's *eyes to see his need of You!*

And even as he drove, leading the little caravan to their destination in San Diego, he imagined that the rest of them prayed similarly, as the usual chatter that accompanied a Rodriguez clan gathering was nearly absent. He could only wonder how much more difficult it was for the others, who, unlike him, had not seen their father in many, many years.

Marty decided he must be crazy. After all, though he'd known Susana for several years now and, in many ways, already felt a part of her family, the realization that he wanted her to be his wife was still very new. Would her family think it was too sudden? Would her parents even agree? Marty certainly didn't want to do anything without Susana's family's blessing, though he knew it was a foregone conclusion that they wouldn't receive one from his mother.

That's all right, he told himself, wishing even as he thought it that things could be different. *My mother has never approved of anything I've done before. Why should this be any different? But Susana's family? What they think is definitely important. Oh, please, Lord, let them agree!*

As he sat on an old bench in the shade beside the house, waiting for the afternoon sun to set and wondering what Susana was doing, he realized that if it were up to him he would march right down to her house this very day and ask Susana's father for her hand in marriage. After all, she had been out of high school for an entire year now and there was no money for her to go to college. It was as if God had arranged the details so there would be nothing in the way to prevent her from becoming Marty's wife. But wisdom restrained him from acting impulsively, as he decided to wait until Hector had returned from visiting his father. Marty felt it would be best to run the idea past Hector first, and besides, he didn't want to hurt his friend's feelings by not confiding in him before acting on his plans.

Will he tell me I'm moving too quickly? Marty frowned. Perhaps he was. After all, it had been only a few weeks since he'd left school and come to Tijuana to seek God for direction for his life. But each time he did, he sensed that direction involved Susana Lopez.

Susana Johnson, actually, he thought, nearly saying the words aloud just to hear how they sounded. But he didn't want to get ahead of himself. First things first, he reminded himself yet again. He would talk to Hector, and then approach *Señor* Lopez before popping the question to Susana.

He felt his eyes widen at the thought. What if she refused him? No. He was sure now that she felt as he did, and though they were young and hadn't really gone on any formal dates, Marty was sure they knew one another well enough to be certain they shared the same values and dreams.

San Juan Chamula. Why was it that every time he considered a future with Susana, the town where Virginia had died loomed in his vision? Was it possible that God was giving him the direction for his life as well as the partner to walk it with him?

Alone in the shade while the rest of the family enjoyed a brief afternoon siesta, Marty felt his grin spread across his face. The certainty he felt in his heart at that moment made it even more difficult to wait for Hector to return, but wait he must. This was too important to run ahead of God, even with one step. Besides, Susana deserved the best he could give her, and Marty sensed that this was a topic he needed to discuss and pray about with Hector before approaching Susana or her family.

La curandera was angry.

Chapter 38

ALBERTO'S DAY HAD NOT GONE WELL. THE PAIN WAS especially intense, and even the increased dosages of medication failed to dull it sufficiently, leaving his faculties more alert than he cared for them to be. It was much easier when he could float away on the morphine drip and forget that he had made such a mess of his life and was now dying alone.

And then they had walked in—all nine of them! His own children, the very ones he had so longed to see just one more time before taking his last ragged breath, had shown up together, with Hector at the lead. Alberto had immediately recognized each one, though years had passed since he'd seen any of them except Hector.

Why now? he wondered. *Why couldn't we have been reunited when I was still healthy, with at least a few good years left in me? Why now, when I must appear to them as the most pitiful example of a man?*

The very thought threatened an outpouring of tears, but he steeled himself against it. He looked pathetic enough; he certainly didn't want them to see him crying on top of everything else. Surely he could muster up just one last glimmer of strength and dignity for his children to take away with them! He must, for it was all he had left to give them.

And so he swallowed his tears and clenched his jaw, determined to show no weakness, though his heart cried within him for forgiveness and mercy.

Hector didn't even try to suppress his smile. It was all he could do not to jump up from his spot on the sand and start dancing in front of everyone on the beach. But he knew there would be time for celebration later. And so he limited himself to clapping his friend on the back and congratulating him on his good taste.

"You have chosen one of the two most beautiful women in all of Mexico to be your *esposa*," he proclaimed. "I got the first one, of course. And she will be so excited when I tell her the news! I know she has long hoped that you and Susana would one day open your eyes and see what God has done in bringing you together."

Marty laughed, the sound merging with the crashing of the waves on the shore and the shouts of children playing nearby. Hector's heart rejoiced that Marty had invited him here to their favorite spot in Puerto Nuevo to tell him the news. It was only appropriate that the young *gringo* who had already captured the Rodriguez family's heart and been christened *"Tio"* by the children should officially join their clan.

And the timing couldn't have been better. After Hector and his siblings had returned the previous day from their trip north of the border, they had all gone to bed with heavy hearts, saddened that their father continued to refuse God's offer of forgiveness and reconciliation. How Hector's chest had ached as they finally gave up and exited the hospital room, leaving Alberto Javier Rodriguez alone on his deathbed.

Hector had felt especially bad, since he was the one who had encouraged his siblings to go to their father in a group attempt to implore him to repent while there was still a chance for him. Hector had been so sure that seeing his entire family together would melt Alberto's heart and open him to the truth of God's love. Instead it appeared to have hardened him even more. And when they had finally told him the news about Virginia, he had turned his face away and refused to speak to them again.

Now there was nothing left but to pray until their father was gone from this earth. They had agreed they would do so, but it didn't lessen the pain and rejection they'd felt after visiting the man who had partnered with their mother to give them life.

Hector shook his head. It was no time now to sink into despair or depression. There was a wedding to plan! And soon there would be new nieces and nephews to welcome into the family. *As it should be*, Hector thought. *Someone leaves this earth, and someone else is born into it. Always new life, always hope...* *Thank You, Lord!*

La curandera was angry. She couldn't remember when she'd felt such intense anger or even hatred toward one of her own people, so much so that her entire chest ached. It had been easy when the offender was an outsider, but now it was the young Imix who insisted on adopting the blasphemous ways of the *evangelicos*, and Evita knew it was up to her to take care of the problem—permanently this time. She had hoped the old woman's demise would frighten Imix enough that she would abandon her traitorous pursuit and return to the ancient ways, but apparently that hadn't happened.

Kawak's visit the previous day had stirred up not only Evita's anger but the fury of the ancient spirits as well. She could feel it. She could hear it, whispering to her heart. And she knew they would give her no rest until she fulfilled her calling.

The resolution to this problem, however, was more than she could handle on her own. With the help of only one other — a powerfully built Mayan warrior who was indebted to Evita for favors over the years — she had successfully eliminated the woman known as Virginia. But it would take several willing warriors to make the same thing happen with Imix and the entire Campos family. And Evita knew exactly where to find such men.

It was obvious to Susana that something was up. First Marty and Hector had gone together to the beach, only to return looking as if they'd been let in on the biggest secret in the history of the world. And then Marty had come to her home and met with her parents. Susana could think of only one reason for such behavior, but she wasn't about to ask any of those involved. She would simply have to pray and wait until God brought Marty to speak to her directly.

It didn't take long. That evening, as Susana finished cleaning up the family's dishes after dinner, Marty arrived at their front door, asking if she would like to take a walk with him. That her father not only gave his permission but encouraged her to go left her with little doubt that she was about to hear for herself what others in the family already knew.

The night was warm but pleasant as they strolled side by side, not touching but close enough to hear the other's breath, speaking only occasionally in order to break the uncomfortable silence. At last they arrived at a small park, deserted now as if making way especially for them. Settling onto a backless wooden bench, Susana marveled at the bevy of stars that illuminated the scene.

"Beautiful, isn't it?" she murmured, daring a glance in Marty's direction.

He nodded in agreement, though his eyes were fixed on her rather than the sky. "Absolutely," he said. "If you were any more beautiful, I don't think I could speak."

Her cheeks warming to the compliment, she dropped her eyes, wishing she knew the proper way to react in such a situation. She had never been comfortable with compliments, though she knew Marty was sincere and would never use flattery to achieve his own purposes.

After a moment, he laid his hand on hers, spanning the gap between them. "You know why I'm here, don't you?"

She nodded, knowing there was no sense pretending ignorance. He was going to ask her to marry him—and she was going to accept. It was just that simple...and that amazing.

"I understand if you think this is too sudden," Marty said, absently rubbing the top of her hand with his thumb. "If you need time to think or pray about it, or—"

Before he could finish, Susana raised her eyes to his and spoke the words that she'd already heard in her heart. "I have prayed about it, and God has assured me that we will be married and that it's what He wants for us. I don't need more time to consider what I already know."

Tears glistened in Marty's eyes as he squeezed her hand. "Susana..."

Leaning toward her, he gently placed his lips on hers, sealing their future and sending a sense of anticipation snaking down Susana's spine, as she wondered how soon God would send them to San Juan Chamula. For it was quite evident to her that it was in that remote little village that their life together would find its fulfillment.

*Why had he been so stubborn,
so hard and unbending—so prideful?*

Chapter 39

ALBERTO HAD SCARCELY SLEPT THE LAST TWO DAYS. He had never felt so crushed or broken as he had since learning the fate of the woman with whom he had once shared his life.

"Virginia."

It seemed the only word he could speak in the midst of his pain. Though he wanted to lash out at whoever had done this terrible thing, as well as those who had allowed her to go to such a dangerous location in the first place, he knew the fault truly lay with him. He was the one who had deserted her, leaving her to raise nine children by herself. What sort of man committed such a heinous crime? Just how selfish and evil was he?

Clutching the beloved letter to his chest, the old man sobbed, as the offers of God's love and forgiveness, spoken to him by his own children, swirled through his mind. Why had he been so stubborn, so hard and unbending—so prideful?

Why hadn't he simply opened himself to them and begged them to help him find the peace that he so desperately longed for?

Now it was undoubtedly too late. His children certainly wouldn't come back again, not after the way he had shut them out. And why should they? What had he ever done for them except abandon and reject them? Now even Virginia was gone. Since receiving her letter he had clung to a shred of hope that she might somehow show up in his room, offering her love and forgiveness in person before he slipped away into a tortured eternity. But now even that hope was gone.

Was it truly too late for him? Had he passed a point of no return with God? Was there such a thing?

His heart racing with dread, he uttered his first prayer since he was a child. *"Por favor, Señor,"* he whispered. "Please, God, if You're there and if there is any hope for me at all, have mercy on me..."

The children were nearly giddy with excitement, and Hector didn't blame them. He felt like twirling and skipping around the yard and yelling right along with them. *Tío* Marty and *Tía* Susana were getting married! What better news could their grieving family possibly receive?

That, of course, had been Marty's primary concern. Should he hold off proposing or making the announcement until more time had passed since their loss? Absolutely not, Hector had assured him. It was just the boost they needed, and no one would have agreed or approved more wholeheartedly than Virginia Correo Rodriguez herself!

Hector smiled at the thought as he sat on the stoop and watched his children play. Second only to the birth of a new baby, his mother had loved weddings most of all. Even if she scarcely knew the bride or groom, she always dressed in her finest clothes and arrived early for a good seat each and every time she was invited to such a joyous occasion.

"New life," she would declare. "That's what this symbolizes. God's plan and purpose for two people, bringing them together and uniting them as one." Hector had marveled each time he heard her speak such words, knowing that many women in her position would have become hardened and embittered over the betrayal and desertion of her husband. The one time Hector had dared voice such a thought she had assured him that one person's wrong choices did not negate God's perfect plan for all mankind.

"Attending a wedding is a privilege," she would explain. "The memory of it calls me to pray for the two people involved, as well as the children whose lives will begin as a result of their parents' love. Marriage is a beautiful and sacred thing, *mijo*."

As always, his mother had been right. Though she had not personally experienced it in the latter years of her life, Virginia had passed on the sacred truth of God's institution of marriage to her children. Hector and his siblings had all married godly spouses, and now Marty and Susana would have the same opportunity.

"*Sí*. You would truly approve, Mama," he whispered, wishing she were there to celebrate with them and wondering if the man who had broken his mother's heart might still find peace before he left this world.

Evita had waited until after dark to steal away from her home and make her way through the deserted streets of San Juan Chamula to the place where she knew she could find those who would gladly do her bidding. Though her chest continued to ache as she walked, she pushed ahead, believing that relief would come once the arrangements had been made and she had satisfied the ancient ones. Perhaps she was suffering now because she hadn't completed her work the last time.

Imix and the Campos family are traitors, she thought, ignoring the pain that seemed to increase with each step. *The stranger named Virginia would never have found a place here if they had been true to the ancient ways. But instead they welcomed her and even joined her in trying to poison the minds of our people. It is up to me to stop this blasphemous talk of the faith of the evangelicos—once and for all...*

With her destination in sight, Evita stopped and placed her hand on her chest, struggling to breathe deeply enough to continue on and complete her mission. She had such a short distance to go now—so close, and yet...

The pain that had plagued her throughout the day now exploded inside her, radiating up her neck and down her arm, even as she struggled to take another step. *I must stop them*, she told herself. *I must...*

But the pain was too great, as she stumbled forward and fell to the ground, lying motionless in the darkness that thickened and swirled around her.

The swelling and discoloration in Celeste's face was nearly gone, and Byron had promised her car would be delivered to her as good as new before the day was out. But none of that seemed to matter when all she could focus on was her son's fate. Whatever was he thinking, throwing his life away on a young woman who obviously had no future? The girl was attractive, certainly, but hardly a compatible companion for someone like Marty. Where had she gone wrong as a mother that her only child would so blatantly defy her and reject the good life she desired for him?

Celeste shook her head as she sat on her patio, overlooking the valley below. The sun was just peeking over the horizon, and she couldn't remember the last time she'd been up so early. From her vantage point she noticed a dark car winding its way up the long driveway toward her house. She was stunned to realize it was her car, the one she'd left for repair in San Diego—even more stunned to see the car stop in front of her home and Byron climb out of the driver's side door.

Her heart melted at the sight. When Byron assured her last night that she would have her car back the next day, she had no idea he was planning to bring it to her himself. No doubt he'd lost another night's sleep to make it happen. How many times had he given up sleep and sacrificed his personal life over the years to help her? Celeste had lost count. In fact, she'd never even considered it before. Why did it suddenly seem important now?

She knew Byron had his own key and could certainly let himself in, but he might not because he wouldn't expect her to be awake. Jumping up from her lounge chair, Celeste hurried to the front door, eager to thank Byron for his thoughtfulness.

But it was more than that, and there was no sense denying it any longer. Her gratitude to Byron and his devotion to her was the closest thing to love that Celeste had experienced since death had stolen her husband from her two decades earlier. It was time to stop mourning and trying to drown her pain in alcohol and meaningless relationships. If Byron's long-standing offer to marry and take care of her was still an option, she would take him up on it. Maybe then she could release Marty to pursue his own dreams, wherever they might take him. And who knew? Perhaps one day she might even begin to understand his need to do so.

Before she could take another step, her eyes widened and her heart seemed to stop within her.

Chapter 40

KAWAK HADN'T SLEPT WELL, AND THE MORNING
found her bleary-eyed and weary as she stumbled from
her home, determined to go to the home of *la curandera*
and beg her not to go through with what Kawak was sure was
a plan to kill the Campos family and Imix. Throughout the
night Kawak had been plagued with dreams of her friend and
what would happen to her as a result of Kawak's last meeting
with the shaman. The young Mayan woman could only hope
that Evita would listen to her—and that Kawak wasn't already
too late to stop what would surely be a great tragedy.

With the sun just rising over the treetops but not yet high
enough to break through the morning mist, Kawak shivered
and pulled her *serape* more tightly around her shoulders as she
turned the corner. Before she could take another step, her eyes
widened and her heart seemed to stop within her. For there,
directly in front of her, lay the shaman, facedown, unmoving,
her ever-present red shawl covering her head and shoulders,
and her hand outstretched as if in failed supplication.

Kawak gasped, clutching her throat to stop the scream that threatened to erupt into the relative silence of the early morning scene. What had happened to stop *la curandera* in her tracks? Kawak's mind darted to her meetings at the Camposes' home, the few words she had heard of a powerful God, written about in the *evangelicos'* Bible. Was it possible there was such a God, that He somehow knew what the shaman had been planning…and that He had miraculously stopped her before she could carry it out?

So many thoughts flew through Kawak's mind as she stood there under the rising sun. And then a sense of terror swept over her, as she realized the implications of being caught alone in the street with the dead woman's body. Spinning as quickly as she could without losing her balance, she raced away from the terrifying sight and didn't stop running until she was back inside her home, leaning against the door and praying it would hold against the spirits of darkness that she was certain had pursued her the entire way.

Marty and Susana had taken Lupita with them on their morning jaunt to the beach, wanting to ensure that even the appearance of their relationship was aboveboard at all times. Lupita, of course, had been thrilled to join them, particularly when they told her they would be bringing a picnic lunch and staying until at least midafternoon. The little girl had chattered all the way to the beach and the entire time they strolled along the sand. Now the couple at last had a little privacy as they sat on a blanket, watching Lupita build sand castles just a few feet away.

Marty never completely removed his eyes from their young charge, but he couldn't help but let his gaze drift occasionally to the beautiful young woman sitting beside him, close enough to touch though they left a space between them. The way her dark hair shone in the noonday sun nearly took his breath away, and the fullness of her lips drew him so strongly he had to forcibly turn away. He still had trouble believing she had so readily agreed to be his wife. Would she want a long engagement, time to plan her wedding? How long would he have to wait to share every aspect of life with her, as he so longed to do? So many questions...

"I—" As abruptly as he had begun, he stopped. What did he want to say to her? They needed to discuss all these details, but should he be patient? Perhaps it was best to let her bring them up.

She turned to him, her dark eyes smiling with a warmth that dwarfed what he felt from the sun overhead. Eyebrows raised questioningly, she asked, "Did you say something, *mi amor*?"

Marty thought his heart would explode out of his chest. *Mi amor!* She had called him "my love." How was it that this young woman could be so humble and yet fearless at the same time? Marty longed to bestow some word of endearment upon her, but he had worried that it would sound too familiar. But after all, they were engaged now—informally, yes, but engaged nonetheless. He thought of the tiny diamond engagement ring that sat wrapped in cloth in his pocket and smiled. Surely it was appropriate to express their feelings through the words they spoke to one another.

"*Gracias*," he said, reaching across the slight distance between them and laying his hand on hers. "Thank you for calling me your *amor*."

She returned his smile. "I am glad to finally be able to say it. I have wanted to for what seems so long now. I love you, Marty Johnson, and it is an honor to know that I will soon be your *esposa*."

Hot tears misted Marty's eyes as he squeezed her hand. "I'm the one who's honored...*mi amor*. I still can't believe you've agreed to be my wife!"

Susana's eyes widened. "But it is of God," she said, a hint of awe in her voice. "He has purposed it and has given us this love to share. Why would I not agree?"

Marty's laugh seemed to surprise him even more than it did Susana. He shook his head, still grinning. "Forgive me, dear Susana," he said, squeezing her hand. "I'm not laughing at you, but at my own ignorance. How can I be so slow to see what you see so quickly and easily? I think you knew what God had in mind for us before I did, and that's why you're so comfortable with it and I'm still getting used to it." He lifted her hand to his lips and kissed her softly. "Is there anything else I should know? Any other plans God has for us that I may not have recognized yet?"

The flicker of surprise in Susana's eyes changed quickly to one of determination, and Marty couldn't have been more surprised if she'd suddenly announced that she could fly. What other surprises were in store for him in his life with this beautiful but amazing woman?

"San Juan Chamula," Susana said simply. "God has called us there."

Marty could scarcely breathe, as the truth of her statement invaded his consciousness. She was right, of course. He'd sensed it all along, but now it was there, right in front of him, the words hanging between them as surely as if God Himself had spoken them from the heavens.

He nodded. "Yes," was all he could bring himself to say.

Apparently it was enough, because Susana nodded. The issue was settled, and they would let God work out the details.

His mind returned to the ring that seemed to call to him from its hiding place in his pocket. Was this the right time?

Marty's glance darted from Susana to Lupita, whose sand castle was now nearly as tall as she, though listing badly to one side. Smiling, Marty turned back to Susana, whose gaze had also drifted in Lupita's direction.

Removing his hand from Susana's, Marty reached in his pocket and pulled out the soft cloth that held his treasure. He wished it could be more, but he wasn't about to use Johnson family money to make that happen. Besides, he knew Susana's heart was pure and she would love what the ring symbolized and never judge it by its monetary worth. She was too fine a lady for that.

Reaching up and laying his left hand against her chin, he gently turned her face toward him. With the cloth-encased ring in his right hand, he smiled. "I have something for you, *mi amor*," he said, his voice husky as he leaned in to brush his lips against hers. When he held up his right hand, she bent her head to see his offering. Slowly he unwrapped it, thrilling to the sound of her gasp when the cloth fell away and the sun sparkled on the miniature gem.

Gently, he placed it on her finger, as she continued to stare at the shiny stone. Then, without warning, she seemed to revive, letting out a squeal of delight and throwing her arms around his neck, quickly pulling him close and covering his face with kisses. "Aye, *mi novio*," she cried, "it is beautiful! Never have I seen anything so beautiful in all my life! *Gracias, mi querido! Gracias!*"

Marty was having difficulty breathing, but he so enjoyed her embrace and kisses that he didn't dare complain. Besides, she had now added "sweetheart" and "dear one" to her terms of endearment, and he was far too happy to complain about anything.

"*Que pasa?*" Lupita asked, doing her best to insert herself between the two lovebirds. "What happened? Why are you so happy, *Tia*? And why are you kissing my *tio* like that?"

Surprised at the interruption, Marty and Susana pulled back from one another, chuckling at their chaperone's timing. The little girl looked perplexed but intrigued at the same time, as her eyes darted from one to the other until Susana held up her left hand and allowed her diamond to shine in the sun.

"Look what your *Tio* Marty has given me," she exclaimed. "Isn't it the most beautiful ring you have ever seen, *mija*?"

Lupita's grin lit up her sand-sprinkled face. "I saw bigger ones in the window of *la tienda* when Papa took me to town," she said, gingerly touching the gleaming jewel, "but none more beautiful than this."

Her grin turned to a full-blown smile then, as her eyes began a joyful dance. "Can I be in the wedding?" She clapped her hands. "My friend Carmenita got to be in her neighbor's wedding, and she told me she got to wear a new dress and carry lots of flowers. Will I get to carry flowers too?"

Marty and Susana laughed as they simultaneously pulled the child down to sit between them on the blanket. "Of course you can be in our wedding and carry flowers," Susana told her. "How could we get married without our Lupita to help us?"

The little girl squealed with joy, and Marty marveled that God intertwined such moments of happiness into a world weighed down with so much grief.

The next morning Hector was in his office early, feeling the need for some quiet time alone with the Lord. He had, of course, thanked God wholeheartedly for the wonderful news of Marty and Susana's wedding, and when the threesome returned from their beach outing, the rest of them had celebrated and exclaimed over the lovely engagement ring. Lupita, of course, had felt quite important about having seen it before everyone else. All of that was good news, and yet...

Hector sighed, sipping what was now a lukewarm cup of coffee and staring blankly at his open Bible. Never before had he felt so torn between what he said he believed...and what he felt in his heart.

Where had this fear come from, this lack of faith and peace? His mother's fate, no doubt, had a lot to do with it, not to mention his father's stubborn refusal to repent and turn to God before it was too late. But now this situation with Marty and Susana! It just seemed more than he could bear on top of everything else.

Their eyes had shone as they talked to him and Mariana about their wedding plans, and Hector had rejoiced right along with them. But then they had moved on to discuss their conviction that they were to go to San Juan Chamula to carry on the work that Virginia had begun. With no answer for how they would support themselves, they had explained how they both sensed the same calling and believed without doubt that it was God's purpose for them, at least for this season of their lives. And how could Hector argue with that? Hadn't he always preached and taught and declared that the safest place to be was right in the middle of God's will? And hadn't his own mother reminded him of that many times?

Yes. And where was she now? In a crude grave outside the Mayan village of San Juan Chamula.

Of course, Hector knew that though his mother's body lay in that faraway grave, she was no longer there. It was just the shell in which she had lived while she was on this earth, and now she was free of that mortal shell and rejoicing in the presence of the One she had loved and served for so many years. Hector *knew* that . . . but his heart still grieved. And now two more of his loved ones felt called to place themselves in the same danger that had stolen Hector's mother. How could he ever find peace in that?

The knock on his office door was tentative. He raised his head but said nothing, waiting. The knock was repeated, and this time the doorknob turned slightly.

Hector rose to his feet as the door opened to reveal *la abuela*, standing in the frame and draped in a black shawl that trailed from her bent gray head to her shoulders and beyond. Her smile was hesitant.

"*Pardone, Pastor,*" she said. "I do not mean to interrupt you. I know you are a busy man who must spend time seeking the Father. But as I prayed this morning, *El Señor* would not stop speaking to my heart to come here and meet with you. And so . . . I am here."

Hector rushed to her side to escort her into the office and to seat her on one of his two folding chairs. "I am so glad you have come, *Abuela*," he said, meaning every word though not

301

sure why. "May I get you some coffee or water? I'm afraid I have nothing else to offer you."

Señora Mesa shook her head. "I need nothing," she said. "*Gracias.* I came only to speak to you about what is in *mi corazon*, my heart."

Hector nodded, anxious to hear what she would say. Rather than return to his chair behind the desk, he took the other folding chair at her side, turning it so they could face one another.

What is it? What has God spoken to your heart for me?" *La abuela* smiled. "Ah, so you know He has a message for you." She nodded. "That is good that you do not doubt."

Hector swallowed the lump in his throat, wishing his faith were as strong as his visitor seemed to think it was.

"As I prayed this morning," she said, "I thought of your mama dying in such a faraway place. It is very sad." She paused before continuing. "And then I thought of my own Roberto, who died right here in his own neighborhood, just a few blocks from his home—on the very steps of this church."

Her pause was longer this time, as her rheumy eyes seemed to search Hector's for a response. When he restrained himself from speaking, she went on. "I sensed then that God wanted me to remind you that we cannot choose the time or place of our death. That is up to Him, and Him alone. We can only choose to obey Him while we are still alive."

Hector felt the tears fill his eyes, as the truth of her words sliced through the hard places of his heart, places he hadn't even realized were there. But before he could answer her, she laid her frail hand on his. "If you desire above all else that *El Señor* keeps your loved ones safe, how will they ever fulfill their calling?" She squeezed his hand with such pressure that it astonished him, and when she spoke again, her words were like fire in his bones.

"If what you say you believe does not govern how you live," she said, her voice nearly a whisper, "perhaps you do not truly believe it."

"Excuse me. Mr. Rodriguez?
Hector Rodriguez?"

Chapter 41

THE CALL HAD COME LESS THAN THIRTY MINUTES after *la abuela* had left his office. Hector still sat at his desk, head in hands, trying to pray and to resolve the conflict that raged in his soul. He knew *Señora* Mesa was right. He knew it was time to start practicing what he preached—or get out from behind the pulpit. But his heart just wouldn't let go of the "what if's" and "if only's" that had plagued him now for many weeks. Marty and Susana's plans to go to San Juan Chamula after their wedding only added to Hector's turmoil.

He had wondered if he might somehow dissuade them from following through on what they believed was God's purpose for them, but then realized how cowardly it was of him even to consider such an attempt. He then mulled over the possibility of convincing them to postpone the trip to the remote village, or even to put off the wedding for several months, rather than moving ahead quickly as they currently seemed determined to do. But he had no sooner entertained the thought than the phone rang—and everything changed.

Alberto Javier Rodriguez had died. Hector's body shook, and his shoulders heaved with sobs at the realization that his father was dead—gone forever, and most likely without having first made peace with God. The realization had struck him more forcefully and painfully than the news about his mother. At least in her case Hector knew she was safe and rejoicing with the Lord. His father, on the other hand...

Hector had quickly called his beloved wife, who had rushed to his side, leaving the children with Susana so the two of them could drive across the border and retrieve Alberto's few personal effects. Hector had opted to wait until they returned to tell the rest of the family; then they would all make the final arrangements together as a family.

Now he and Mariana stood in the empty room that had so recently witnessed a soul's passing into eternity. How many such passings had taken place in that very room, Hector wondered, eyeing the bed that no longer bore the frail frame of the man who had been his father. How many of the souls who had occupied that bed had passed peacefully into the arms of Jesus, and how many had moved on to a fate far worse than anything they had experienced on earth?

Only three hours ago, Hector thought, stepping toward the bed and laying his hand on the plastic-covered mattress, already stripped of the soiled linens. He would like to have been able to touch the sheets and to smell the pillowcase where his father's head had lain when he took his last breath. But it was too late now. Too late...

Mariana moved to his side, silent but supportive, laying her hand on his shoulder. How grateful he was for her presence! He doubted he would be able to get through what must be done without her. He knew, too, that she was aware of the thoughts that danced through his mind—unspoken prayers that begged for God's mercy and yet expected little in this situation. His father had made his choice. He had hardened his heart toward God and refused every offer of reconciliation, even up to the moment Hector and his siblings had come to beg him to reconsider. There was nothing left to do now but to ask God to somehow bring good from this heartbreaking occurrence.

"Excuse me. Mr. Rodriguez? Hector Rodriguez?"

The voice interrupted Hector's thoughts, and he and Mariana turned simultaneously toward the nurse who stood behind them in the doorway. Her middle-aged, chubby face was lined with what appeared to be fatigue, but even beneath the weariness Hector sensed concern and compassion. For that he was grateful.

"*Sí*," he said. "Yes. I am Hector Rodriguez."

The warmth of her smile reinforced her caring demeanor. "I'm Jeanette Thomas. I was with your father when he died."

The word ripped through Hector's heart, and he sensed the blow had impacted Mariana as well. It was then he noticed for the first time the large plastic bag that hung from the nurse's right hand.

Jeanette's eyes followed Hector's gaze downward toward the bag, and she raised her hand and held it out to him. "These are your father's things," she said. "He wanted you to have them."

Hector swallowed and nodded, telling himself he needed to take the bag from her but dreading what he might find inside. How was it possible that the entire remnants of a man's life could be contained inside one plastic bag? And what could there be of any import? The clothes he wore when he was admitted to the hospital? A few toiletries? A book or two, perhaps?

Hector sighed and at last received the package from the patient woman, nodding again as he mumbled a polite word of thanks. Tears pricked his eyes, and he wondered if his knees might buckle.

Obviously recognizing his dilemma, the nurse excused herself, promising to return in a few moments. Gratefully, Hector sank down into one of the two plastic chairs in the room, knowing that Mariana would take the other one. She did, pulling it up next to him and this time laying her hand on his forearm.

307

"I need to open this," Hector said, staring down at the bag in his lap as a lone tear escaped and dripped down onto his hand.

"I know." Mariana's voice soothed and encouraged him. So long as she was at his side, he would get through this. He considered waiting to open the bag until he was back across the border, in the comfortable familiarity of his own home or perhaps even surrounded by his siblings.

No. He knew in his heart he must open it now. He would share the contents with his brothers and sisters later.

His hands trembling, he opened the bag and peered inside. Everything was pretty much as he had expected. A faded shirt and pair of pants, neatly folded. A pair of dingy white socks tucked into scuffed black leather shoes. Dentures in a small container—nearly undoing Hector's resolve.

And then he saw it. A letter, worn and folded, the handwriting smudged from abundant handling. But even in its tattered state, Hector recognized the penmanship. It was his mother's—a letter from Virginia Correo Rodriguez to her husband. When had it been written?

The trembling in his hands increasing, he pulled it from the bag and stared at it, stunned to see the date at the top of the letter. It had been written just before his mother disappeared! No doubt it was the last letter she had mailed before that fateful day. How was it possible...?

Tears flowed freely from his eyes by then, and he knew he could never read the letter himself. He handed it to Mariana, who hesitated only slightly before beginning to read:

Mi esposo:

My dear husband, it has been far too many years since we have spoken, too long since we have looked into each other's eyes and expressed what is in our hearts. Now I fear it is too late and we will never have the chance to do so on this earth. I sense that one or both of us will leave this place very soon, and my heart aches to think you will do so without first receiving God's love and forgiveness.

Before I speak to you of God's forgiveness, Alberto, let me first tell you of mine. Though I struggled for many years to let go of the hurt and pain in my heart, I have done so now—completely and without reservation. I want only what is best for you, mi amor, and that is that you would at last reach out to the God you have so long rejected and receive the love and forgiveness He offers you through His only Son, Jesus! Por favor, querido, please, I want to know that we will be together in eternity! Do not wait another minute, Alberto. Do it now! Hector will help you. Just ask him. The time is short...for all of us.

Your loving esposa, Virginia

By the time Mariana finished reading, both she and Hector were weeping softly, as Hector agonized over not being at his father's side at those last moments. Perhaps if he had been there, the stubborn old man might at last have broken down and turned to the Lord. As it was...

"Mr. and Mrs. Rodriguez?"

The nurse's voice once again interrupted Hector's reverie. He raised his head, and through his tears saw the kind-faced woman smiling down at them.

"I have a message for you from your father," she said. "One I couldn't put inside a bag. It happened in his last hour of life, when he showed me the letter from his wife—your mother. He asked me to read it to him one last time, so I did." The words caught in her throat, but she continued. "He asked me if I was a Christian. I told him I was, and then he asked if it was too late for him to make peace with God. I assured him it wasn't, and then he...he prayed with me to receive Christ as his Savior."

Hector heard Mariana's gasp, even as he felt an explosion of joy in his chest. Was it true? Was it possible?

Jeanette stepped closer to Hector and Mariana, her next words falling upon them like the warm oil of a benediction. "Alberto Javier Rodriguez died with words of praise and thanksgiving to God on his lips. He left this place in peace, and his last wishes were that I would be sure you knew that."

Hector felt Mariana's arm slip around his shoulders as she leaned against him, sobbing with the same joy that surged through his veins with every beat of his heart. The faithful Lord, in His great mercy, had reached the hardened old man while there was still time. And now Alberto and Virginia Rodriguez had been reunited at the foot of God's throne.

Imix thought her heart would stop beating when she heard the faint rap on the door. With only a candle to light the opened Bible that lay on the table between her and Diego and Eldora Campos, the trio had hoped their midnight study would remain undetected. Quite obviously that was not the case, and Imix felt a snake of terror slither up her spine and wrap itself around her throat.

Quietly and carefully, Diego Campos rose from his spot on the floor and stepped to the door, pressing his ear up against it as he waited. When the knock came again, slightly more insistent this time, he called out, *"Quien es?* Who is it?"

After only a slight hesitation, the answer came. "It is Kawak. I know Imix is in there with you, and I want to talk to her—to all of you."

Imix tried to swallow, but her mouth was too dry. Kawak was here? Imix thought she had been so careful. Obviously not careful enough, as Kawak must have been watching and waiting...

Diego whispered to Imix in the darkness, asking what she wanted him to do. Imix's first thought was that she wanted him to barricade the door until Kawak went away, to somehow make Kawak disappear and never come back. But of course that would never work.

"It is your home," she whispered in return. "You must decide. But I am so sorry to have brought this trouble upon you."

Eldora, who sat beside Imix, laid her hand on the girl's arm. "God is our Protector. Nothing happens apart from His perfect will. Virginia taught me that. He is here with us now, and He will not leave or forsake us."

Imix, though new to the faith of the Scriptures, knew Eldora spoke the truth. She felt her shoulders relax then, and she said, "If you want to let her in, I will speak with her. And I will trust that God is in control."

Seemingly satisfied with her answer, Diego cracked the door open and peeked outside before opening it wider to allow Kawak entry into their modest home. As Imix saw her friend's outline in the doorway, she sensed a peace wash over her, replacing her fear with excitement at Kawak's possible reasons for coming.

Hesitantly, Kawak accepted Diego's invitation to join them at the table, and soon she was seated on the floor to Imix's right. Even in the candlelight, Imix could detect the mixture of fear and curiosity in the young woman's eyes. Why had she come? Could it have something to do with the death of *la curandera*? It seemed the entire village had spoken of little else since her body was discovered the previous morning.

As if reading her thoughts, Kawak said, "It was me. I'm the one who found the shaman in the street. But I . . . I was afraid. I ran back home and said nothing until others found her and reported it."

Imix frowned. Why was Kawak telling her this? They were friends, yes, and they shared many secrets. But to come all this way under cover of night . . . ?

Tears pooled in Kawak's dark eyes then, and Imix wondered at the reason. Surely she hadn't been that close to the woman named Evita who for years had nearly ruled much of San Juan Chamula with her superstitions and practices. Why would the woman's death cause such distress for Kawak?

"It was also me who caused it," Kawak said, her voice cracking as the tears spilled over onto her cheeks. "I went to her and told her . . . first about the woman named Virginia and how she was drawing you away from your people with her

311

false teachings." She dropped her eyes before raising them again to continue. "And then about you, when I...saw you coming here at night, even after Virginia was...gone."

Imix heard the collective gasp from Diego and Eldora, even as she realized what they, too, had just come to understand: it was Kawak who was behind the fate of the woman named Virginia, and *la curandera* had somehow been involved. Questions swirled through Imix's mind, as the meager pieces of the puzzle began to fall into place. Kawak had gone to Evita not once, but twice! The first time had resulted in Virginia's death, but what had Kawak hoped to accomplish with the second visit? The implications exploded in Imix's mind, even as she tried to form words to respond to her friend's revelations.

"You...you went to the shaman about Virginia?" Imix swallowed the bile that threatened to rise in her throat. "And...about me?"

Still weeping silently, Kawak nodded. "I thought...I could rescue you..." Her voice trailed off and she darted a glance toward Diego and Eldora. "From them...and from all those who believe like them and try to steal our way of life."

Imix was sure her heart would shatter in a million pieces. Her friend had been trying to win her back to the old ways of her Mayan people, but instead had caused the death of the woman named Virginia, a kind and gentle lady who had taught them about the markings in the Bible—and about the true faith contained within its pages.

Before Imix could answer, Diego laid his hand on the still open Bible and said, "Kawak, this is not the book of people who want to conquer or destroy you or your Mayan ways. It is the book of the God who loves you so much that He died for you—and of the people who love that one true God in return."

Kawak's eyes mirrored her confusion, as Imix watched her closely and waited to see how she would respond. At last she said, "I heard the woman named Virginia speak of *los conquistadores* from the markings in the book. 'We are more than *conquistadores*,' the book says. If it is not the book of *los conquistadores* and others who tried to destroy our people, why would it contain such words?"

Imix turned from her friend and looked back at Diego. Eldora, too, appeared to be waiting for his answer.

In the glow of the candle, Diego smiled. "We are more than *conquistadores* through Him who loved us," he recited. "That's what it truly says. And it means that no matter what happens to us or who fights against us in this world, we will not be defeated in our faith because God's love protects us. Even if we are killed for our faith, we will still be safe in His love."

Imix felt her heart leap with joy at the simple truth in Diego's statement. Turning back to Kawak, she prayed her friend would recognize it as well.

Kawak appeared thoughtful, if not fully convinced. But, Imix reasoned, at least she wasn't openly rejecting his words. The thought brought a smile to her lips, and she knew it wasn't lost on Kawak.

"I will consider it," she said, directing her gaze and words to Imix. "When the woman named Virginia died, I thought you would abandon these teachings. Instead I saw you coming here at night, and I wondered why you would take such a chance. It is very dangerous, you know."

Imix nodded, realizing that if Kawak was aware of their nighttime meetings, others could know as well. *La curandera* might be gone, but there were other shamans in the area who would gladly step in to avenge her death if they believed it had come as a result of the interference of outsiders and *evangelicos*. Even a descendant of the Mayan people, such as Imix, would not be spared if it was believed she was involved. She would, in fact, pay the ultimate price as a traitor of her people.

Imix closed her eyes. What would happen to them, she and the Campos family and the handful of other Christian believers in San Juan Chamula? Surely God would not abandon them! Was it possible He might even send someone to take Virginia's place, someone to teach them more fully from the Scriptures that had only recently become so precious to Imix? She could only pray it would be so—and that God would also show Kawak the truth so that she, too, could join their little band of followers.

Hector couldn't remember a time in his life when he had been more filled with joy. As he stood at the door of the little *Casa de Dios* church and welcomed the wedding guests, he marveled at what God had done in such a short time. Though he still missed his beloved mother, Hector had finally been able to let her go, knowing she was safe with the Father and basking in the presence of her beloved Savior. Hector knew, too, that his own father was there with her, and that was a miracle nearly beyond his comprehension. Oh, the mercy and faithfulness of God that would orchestrate such events and bring them all together so that good could come from such seemingly tragic circumstances!

Hector was technically an orphan now, with no parents on earth to love and protect him. But God had given him so much in return—most of all the peace to release Marty and Susana to follow their calling to San Juan Chamula. Their letter to the Campos family had already been mailed and would no doubt be received within a few days. Hector had no doubt that the same family who had so lovingly welcomed his mother would do the same for these newlyweds.

A slight tug on his suit jacket interrupted his musings, and he glanced down to see a bright-eyed Rosa Diaz staring up at him, her excited smile nearly engulfing her face. "Pastor Rodriguez," she said, glancing from Hector to the couple standing behind her, "*mi papa* came with us!"

Hector smiled at Rosa's mother, who stood beaming beside the man whom Hector had seen in the neighborhood but never formally met. As Hector introduced himself and shook the man's hand, he sensed that this would not be the last time *Señor* Diaz would cross the threshold of their humble church.

Then, behind the Diaz family, Hector was astonished to see Marty's mother, Celeste, approaching arm-in-arm with a well-dressed gentleman whom Celeste quickly introduced as her lawyer and new husband, Byron Moore.

Hector felt his eyebrows shoot up in surprise. "Husband?" His eyes darted back and forth between the two. Their unannounced attendance at the wedding was shock enough, but...a wedding of their own? "You two are...?"

Byron laughed, warming Hector with his genuineness. "Yes," Byron said, shaking Hector's hand. "It took me nearly twenty years to talk her into it, but now that Marty is taking the plunge, I finally convinced her to do the same. We were married in a small, private ceremony just last weekend." He turned to his bride and smiled down at her. "I've never been happier."

"Nor have I," she answered, shifting her gaze from Byron back to Hector. "I can't imagine why it took me so long to see what was right in front of my eyes." She smiled. "Maybe now I can stop trying to control Marty's life and just concentrate on enjoying my own."

Hector laughed, watching the couple make their way to a couple of vacant chairs, delighted at the thought of how this news would impact Marty and Susana. Now, instead of praying only for Marty's mother, they could pray for his stepfather as well. What an amazing God they served!

"It's time," Mariana whispered from behind, laying her hand on Hector's arm. "The guests are all seated, and the wedding party is ready to enter."

Hector turned and looked down at his *esposa*, stunned yet again that he had been blessed with such a beautiful life partner. As she smiled up at him, he leaned down and kissed her lightly on the forehead.

"*Gracias a Dios*," he said. "*Gracias a Dios...por todo*."

"*Sí*," Mariana agreed, her dark eyes glistening with sudden tears. "Thank You, God...for everything."

The End

More than Conquerors:

The movie *2012* brings to the screen the images and horror born out of the predictions that have their roots in Mayan prophecy. The Mayan culture is both ancient and superstitious, having accepted some aspects of Christianity, but only in such a way that it could be tweaked to fit its own lifestyle and beliefs. As such, the remnant of the Mayan culture clings fiercely to its particular form of faith and fights ferociously to preserve it, rendering outsiders, particularly Evangelical missionaries, most unwelcome.

—◦∞◦—

Red Ink

Book Three of the "Extreme Devotion" Series
Kathi Macias

Prologue

YANG ZHEN-LI WAS NEARING THIRTY BUT AT TIMES she felt twice that old. Her back was becoming permanently bent forward from the heavy pails she carried daily, one attached on each end of the thick bamboo rod that stretched across her shoulders, mirroring the heaviness of her heart. There had been a time when she'd been acclaimed as a beauty, but she could scarcely remember why...or imagine that it would matter.

She tried to fight the encroaching darkness, tried to hold fast to what she knew was true, but the constant lies and propaganda were taking a greater toll even than the physical labor and abuse or the burning, gnawing hunger. If her situation didn't change soon, she knew she would never live long enough to see her husband or son again. And with nearly eight years of her ten-year sentence left to serve, the possibilities of her emerging from prison alive grew dimmer by the day.

For to me, to live is Christ, and to die is gain. She forced herself to focus on one of the scripture verses she'd had opportunity to memorize between the time she accepted *Zhu Yesu* as her Savior and her arrest by members of the Public Security Bureau (PSB) on charges of teaching religion to children, including giving them papers containing religious writings. Even before her arrest, her parents had warned her, begged her, threatened her—and finally had her kidnapped in an attempt to convince her to go along with the government rules, especially the one limiting each family to one child. After all, she already had a healthy son. Why would she want another baby when they could scarcely afford to feed the first one? But though her abductors had forcibly aborted her second child, they had not succeeded in convincing Yang Zhen-Li to abandon the faith she had adopted before marrying her Christian husband. If anything, the ordeal had only strengthened her resolve to take a stand for the meaning of her name—Zhen-Li, "Truth"—and spurred her to begin actively sharing the Good News of Yesu every chance she got. As a trained teacher, that quite naturally included talking with children about the gospel, a practice expressly forbidden by the government.

And now she was paying the price. Separated from her family and sentenced to ten years of hard labor and "re-education," Zhen-Li struggled to survive against pain, exhaustion, and bitter loneliness. Worst of all were the times she felt God had abandoned her. It wasn't enough to know in her mind that He promised never to leave or forsake her. She needed a visible reminder—soon—if she was to continue to remain faithful behind these prison walls.

New Hope® Publishers is a division of WMU®, an
international organization that challenges Christian believers
to understand and be radically involved in God's mission. For
more information about WMU, go to www.wmu.com. More
information about New Hope books may be found at www.
newhopepublishers.com. New Hope books may be purchased
at your local bookstore.

If you've been blessed by this book, we would like to hear your story.
The publisher and author welcome your comments and
suggestions at: newhopereader@wmu.org.

WorldCrafts

You can join other caring people to provide income, improved lives, and hope to artisans in poverty around the world.

Own handmade items produced by people in fair-trade, nonexploitative conditions.

Share your passion for the world. Use WorldCrafts[SM] products with this book:

Leather Bookmark (Burgundy)
H094162 • (North Africa) • $4.99

Henna Bag
H064173• (India) • $14.99

Change the World Saree Coin Purse
H084110 • (Sri Lanka)• $12.99